T0123408

The Arimathea Series -

Book 1 – Be My Witness
Book 2 – Whither Thou Goest
Book 3 – Whom Will You Serve
(Future Publication)

WHITHER THOU GOEST

A Christian Historical Fiction Novel

Book 2
of the Arimathea Series

BEN F. LEE

WESTBOW
PRESS®
A DIVISION OF THOMAS NELSON
& ZONDERVAN

WestBow Press books may be ordered through booksellers or by contacting:

WestBow Press
A Division of Thomas Nelson & Zondervan
1663 Liberty Drive
Bloomington, IN 47403
www.westbowpress.com
1 (866) 928-1240

ISBN: 978-1-9736-5600-5 (sc)
ISBN: 978-1-9736-5599-2 (e)

Print information available on the last page.

WestBow Press rev. date: 04/01/2019

ENDORSEMENTS...

Be My Witness, Ben Lee's first book, was truly captivating and gave me glimpses of hidden and forgotten corners of our Biblical past. In the mind's eye, I could see the streets and alleyways of Jerusalem where our King walked. *Whither Thou Goest* not only continues that tradition but also creates a wealth of feeling that surges forth from Ben Lee's living characters. Your mind's eye will see and your heart will feel that you are privy to unknown history. Come on this journey, and you may feel that you are closer to the King of Kings.

Doug Turnage, Living history re-enactor

Ben Lee does it again. I can see the movie already. With the heart of a deeply spiritual man, the mind of a classical theologian, and the spirit of a conspiracy theorist, Lee weaves this story in and out of the historical narrative with great intrigue. I could not put the book down. Like a Dan Brown book that attempts to keep to the truth of Scripture as its primary source, *Whither Thou Goest* captures the reader within its pages of history, danger, conspiracy, pilgrimage, theology, scenery, dialogue, and inspiration.

Dr. Christopher Moody, Assistant Professor of Systemic Theology, Instructional Mentor, Library Baptist Theological Seminary

I have read Ben Lee's "*Whither Thou Goest.*" This is an incredible volume filled with intrigue and compelling narratives. Ben Lee is a remarkable author and experienced in the art of storytelling about Biblical times that are so real, one has the feeling that it really happened. The story that unfolds is fiction, but the setting is remarkable as it is a glimpse of what may have occurred during the early Christian era. Pick a good day when you have an open day. You will not want to put this book down!

Dr. Jimmy Draper
President Emeritus, LifeWay

DEDICATION:

There is something to be said for taking a stand, doing the Lord's work. I know older men who did and who do.

This book is dedicated to the memories of our fathers, Ben Lee and Jack Gardner.

These men in great part molded me and my wife Liz, their children. They were born over 100 years ago. Unfortunately our son, Zane, did not meet either one of his grandfathers. We hold the Hope that one day he will. Zane's older brother Aaron [lost just shy of his sixteenth birthday] played at his grandfather Jack's feet.

Also, this book honors a group of senior gentlemen in the Friendship Class of First Baptist Church Beaumont with whom I had the pleasure to meet on Sundays and facilitate their Bible Community discussions. These gentlemen were far more knowledgeable about Scripture than I, some of them my teachers in years gone by, staunch followers of our Savior now gone on to their reward....

To our dear friend, a copy editor, Robin Griffin Ridgeway, in honor of her only daughter, Marissa Kennedy (9-1-1986 – 11-22-2012)

And to Doug Turnage...who knows miracles happen.

Acknowledgements

Scripture references are from the New American Standard Bible and are consistent and true to the original Hebrew, Aramaic and Greek.

Continuing thanks to *and* appreciation for my early mentors who have gone on to their reward: Ruth Garrison Scurlock and Violette Newton (Poet Laureate of Texas) who inspired a young writer.

Special thanks to: Dr. Ben Stafford who continues to be my Gamaliel; Robin Griffin who still reads for me in tough times; Doug Turnage [my Society for Creative Anachronism Brother-in-Arms who inspired my Dominus Airakles in future books] and is my sounding board; D.J. Resnick, Kay Resnick [deceased], and Jeane-Marie "Loy" White, dear friends and often, my copy editors; the Golden Triangle Writers Guild, which nurtured me; and the many friends over the years who provided and provide inspiration and help.

Lastly...to the Society for Creative Anachronism for the fundamental and lasting relationships I developed over forty-two years and continue to develop, for the wonderful in-depth knowledge and opportunities the group provided and provides to experience medieval history in action, and for all those who cross my path and touch my life in the pursuit of honor....

Book One & Two - Place Names

Judea / Samaria / Galilee

Damascus: Possibly the most ancient of Oriental cities. It is first mentioned during the time of Abraham. [Modern name: Damascus, the capital of Syria]

Bethany-beyond-the-Jordan; Also known as Bethabara. Where John the Baptist preached and performed baptisms.

Bethany: Bethany has traditionally been identified with the present-day West Bank city of al-Eizeriya, site of the reputed Tomb of Lazarus, about 1.5 miles east of Jerusalem on the southeastern slope of the Mount of Olives.

Jericho : The city of Jericho is in an oasis in Wadi Qelt in the Jordan Valley [which makes it the lowest city in the world].

Scythoplis: [Modern Name: Beth-shan]. The city was located at the east end of the Jezreel Valley.

Joppa: Ancient port city in Israel. [Modern Name: Jaffa]

Sidon: A ancient Phoenician city on the Mediterranean Sea coast north of Tyre.

Tyre: An ancient Phoenician port city on the Mediterranean Sea south of Sidon.

Ptolemais: A prominent town and sea port on the Phoenician seacoast, across the bay from Mount Carmel [Modern Name: Acre, Israel]

Sapphris: 'The Ornament of all Israel' - Herod Antipas chose this site in 4 BC to be the capital of his government. It was the largest city in Galilee.

Cana: Exact Galilee location of Cana is unknown. Possible locations: the modern Arab town of Kafr Kanna, Kenet-el-Jalil, Ain Kanaand Qana, all near Nazareth. The exact location may never be identified.

Nazareth: A small Jewish town is situated on a hill in the Plain of Esdraelon in Galilee.

Ginea: A Samaritan town. The country of Samaria lies between Judea and Galilee. It begins at a town called Ginea, lying in the Great Plain, and ends at the Toparchy of the Acrabateni.

Pella: A city in the Decapolis prominent in the Roman era. It is nestled within the lower foothills of the eastern slope of the Jordan Valley, south of the Sea of Galilee and southeast of the Bet She'an.

Capernaum: An ancient Jewish fishing village on the north shore of the Sea of Galilee in Israel, and the first town encountered by travelers on the west side of the upper Jordan. It was equipped with a Roman customs office and a small garrison overseen by a centurion. The village was apparently poor, since it was a Gentile centurion that built the community's synagogue (Luke 7:5). The houses were humble and built of the local black basalt stone.

Sea of Galilee: The Sea of Galilee (Kinneret) is situated in northeast Israel, near the Golan Heights in the Jordan Rift Valley, and is the largest fresh water lake in Israel. It is approximately 33 miles in circumference, about 13 miles long and 8.1 miles wide.

Jabbok River: The headwaters of the Jabbok begin in Amman (ancient Rabbath-ammon), and the river flows to the north before heading west to the Jordan River.

Decapolis: A group of ten cities on the eastern frontier of the Roman Empire in Judea and Syria. The ten cities were not an official league or political unit, but they were grouped together because of their language, culture, location, and political status.

Samaria: A mountainous region in the northern part of the geographical area to the west of the Jordan River. The name derives from the ancient city of Samaria, the old capital of the Kingdom of Israel.

Baqaa Valley: A fertile valley in eastern Lebanon. For the Romans, the Baqaa Valley is a major agricultural source. It is situated between Mount Lebanon to the west and the Anti-Lebanon Mountains to the east and forms the northeasternmost extension of the Jordan Rift Valley, which stretches from Syria to the Red Sea.

Mount Hermon: Mount Hermon is a mountain cluster in the Anti-Lebanon mountain range whose summit straddles the border between Syria and Lebanon.

Gaul

Massilia: A seaport city in the first century AD [Modern name: Marseilles – Second Largest City in France]

Bononi-by-the-Sea: A Roman seaport in Gaul (across the Strait from Dover). [Modern Name: Boulogne-sur-Mer, a city in northern France]

Burdigala: A seaport city on the Garumna River. [Modern name: Bordeaux on the Garonne River]

Britannia

Belerion: Ancient Celtic name for England. Oldest known name: Albion. Roman name: Britannia.

Avalon: Also known as *Ynys Wydryn*, 'the Isle of Glass.' Sacred to the Celts, it is considered the "Gateway to the Netherworld." Here stands the '*Tor*,' a five-hundred-foot hill. '*Tor*' is a local word of Celtic origin meaning 'rock outcropping' or 'hill.' In the first century AD the *Tor* was situated on a peninsula/tidal island. After the Romans drained the swampy area, the *Tor* today is a striking location, a very high hill in the middle of a plain called 'the Summerland Meadows.' It is associated with both the 'Grail Sagas' and the 'Athurian Legends.' [Modern name: Glastonbury, Somerset, England]

Ictis: Celtic seaport on the Southwest coast of England. Named by the Romans 'Ictis.' Celts first called it '*Karek Loos y'n Koos*,' - 'Gray Rock in the Wood.' Later called 'St. Michael's Mount.'

Wolmecoma: A small fishing village on the southwestern coast of Belerion [England]. Celtic name means "Wolves Valley" for a pack of wolves which dominated the coast region at night near the village.

Mynedd: A Celtic fishing village on the Sabrina Aest [the Bristol Channel].

Camulodunum: The capital of the Catuevellauni, the most powerful British Tribe in Celtic Belerion. [Modern name: Colchester]. Prior to the Roman invasion of 43AD, the Tribe was ruled by Kimbelinus ap Tasciovanus, who styled himself as '*Britannorum rex*,' 'King of the Britons.'

Northwestern Mediterranean

Sea of Crete: The Sea of Crete is the sea south of the Aegean Sea north of the island of Crete and south of Cyclades. It also stretches from Kythera east to the Dodecanese Islands of Karpathos and Kassos. Bounding seas to the west are the Ionian Sea and the Mediterranean Sea.

East African Coast

Carthago: A major port on the African Coast. Ancient Roman name: Colina Julia Carthago. [Modern name is Carthage]

Misenum: Ancient seaport of Campania, Italy.

Abyla: A seaport city located on a peninsula whose promontory is opposite the Rock of Gibraltar. It formed one of the 'Pillars of Hercules.' [Modern name: Ceuta]

Tingis: A seaport city on the Western African Coast. [Modern name: Tangiers, a city in northern Morocco]

Melita Islands: Islands in the Mediterranean Sea between Sicily and Africa. [Modern name: Malta]

Cyrenaica: The historical name for the eastern region of Lybia. Also known as *Pentapolis* in antiquity.

Tripolitana: Historical region in Lybia on the Mediterranean coast of Africa. Founded by the Phoenicians in the seventh century BC. Conquered by the Greeks and lster by the Romans. Name means 'Three Cities.'

Numidia: Part of an ancient Berber Kingdom along the African Coast [Modern day Algeria and a small part of western Tunisia in North Africa]

Traducta Julia: A small part of the Southern Spanish Coast [West of Gibraltar], founded by Greeks in the sixth century BC, who established colonies along the coast. Years later, Rome established dominance over the area, and it received a Roman name.

France/Spain

Galaecia: A Roman province that comprised an area in the northwest of Hispania [approximately present-day northern Portugal, Leon, Asturia, and Galicia in Spain].

Sinus Cantabrorum: A body of water named by Romans in the first century BC. Name means 'Bay of the Cantabri.' More frequently known as 'Mare Gallaecum.'

Oceannus Britannicus: Narrow arm of the Atlantic Ocean separating the southern coast of Belerion [England] from the northern coast of Gaul [France]. [Modern name: the English Channel]

Fratum Gallicum: Turbulent strait separating Gaul [France] and Belerion [England]. [Modern name: Strait of Dover]

Victis: An isle off the coast of southern Belerion (England). [Modern name: Isle of Wight]

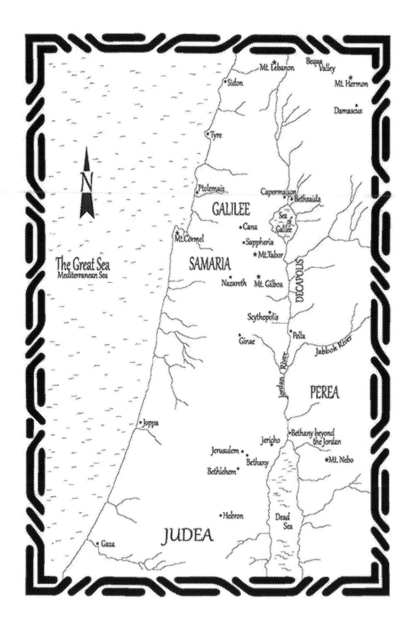

FOREWARD

In 1989 I wrote a poem, "The Cripple," that did well in contests and won several awards. It remains a showcase poem of my portfolio, often read. After Thanksgiving 2009, in the course of working on a Medieval Fantasy sequel, this poem grabbed my attention, told me it needed to be a novel. Two months later I had researched and completed the 62,000 word novel, *Be My Witness*. I have written longer. But never as quickly.

Over the following ten years the Arimathea Series now numbers [roughly 700,000 words]. Undeterred, I continue to work on the Arimathea Series, which is now two printed books as well as eleven completed manuscripts with a twelfth manuscript in progress. During this time period my wife, Liz, broke both bones in her lower left leg, I had three-way bypass heart surgery [12-2010], and I was diagnosed with throat cancer [2014]. By the grace of God, I am a cancer survivor.

In my research, I stumbled on a man I believe is one of the unsung heroes of the New Testament, Joseph of Arimathea....

All four New Testament gospels mention Joseph of Arimathea. New Testament Canon Scripture says of him:

- A good and just man
- who was waiting for the kingdom of God
- who went to Pilate, the Roman governor, and asked for Jesus' body

- A member of the Council [The Supreme Jewish Council, the Sanhedrin]
- the rich man [along with Nicodemus] who laid Jesus to rest in his own tomb

Joseph of Arimathea is venerated as a saint by the Catholic, Lutheran, Eastern Orthodox and some Anglican churches.

The Jewish Talmud has Joseph of Arimathea the younger brother of Heli, who was [according to Luke's Gospel] the father of Mary, Jesus' mother, which makes Joseph of Arimathea Jesus' great-uncle.

Additionally, Joseph is referenced in apocryphal and non-canonical accounts such as the Acts of Pilate, given the medieval title Gospel of Nicodemus, and The Narrative of Joseph, and in early church historians such as Irenaeus (125-189), Hippolytus [170-236], Tertullian [155-222], and Eusebius [260-340], who added details not in the canonical accounts. Hilary of Poitiers (300-367) enriched the legend, and Saint John Chrysostom [347-407], the Patriarch of Constantinople, was first to write that Joseph was one of the Seventy Apostles appointed in Luke 10.

St. Jerome [340-384] lists Joseph of Arimathea's official Roman title as 'Noblis Decurio,' a minister of mines for the Roman empire with direct access to Pilate Himself.

English history indicates Joseph was well acquainted with the British kings Beli, Lud, Lylr, and Kimbelinus, who gave Joseph and his companions twelve 160-acre parcels of land tax free. Joseph's sister or his daughter [depending on the quoted historian] is said to have wed Bran the Blessed, the Arch Druid of Belerion [and the first Celtic convert to Christianity on the island] and became the mother of Caratacus whose children were prominent in the early Christian Church in Rome.

Legend and Lore credit Joseph of Arimathea with establishing the first Christian church in Britain in AD 37.

Legend says Joseph's Hawthorn staff, thrust into Wearyall Hill in Glastonbury, immediately flowered and became a tree. The original tree has been propagated several times, with one growing at

Glastonbury Abbey and another in the churchyard at the Church of St. John. The original Thorn was cut down and burned as a relic of superstition during the English Civil War, and a graft was replanted on Wearyall Hill in 1951 to replace it. That replanting had its branches cut off in 2010 but survives. The Queen of England uses Glastonbury Thorn's blossoms to decorate her table at Christmas. Unlike other typical Hawthorns which flower once-a-year, the Glastonbury Thorn flowers...twice-a-year, at Christmas and again at Easter.

Other legends say Joseph hid the Holy Grail in the Chalice Well, a Glastonbury spring, and King Arthur and Guinevere are said to be buried in Glastonbury Abbey.

Many consider Joseph of Arimathea to be the forefather of the Grail Sagas and the Arthurian Legends.

PROLOGUE

Death came in blood and agony.

But on the third day, the earth shook, rocks split, and the veil of the Temple in Jerusalem split from top to bottom. Death had lost its sting!

Throughout Judea, into Galilee and beyond, the word of Jesus Christ's resurrection spread. The risen Son of Man appeared to many, His Apostles and others, and they believed. Many more, who had not seen, also believed....

In the second watch of the night after Pentecost, lamps burned late in the House of Arimathea. The head of the house, Joseph, a Pharisee, and his minister, Reuben ben Ezra, poured over shipping accounts and prospective trading ventures, reconciling and planning for the days after Joseph's departure. Joseph soon would take ship for Britannia, answering the call of the risen Savior Jesus Christ to spread His ministry on those northern shores.

Reuben, at his master's direction, would remain in Jerusalem, overseeing the House of Arimathea's commercial empire, its trading interests with Rome and its provinces. Like Reuben's, Joseph's hands were ink-stained from penning missives and lists with reed pens. In the privacy of his own home, the master had laid aside the shawl and *talis* of his order. He wore only his inner robe and yarmulke, following the Jewish custom of covering his head to show that he was a servant of God. Reuben, as was his want, chose unbleached linen tunic, breeches, and girdle.

"Master...?" a servant called from the doorway, "two men come.

I have told them it is late, and you had retired for the night, but they insisted the matter is urgent."

Joseph lifted his pen from the parchment, looked up from his scroll. "Do they have names, Jonas?"

"They said to tell you they were His Disciples," Jonas said with some hesitation, "that you would know them."

"I will go to the gate, Master," Reuben offered. "If they are not His own, I will turn them away."

In the shadows between the main house and the gateway, Reuben paused. Jonas spoke truth. Two men waited patiently with the guards just outside the estate gate. Clearly illuminated by the torchlight, they were clad in unbleached linen tunics and breeches of common laborers. One was square-shouldered, his face, framed by dark hair and beard, was weathered, older than the other who was more slender, young face unlined, with sparse beard brown like his hair.

Reuben recognized them both: Peter, the Capernaum fisherman, who was considered first among Jesus' disciples, and John Boanerges, one of the Sons of Thunder, who stood beside Mary, the mother of Jesus, at Calvary.

"Peter! John," he exclaimed with a wave of friendship. To the guards, he acknowledged the visitors and ordered, "Let them pass."

They embraced Reuben warmly, almost as one of their own. Joseph had been unsparing in his praise of his minister and scribe, the one who made him understand and see that Jesus was indeed the Messiah.

"Your Master——" Peter asked hurriedly. "Is he well? He has not retired for the night as the servant reported?"

"He is well," Reuben verified, "and still up. He works with me in the study."

"We would see him tonight, John and I," Peter pressed, urgency in his voice. "It is important."

Reuben was puzzled, but he did not keep them waiting. "Then come. I know he will see you."

When they approached the library door, Reuben called out, "Joseph, it is Jesus' disciples, Peter and John."

Discarding the scroll he held, the Pharisee hurried around the table and embraced them both. "All is well with the Eleven?" he asked them. "You have encountered no trouble?"

"No, Master Joseph, we are all well," Peter said quickly, but to Reuben's ear, there was an edge to his tone. He was troubled and sought to hide it. He shifted his bundle from one arm to the other. "For now, the Council has left us alone."

Joseph ushered them both to cushions, saw them seated and sat with them, Reuben near his shoulder. "Can my servants bring you wine? Refreshments?"

"If it please you, Master, no," John spoke for the first time. "Our stay cannot be over long. We do not want our presence missed by the others."

At a loss to understand, Joseph glanced at Reuben, who shrugged his lack of knowledge over the secretive visit.

"We fear that any moment we will be arrested," Peter said quickly, "and we do not want what we bring to be lost."

Intrigued, Joseph leaned forward. "What is so important that you must bring it by night?"

With patient fingers Peter drew the folds of a cloak from the object. It was a simple wooden box. Clearly wrought by the hands of a master craftsman, roughly two-thirds cubit long by one-half cubit wide and high. From its rich grainy mix of red and creamy hues interspaced with gray, brown, and wild black lines, Reuben knew at a glance the box was made of olive wood.

Peter opened the hinged top with reverent hands. Within lay a swath of white woven fabric, and nestled at its heart was a nondescript earthenware cup of fired clay about seven-fingers tall by five-fingers across the mouth. It was a cup of no marked significance, its simple design devoid of handle, its sides unadorned, a cup commonly found in the poorer homes throughout Judea and Galilee. When Peter drew it forth, he held it reverently. In his hands the fired clay seemed to glow from within. An inner fire burned in the heart of the vessel. For all its simplicity, it drew the eye, held it.

Joseph gazed at the cup appraisingly. "What makes this box," he asked, "and this cup so important that you must bring them to me by night?"

An unmistakably intimate look passed between Peter and John before the younger disciple answered softly, "The touch of the Master's hand."

Reuben saw the shared glance, then he, like Joseph, faced Peter openly, their eyes full of questions.

Peter sighed deeply. "Our Master held this cup to the lips of each of His disciples so that we might drink at our Passover meal on the night He was taken."

He extended his arms, held the cup cradled in his palms, and said in soft tones, but all in the room heard it. "And when He had taken a cup and given thanks, He gave it to each of us saying, *'Drink from it all of you; for this is My blood of the covenant, which is poured out for many for forgiveness of sins.'*"

When Peter's voice broke, John continued reverently, "He told us also, *'But I say to you, I will not drink from this fruit of the vine from now on until that day when I drink it new with you in My Father's kingdom.'*"

Joseph sat awestruck. "And you bring *such* to *me*?"

Peter drew himself from his memories, captured Joseph's eyes with his in a bridge of trust. "Who better to guard the cup than he who laid our Master to His earthly rest when all of us deserted Him?"

The Pharisee shook his head. "Reuben should have——"

"*No!*" Reuben interrupted. "It matters not how you came to fulfill prophecy. You obeyed willingly."

"Once I believed," Joseph acknowledged. He saw the puzzlement in the disciples' faces. "I tried to force Jesus into the Messiah our people wanted," he said apologetically. "Only when He healed Reuben's legs on the way to Calvary and the lad came and witnessed to me did He open my eyes to the fool I had been."

Peter's face clouded with grief. "Do not rebuke yourself. We were with Him three years, and *we* did not understand even when He told us," he said in a broken voice. "Before He was taken, He told me I would deny Him three times that night before the cock crowed. It broke my heart, but not understanding and fearing for my life, I did what He said I would."

The disciple looked longingly at Reuben. "But you knew when He was laid in the tomb that He would rise again."

Reuben slowly nodded. "I believed, but only because He prepared me beforehand, prepared me to go to Joseph. His words to me were, '*Be My witness*,' and He spoke to His kinsman through me. The Messiah healed my legs to bring me to the moment I could go and be His witness to Joseph."

"You must guard the cup," John said to Joseph, bringing them back to the moment at hand. "We——" he hesitated, "Peter and I do not know what importance the cup holds, yet we know we are not its guardians. You possess the resources to prevent the cup from being lost." He stared hard at Joseph. "With you we know it will be safe. We know this because the Spirit of the Master led both of us here, to this moment of passage."

Joseph sat transfixed. His eyes met Peter's, then John's. His mind awhirl, he offered the only thought that came to mind. "But I will leave Judea soon," he told them. "I feel called by the Christ to take His gospel to a distant land, to Britannia, an island in the far north."

He felt compelled to make them understand the dangers. "On a long sea voyage, the ship could go down, brigands may attack, and the cup might be lost."

Panic seized Joseph. He saw no agreement in their faces. They had to understand. He could not be the cup's guardian. "Britannia is a barbarian land——" he protested, "where the tribesmen serve foreign gods."

Peter was not swayed. "You go to carry the good news. That is enough."

With gentle hands the disciple gently replaced the cup within the fabric before he pushed to his feet, began to pace. "You think there is no danger here in Judea?" he pointed out. "Did He not say to us about Herod's Temple——'*Do you see these great buildings? Not one stone shall be left upon another which will not be torn down.*'"

Peter stopped, faced Joseph squarely. "The Master has said it; so it will come. When this happens to our most sacred site, what will happen to all Judea? Do you even want the cup in this land when this disaster befalls us?"

Beside Joseph, John was nodding. The Pharisee looked to Reuben for support, but the young man reluctantly nodded.

Joseph looked at the cup. "May I touch it?"

John tenderly lifted it from the olive wood box, placed it in the Pharisee's hands. Joseph turned it carefully studying the baked clay. He did not know what to expect, but the cup felt warm against his skin. Like living flesh.

"What is this within the cup?" Joseph asked, turning the throat toward him. "It looks like bloody cloth."

"It is," John confirmed. "The cloth in the cup is stained with blood and water from the spear that pierced our Master's heart. Before I took Mary away from Calvary, the centurion came to me, offered what the bloody spear held."

Reliving the moment, John paused. "He handed me his *pugio*, his dagger, to cut a swathe from the hem of my tunic. Carefully I wiped the mingled blood and water from the spearhead and shaft. Then I looked up at him and asked, 'Why have you done this?'"

John swallowed hard. "He answered me, saying, 'In Capernaum the Nazarene healed the servant of a brother centurion. I heard the crucified One address you as family. I felt led to offer this——' and he motioned to the spear. 'It is small recompense.'"

The disciple's voice broke, but his hand lifted, indicating there was more. In a forced tone, he added, "Before the centurion turned to go, he leaned close, said softly for my ears alone. 'He did not deserve this. I would have stopped this if I could.'"

Silence settled in the library. How long it lasted Reuben could not say, only that Peter broke it.

"John and I have spoken together," he began. "In times to come, we who were close to Him will share our memories with other believers. We have agreed between us, John and I, that for now the cup and the blood-stained cloth must be protected. Outside of the four of us here in Judea, no one will know they exist. In the presence of others, we will not mention these precious items, and no chronicle is to be written about them."

His commanding gaze searched them all. "Do we agree?"

One by one, they voiced their agreement.

Then Peter sighed. "John knows, but I would have you see as well."

With great care the disciple withdrew the stained cloth from the cup's mouth. When it slid free, the cup's throat was darkened, indelibly stained where the wet blood had lain against the fired clay.

With reverent hands he showed them. "When He shared the cup with us, it held wine," Peter said. "Now it holds the stains of our Master's blood, the blood of the covenant...."

Chapter I

Servants and bond-servants of the House of Arimathea chose to forget Reuben ben Ezra had been a bond-servant, one of their own. Joseph raised him to be minister of the household and overseer of the Pharisee's vast commercial empire. In their eyes he became the young master, and they served him with the dedication reserved for their patron. Healed of his lameness by the Christ, they held him in awe, and for them, his word was law unto the household.

"Young Master——" a servant said from the doorway, hesitating to disturb Reuben while he was ciphering.

Pentecost had come and gone, and the city still echoed with stories of the Son of Man's ascension. Then from heaven had come the noise of a violent rushing wind, and the Christ's Apostles and followers began speaking in various foreign tongues, witnessing about the Messiah to the Jews in Jerusalem and those from afar, each in his own language.

But there were those who did not believe. Who claimed Jesus' followers were drunk on sweet wine. Reuben and Joseph had been among those witnessing about the Son of Man.

Now with work to be done before Joseph departed for Britannia, Reuben focused on the cargo figures and did not look up. "Yes," he said absently, "what is it?"

"A man with several retainers has come to see you," the house servant said, "and by his dress, he is not Judean, Roman, or Greek."

Interested in spite of his pressing duties, Reuben laid aside his reed pen. "Did he ask for me by name?"

"Yes, young Master," the servant responded quickly. "He said you would know him." The young man frowned, uncertain about the message. "That he had once given you an arm ring."

Reuben's eyes widened. Only one man had ever given him an arm ring. The Britannian chieftain Damhan Mawr of the Dumnonii. How could he be in Judea?

The servant hesitated. From his master's joyful countenance, he knew the man. "Shall I escort him here?"

"No," Reuben exclaimed. "I will go to him."

The servant drew a quick breath. This visitor must be of some importance indeed for the young master to set aside his responsibilities and go to the gate himself.

Reuben quickly ordered his desk. His mind rushed back the three years since he had seen Damhan. In those days he had been lame from birth, his twisted legs unable to bear his weight. Joseph of Arimathea had given him Gwyr, a giant of a man, an Iceni, a Britannia tribesman, a mute, to be his legs. Gwyr who became his boon companion. Gwyr who gave his life to allow Reuben, Joseph of Arimathea, and Damhan and his retainers to escape a treacherous ambush.

Damhan here? Reuben's thoughts repeated as he pushed to his feet. *What would bring him all the way to Jerusalem?*

Again his thoughts ran to Gwyr. The Iceni had carried him everywhere, and after his death, Simon. But Reuben needed no one to carry him now. *Jesus the Christ healed my twisted legs*, Reuben reasoned, *that I be His Witness in Judea and beyond. And now Damhan comes.*

His feet almost grew wings as he hurried to the gate. Becoming Minister of the House of Arimathea had little changed him. He discarded tunic for robes, but they remained unbleached linen like his headpiece.

I am older, Reuben admitted, *and I have functioning legs. Will Damhan know me?*

Near the gate Reuben slowed his pace. Damhan stood with crossed arms, dark head high, his opaque observant eyes surveying the estate. He stood chatting with his two tribesmen companions when the Minister of Arimathea approached.

"Damhan Mawr?" Reuben asked, struggling not to grin. "I see you."

The Dumnonii chieftain nodded. "I am pleased he remembers." Then his eyes widened, his mouth gaped. "Reuben——?" he murmured incredulously, recognizing him. "This cannot be!"

"But it is, my friend, it is," Reuben affirmed, opening his arms to Damhan. "I was healed not long ago by Jesus who is the Christ anticipated by my people."

With a glad cry Damhan rushed into the embrace, crushing the air from Reuben's lungs. Not caring who saw, the Dumnonii spun him off his feet, whirled him about.

Setting Reuben down, Damhan pushed him to arm's reach. "I shall thrash Gwydion for not warning me," the Dumnonii threatened, but he was smiling. He drew a quick awed breath, said joyfully, "You must tell me all."

Reuben dispatched a servant to lead Damhan's companions to the kitchens where they could dine. Then, while he and Damham walked, Reuben told of Simon of Cyrene who took Gwyr's place and became his legs. He spoke also of Jesus and the healing on the road to Calvary, his personal witness to Joseph. All that happened following the Christ's death, burial, and resurrection.

"And he lives, this god?" Damhan countered, not quite convinced. "You have seen him?"

"The Son of God," Reuben corrected. "Not only seen Him, but I have touched Him, and because of Him, I walk. He lives, Damhan. On my life, He lives."

"Having carried you when you were lame," the Dumnonii said. "Having rubbed salve onto your twisted legs when you could not do it for yourself, I say you almost persuade me to believe in this Jesus."

Reuben ushered the Dumnonii into his work chamber, waved him to cushions near a window. When they reclined, Reuben said, "I am glad to see you, my friend. It does my heart good. But you are far from Britannia. Why come to Judea?"

3

"To pay homage to a prophet," Damhan answered with all sincerity and a knowing smile Reuben was at a loss to interpret. "Had we not heeded your counsel, the Dumnonii would have been almost destitute."

Baffled, Reuben shook his head. "I do not understand?"

"When the Tribes held the moot on building tin furnaces near the shore," Damhan explained, "you said to me, 'My lord, if you build them here and the sea rises, you will lose the coin you invest.'" He glanced aside at Reuben. "Do you remember that moment and those words?"

Reuben nodded. "Of course I do. You praised my insight and gave me the arm ring."

Damhan grinned. "You gave sage counsel. This year the sea has come to *Karrek Loos y'n Koos.*"

Reuben blinked his surprise. He pictured the high hill, *Karrek Loos y'n Koos.* 'The gray rock in the wood' was almost half the height of *Ynys Wydryn*, 'the Isle of Glass,' which the tribesmen council gave to Joseph of Arimathea. A lush green meadow and old forest surrounded 'the gray rock in the wood.' The small tor had been almost two leagues from the seashore where Gwydion beached *Judah's Hope.* "Surely you jest...?"

"I do not," Damhan said profoundly. "The earth shifted and rolled and sank, allowing the Great Sea to surge inward and claim the land almost to *Margas Jew*, your Roman port of Ictis. What once was dry land now is submerged twice a day with the rise and fall of the tides. All but *Karrek Loos y'n Koos.* It becomes an island at high tide."

Leaning against a cushion, the Dumnonii seemed greatly amused at his friend's discomfiture. "The meadow where we would have constructed the new tin forges is a morass, a tidal swamp. Had we built where we first intended, our four Tribes, the Dumnonii, the Dobunni, the Durotrigues, and the Belgiae, would have lost all we invested in the forges, been beggared, and become prey to our enemies."

Reuben started to protest, but Damhan lifted a restraining hand. "There is more," he said, barely able to restrain his mirth. "My people and the other Tribes have taken to calling you '*the Lame Prophet.*' Bardds sing the praises of '*the broken man touched by the gods.*' The man I see now, they do not know how right they are."

"Damhan——" Reuben glared at the chieftain. "Do not jest on my account."

The Dumnonii shrugged. "What will you do?" he challenged. "Kill the messenger?"

With a grimace, Reuben protested, "I am no prophet."

Damhan sat up. "Did you not predict winds to bring your fleet home when your shipsmaster believed there would be none? Did you not tell him when to change course without the aid of charts? You who had been almost deranged from the loss of your beloved Gwyr."

Reuben pursed his lips. "Gwydion talks too much." He shook his head. "What must I do about these tales?"

"What all men of renown do," the Dumnonii replied without humor. "Accept your fame. Live with it."

Damhan's smile quickly returned. "And I see your legend only growing greater when the four Tribes discover a living god has healed your legs."

Growing increasingly uncomfortable and frustrated, Reuben wrung his hands, echoed, "What must I do?"

Damhan rested his palms on his thighs. "Truth or not, in the eyes of my people, they hold you up as '*a Holy One.*' Naught can change that. When they craft songs about Gwyr, they also sing of his companion, the Lame Prophet."

Reuben's face changed instantly. "What of Gwyr?"

"I do not know," Damhan said honestly. "I know the Atrebates' tales. Because Gwyr killed silently, they branded him a scion of the underworld. When the Iceni slew every one of the armored warriors, he turned on the archers. They put three arrows in him but, one by one, he still ran down those brave enough to face him. The few who remained alive fled, left the *tor* in a single boat. When last they saw him, he roamed the shore wildly waving his swords."

"What happened to him afterward?" Reuben pressed. "I must know."

"While I carried you and Joseph safely away, my people returned in force to the *tor*," Damhan said quietly. "They found the bodies of my retainers amid the corpses of the Atrebates' dead. Gwyr was not among them. At first some believed he was mortally wounded. That he collapsed into the dark waters surrounding the *tor* where the weight of his armor pulled him down, never to be found again."

Damhan paused, but Reuben could tell from the Dumnonii's face there was more. "They believed the waters claimed him," he said softly, "until they found a blood trail leading to the *tor's* summit. At its highest point my people found his battered helmet and those beautiful twin swords in their scabbards."

He shook his head. "There was no body. No blood trail leading down, no trail whatever. There was just no Gwyr. He had vanished."

Damhan sighed. "Some say the gods took him up. Others believe he stepped from the summit into the underworld from whence he came." He shrugged. "More tales spread that he is sleeping, recovering from his wounds, regaining his strength. That one day he will return when the Dumnonii and the other Tribes most need him."

Reuben saw unashamed tears in Damhan's eyes. His own eyes were wet.

"What is the truth? I can not say," the Dumnonii admitted. "I have the witness of my own eyes that he fought like a god, that none who faced him lived. Even though he urged us away, I bear guilt that I fled when he stayed and fought to grant us life."

Silence answered the chieftain. Sill Reuben knew the tale was still not done, so he waited patiently.

"The Atrebates will not set foot on the *tor*," Damhan said at last. "They fear it. They fear to draw the silent demon back to wreak havoc in their own lands. Other Tribes outside our Council have taken up the tale, and now only the Druids and their students, and those who come from afar to learn their ways, walk the *tor's* summit, slopes, and shores or brave the dark tidal waters surrounding it."

Damhan spread his hands in a gesture indicating it was outside his ability to control. "They draw students from every Tribe across

Britannia. The Arch Druid Bran the Blessed oversees their instruction, but even he gives way to Arawn Doelguss, the Lady of the Lake."

"Quintus Marcellus Gota said you gave her Gwyr's long sword," Reuben said. "Why did you?"

"She also claimed Gwyr's short swords," Damhan explained. "She says she holds them against his return." His eyes sought Reuben's. "The bardds forget he is Iceni; none of their tales claim his Tribe. In time, perhaps, when the tales are told and retold, all of the Tribes will embrace him as their own."

Reuben chewed his lip, followed the trail of his own thoughts. "What is she like, the Lady of the Lake?"

A chuckle answered his question. "Oh no, my friend. No tale I could tell, no picture I could paint with words, would do the Lady justice. For that answer, you must come again to Britannia and to *Ynys Wydryn, 'the Isle of Glass.'*"

CHAPTER 2

In Jerusalem, the day was gray with wind-blown dust and grit from the wild storms across the east desert. Through the winding streets, intermittent whirlwinds swirled in the manmade canyons formed between buildings and homes. Pilgrims in the city for the Jewish harvest festival of *Shavuot* had long since departed, but many who celebrated the Pentecost remained. While they drew joy from one another, the Jews watched them and debated.

In the home of a mutual friend, beyond suspicious and prying eyes, Joseph of Arimathea sat with Gamaliel ben Simeon, a brother Pharisee and leader of the Sanhedrin, a close companion of many years.

"Soon I shall leave Judea," Joseph told Gamaliel, "for Britannia. I am called by God to those shores."

"I mourn your going, old friend," Gamaliel said with a heavy heart. "There are so few who know me well, with whom I can be myself."

"I would think," Joseph began with a smile, "that the greatest teacher in all the annals of Judaism would have so many about his feet that he would be unable to walk from here to there."

"And my face so brightly shines," Gamaliel retorted snidely, "that I am unable to see my reflection in a bowl of water because of the glare."

They both laughed, then Gamaliel added soberly, "Beware of fame, my brother. It is a burden I heartily dislike."

Joseph nodded. "While I do not have your renown, there are many who look to me thusly."

"And who would not?" Gamaliel objected. "Look at you: a Pharisee of Pharisees, a Roman citizen and a *Nobilis Decurio*, a Minister of Mines for the Roman Empire, with direct access to the Governor himself. More, a rich merchant with the resources of a vast commercial empire."

A faint smile played across Joseph's features. "We both have outlived our humility."

Trembling with suppressed laughter, Gamaliel fought to catch his breath. Then he nodded to Joseph, "I could not have said it better."

Then Joseph sobered. "But I have become more," he added humbly. "I am a follower of Jesus the Messiah."

Gamaliel's face grew stormy. "I dispute that Jesus ben Joseph is the Messiah, that he who was crucified is alive."

"When over five hundred of our people in Jerusalem have seen Him, I among them?" Joseph countered. "When our Jewish courts recognize two witnesses' statements as fact, when even you have ruled in the Law that it takes but one witness to verify a woman's husband is dead?"

"You dispute the Law," Gamaliel retorted, "turn it against faith in God."

Joseph stared at him in open question. "Is not God the author of the Law through Moses?"

For long moments Gamaliel stared at his friend. "Are you now rabbi and scribe to challenge what the Law is and what it is not?"

"Someone must challenge the interpretations of the Law for the sake of the Son of Man," Joseph challenged. "For the sake of the Law, I was imprisoned by the high priest simply for doing a kinsman's duty and begging for Jesus' body, laying Him in my own tomb before the Sabbath."

Gamaliel shook his head. "I had no part in that," he attested. "But I will tell you truly, your escape from a locked and sealed cell in the Temple certainly left tongues wagging and set those in power accusing one another of complicity in the act."

"Where do we go from here, you and I?" Joseph asked earnestly. "Do we now become enemies?"

"We do not," Gamaliel affirmed. "Although I cannot bring myself to abandon my faith and accept your Jesus as Messiah, I will not oppose your practice of that faith."

For heartbeats the Sanhedrin leader hesitated. "More, I must warn you about one of my students. Saul of Tarsus, a young Pharisee, a Roman citizen like yourself, does not share my moderate views. He is full of zeal for the Lord's work and already voices his opposition to the Temple leaders concerning the followers of the Nazarene."

He gestured with a pointed finger. "You beware of him, Joseph. There are those within the Temple who would use him as an instrument of their retribution."

Joseph nodded his acceptance of the warning. "You do not share his beliefs?"

"If your Jesus is from God, our best efforts will not prevail." He grimaced. "But others are not so lenient. Beware of Saul; he is your enemy and enemy of all who share your faith. For the moment he is only a firebrand, but if the Temple recruits him, he will become dangerous, even to you in spite of your highly placed Roman favor."

"I will remain watchful, my friend," Joseph assured him. He smiled warmly and pushed to his feet. "And I shall depart by the alleyway to confuse anyone who is watching whom the leader of the Sanhedrin meets."

Gamaliel rose also, embraced his brother Pharisee. "Peace be with you!"

"And with you," Joseph responded. "I shall remember our laughter."

"Remember my warnings most of all," Gamamiel cautioned. "If they seize you again, departure from a cell might not be forthcoming."

Joseph smiled in spite of the tension, remembering it was Jesus who spirited him away from the cell in the Temple, who took him through walls, and set him in his own bed. Returning to the moment, he told Gamaliel in all faith, "I am in the Messiah's hands."

The Sanhedrin leader only shook his head. "I will not debate you again," he stated. Giving Joseph a kiss of peace, he shooed him away with a benediction, "Go with God."

Joseph found Simon where he almost expected. "Reuben sent you," he accused. "Can I go nowhere alone?"

Simon shrugged. "You appointed him my Master," he reminded the Pharisee. "He says '*go*,' and I go; '*come*,' and I come, '*guard him*,' and I guard. I am just a faithful and obedient bond-servant."

"Most certainly an infuriating one," Joseph murmured, intending for the Cyrenian to overhear. Simon only nodded his head differentially, allowed the Pharisee to lead, then followed an obedient and watchful three-steps behind.

At the Arimathea estate, Joseph placed himself in Reuben's doorway, arms crossed at the chest. When his minister looked up, the Pharisee stated matter-of-factly, "I need no nurse-maid."

Without pause, Reuben nodded his head respectfully, said in return, "Then, Master, since you know the dangers, stop behaving like a willful, disobedient child."

Lifting an eyebrow at his minister's response, "You take your role most seriously."

Again Reuben did not pause. "When you made me Second, I asked you why? You answered, 'Who would care more about my interests than you?'"

Perplexed, Joseph threw up his hands. "What am I to do? My own words come back to haunt me."

Assuming a half-smile, he strode forward, stood before Reuben's table. "I should feel blessed," he said in a neutral voice. "Your reputation as an able administrator grows, along with your fame. I salute '*the Lame Prophet*.'"

"Damhan talks too much," Reuben grumbled, returning his eyes to the neat rows of figures, ignoring his master.

Joseph covered his mouth with his hand, chuckled softly behind it. Then he sobered. "Gamaliel sent me with a warning. He believes the Temple will employ one of his own students against the followers of the Christ. A young firebrand named Saul of Tarsus."

Reuben looked up, nodded. "I recognize the name from your agents' reports. But they did not warn he had trained under the Rabban, the leader of the Sanhedrin."

"Send word immediately to the Apostles about Saul of Tarsus," Joseph ordered, "and then to the Seventy. Let them warn the other followers of the Messiah that the Temple plans to move aggressively against us soon."

Joseph turned to leave, paused and turned back before he reached the door. "Oh, since this crisis looms——" He stared back, making sure he had Reuben's attention. He let the tension and the young man's curiosity build almost to a breaking point. "I do not intend to leave for Britannia right away."

Then, a satisfied smile on his lips, the Pharisee slipped away before his startled minister could catch his wind and reply.

Full night with no moon blanketed Jerusalem in darkness. Reuben studied reports from the Arimathea agents both in the Temple and in Fortress Antonio. Now that Quintus Lucius Carus had retired from the Roman army, Reuben's reports were less reliable, but sufficient for his needs.

Hoping to pressure Jesus into claiming the throne of David, the Zealots took advantage of the turmoil within the city and revolted. Under Judas of Galilee's orders, Zealot militia sealed the roads in and out of Jerusalem and the perimeter of the city as well. Loyalists, armed with weapons and armor supplied by Joseph of Arimathea, tried to storm Fortress Antonia and the garrison barracks, only to be beaten back with great losses.

The Zealots' success had teetered on Jesus using his supporters in Jerusalem to seize control of the Temple complex and the Roman barracks. But the Son of Man staged no revolt; He began healing and teaching instead. Without the thousands of supporters the Zealots expected, without the Essenes joining them, the Romans quickly crushed the Zealots within the city and ended their rebellion.

Reuben sighed. Fortunately for his master, Judas the Galilean and

Zadok the Pharisee escaped the Roman net and fled into the hills. Zealots who were captured and tortured had no knowledge their weapons came from Joseph of Arimathea's storehouses. Without the Zealot leaders to implicate him, there was no link back to Joseph.

But it had been a near disaster. One by one Reuben emptied and closed the secret warehouses, channeling the remaining hidden arms and armor into regular lines of supply for the Roman army in Judea, salvaging what coin he could. In the end, Joseph lost a small fortune, but nothing that normal Arimathea revenues would not replenish over time.

Reuben rang the table bell, a holdover from his time with Simon, but it served his needs to summon his servants.

When the man came, Reuben pointed to the stack of incriminating parchment on his table. "Get Simon. Take him with you," he ordered. "Burn every last piece. When it is done, you are to stir the embers until all is ash." He met the man's eyes, silently impressing upon him the importance of his compliance. "Do you understand my orders?"

"Yes, young Master," the man nodded. "We are not to leave the fire untended until all is ash."

"Then go," he waved the man away. "Make it so."

Reuben rose, went to the cushions, slumped down weary to the bone. It had been a Herculean effort, hiding his master's complicity in the revolt. Now Judas and Zadok were the only links to Joseph's involvement, and Reuben could not bring himself to have them killed. His new faith would not permit it. So the worry of exposure remained.

He stared out into deep darkness that the lamps could not penetrate. Saul of Tarsus had thwarted his plans for Joseph to be safely on the way to Britannia, and for a time out to the Romans' reach.

Now I must live in dread of his secret eventually coming to light, Reuben thought dejectedly. He forced his body to relax, his eyelids drooped and he slept.

Even in his dreams he found little peace. Even there, a nameless dread pursued him. And he ran forever....

CHAPTER 3

Jerusalem, with Herod's Temple as its gem, boasted the magnificence of the Herodian age. Herod the Great devoted himself to developing and beautifying the city, building walls, towers and palaces. He expanded the Temple Mount, buttressing the courtyard with huge blocks of stone and doubling the area of the Temple. After his death, his sons continued Herod's building, but they lacked their father's dreams and grand design.

When the inner city expanded, so did the outer city. That seedy "Jerusalem outside Jerusalem" became home to the less fortunate, the poor, and the destitute. A shadow world based on slavery, bondage, poverty, and cruelty, it existed to support its Roman rulers, the Temple hierarchy, the Jewish elite, and those who basked in Rome's favor.

Like all cities, rats infested the poorer warrens. But these were not common four-footed rodents. They were the real power in Outer Jerusalem, the shadow rulers, *"the wolves within the sheep."*

Prominent among the princes of shadow was the Brotherhood of Faceless Men. Common cause, loyalty and a covenant of strong oaths bound the Brotherhood into an iron chain linking the shadow realm to its more prosperous counterpart. Trading information for coin, members of the Order infiltrated all areas of Jerusalem and Roman society, and few secrets escaped their notice. Chief among the Brotherhood elite were those with even stronger ties to the House of Arimathea.

"Find me a house near the Temple," Reuben asked of his faceless agent, "a house with secluded entrances that allows one to easily come and go without scrutiny." Arimathea's minister paused. "Is there such a place?"

His man nodded. "I know several that suit. The one best suited is derelict because its title of ownership is disputed. Its walls conceal tunnels joining it to dwellings on other streets. Because of this feature, it is reserved for the Brotherhood," he grinned wryly, "and Arimathea."

Reuben nodded his satisfaction. "You shall convey my instructions to your brothers." He gazed resolutely at the agent. "But I want it known in advance, no harm must come to my visitor."

"It shall be as you say," he responded. "Now, how may I serve you?"

On the following morn, on a street leading to the Temple, shadow men erupted from an alleyway, draped canvass over a pilgrim's head to muffle his cries, and bore him into their shadow world. In time they wrestled him with great care into an isolated room and departed silently. Finding the knots on his bindings loosely tied, he wriggled free and jerked the imprisoning fabric from his head.

"Are you uninjured, Saul of Tarsus?" Reuben asked from his perch across the room. He reclined on cushions set on a low dais, a cripple's shawl wrapped about his drawn-up legs. "I instructed them to deal with you gently."

Greatly angered, Saul glared wildly about. "Who are you?" he demanded. "Why have you abducted me?"

"You were invited here so we could converse in private," Reuben explained. "As to my identity, for now that shall remain my secret."

Saul shook his fists. "I shall see you flogged!"

Reuben met his tirade with silence. By degrees Saul's temper ebbed, and he surveyed the room more calmly. Perhaps ten strides away, a hallway loomed.

"It leads to a door, which opens onto a well-traveled street. Not far beyond that is the Temple," Reuben advised him. "You are free to go at any time." He gestured at the linen leg shawl. "How could I stop you?"

"If I choose to leave?" he questioned. "What then?"

"You leave. No one will hinder you," Reuben told him. "But when you return with Temple guards, I will be gone." He made no attempt to evade Saul's eyes. "It will be as if this never happened, and you will forfeit all chance of learning why you are here?"

"Why have you abducted me?" Saul repeated, but there was curiosity in his tone. Curiosity and interest.

"Surely Gamaliel's student can pose a better question."

Saul frowned. "You named me, and you named me the Rabban's student, so you know me——?"

"Know *of* you," Reuben countered. "To my knowledge, our paths have never crossed."

A hint of recognition flickered in Saul's eyes. "You are the one Gamaliel quotes often. His Lame Student!"

Reuben nodded humbly. "I am honored he remembers me."

"I could ask him——" he challenged anew, "who you are."

"You could ask him, but I have my doubts that he would break the integrity of his vows before God," Reuben chided, "even for you, a favored student."

Saul paused, eyes narrowed in thought. "You spoke of talking privately. Why?"

"I would know your thoughts," Reuben responded truthfully, "and you know mine. Tell me, since the Scriptures say because of Adam all men sin and fall short of the glory of God, how was Abraham justified righteous in the eyes of God?"

Saul smiled and responded quickly, "Abraham believed in the Lord and He reckoned it to him as righteousness."

"And circumcision?" Reuben pressed.

"It is an outward sign of an inner commitment," Saul again answered quickly, "a commitment of faith asked of His Chosen people, the seed of Abraham."

Reuben changed tactics. "What is the purpose of the Law of Moses?"

Saul pursed his lips. "The Law was given to Moses that man might be convicted of his sin. And it is incumbent on man to obey the Law."

"Does obeying the Law absolve a man of his sins," Reuben

questioned, "and make a man righteous before the Lord? Can any man earn the righteousness of God through good works?"

When Saul hesitated, Reuben challenged him again. "What did Abraham find with regard to the manner in which God justifies a person. Was it by faith or by works?"

Again Reuben pressed, "Our people boast in the Law. But through the breaking of the Law, do they not dishonor God? Do they not condemn themselves?"

Reuben shook his head. "If keeping the Law condemns us, since no man is perfect, the Law itself condemns us. In the Law there can be no justification in the eyes of God for man, except through faith in Him."

Reuben extended his arms, palms open. "Abraham was reckoned justified by God because of his faith, not his works, that he could boast."

Saul remained silent, considering what he had heard and formulating his rebuttal. But Reuben gave him no opportunity.

"Did not Jeremiah write these words...?"

> "*Behold the days are coming,' declares the Lord, 'when I will make a new covenant with the house of Israel and the house of Judah, not like the covenant which I made with their fathers when I took them by the hand to bring them out of the land of Egypt, My covenant which they broke, although I was husband to them,' declares the Lord.*"

Reuben drew a deep breath. "And the prophet Ezekiel. Does he not say of the Lord...?

> '*I shall give you a new heart and put a new spirit within you; and I will remove the heart of stone from your flesh and give you a heart of flesh.*'"

Again Saul hesitated. Reuben did not. "There has long been the hope among our people for the coming Messiah," he said. "A great number looked to Jesus ben Joseph as the fulfillment of that hope, the Messiah who would redeem Israel. But many of our people are foolish men and slow of heart to believe all that the prophets have spoken."

With that, Reuben began to explain all that he had learned and been taught at the knee of Gamaliel ben Simeon and Joseph of Arimathea, although he forebear mentioning his own master by name. Beginning with Moses and with all the prophets he described at length the things concerning the Son of Man contained in all the Scriptures. He spoke also of all that he had discerned from being with the Son of Man and what he had heard of His message to the people.

Reuben described as well the healing in His hands: the deaf receiving their hearing, the blind seeing, the lame walking, the lepers cleansed, the demons cast out.

"Was it not necessary for the Christ to suffer these things and to enter into His glory?" Reuben asked Saul. He knew from eyewitness accounts that the Christ had spoken so to a few of His followers on the road to Emmaus.

"Each year as you know," he told Saul, "at *Yom Kipper* the high priest goes into the Holy of Holies in the Temple to sprinkle blood on the altar in atonement for the sins of our people. But only one perfect sacrifice can restore man's righteousness before the Lord God. One perfect substitute. One unblemished lamb."

Clasping his hands on the blanket covering his legs, Reuben sighed. "Our people looked for a sign that *He* was the One. He gave it to us. We have it. He came and bled and died, and I tell you, if that was the end, I would agree with any argument you would attempt."

He shook his head with a joyous smile. "But it was not the end. On the third day God Almighty raised *Him* from the dead. That *He* lives is the Messiah's sign to an unbelieving nation that all *He* said was true."

"I hear your words," Saul said at last. "They are masterfully crafted. I even concede your correlation of prophecy in Scripture. What I do not accept is your broad application of those prophecies to Jesus ben Joseph's life and death. If he is alive as you say, show him to me."

"I cannot," Reuben countered. "*He* was with us forty days after *His* resurrection, then *He* ascended to *His* Father where *He* sits at the right hand of God."

"You speak blasphemy!" Saul exclaimed and pushed to his feet. "I will not listen to any more of this blasphemy."

Reuben heard denial in the Pharisee's words, but it was denial without passion. "Or is it that you will not listen because you fear to hear and accept the truth?"

"You offer a scholarly argument," Saul conceded, "but that is all it is. You have no evidence to offer. No proof. So I must reject this case you make."

"No proof?" Reuben retorted. "I had to be carried north to Capernaum to hear The Christ. *He* charged me then to be *His* witness and stand for the truth."

Reuben's voice rose, grew more animated. "But how could I do that? All the days of my life, my legs were twisted. Gamaliel bears witness to that, for even you acknowledge him speaking of his Lame Student."

With a firm hand Reuben pulled the linen leg wrap away, uncovered his legs. Then he stood up. He watched shock register in Saul's eyes, on his face.

"On the road to *His* crucifixion, Jesus ben Joseph, the Son of Man, the Messiah, fell," Reuben said passionately. "I was there. I crawled to *Him*, tried to lift the cross. But I could not. I was a cripple. The Romans kicked me aside, put another to that task. But *His* shed blood matted in my hair, soaked into my clothes, and ran across my twisted legs."

Reuben's palms rested against healthy thighs. "*Here is my proof.* Jesus Christ's blood healed my twisted legs. I climbed from the gutter and followed *Him* that day on two good legs to that place of death. Where they drove nails through *His* hands, *His* feet. Hung *Him* from a cross."

19

Saul stood rigid, barely breathing, unable to move, unable to stem Reuben's testimony.

"I was in the garden after *His* resurrection," Reuben pressed. "*He* appeared to me, embraced me, charged me again to be *His* witness. And Saul of Tarsus, I stand before you now as *His* witness."

In a voice of calm authority, Reuben spoke the words that came into his heart, "Verily, verily, I say to you, the day will come when you, Saul of Tarsus, will no longer deny *Him* before men."

Reuben's declaration freed Saul of his immobility. With a choked cry, he turned and ran from the house.

A short time later, the young Pharisee returned, showed Temple guards the house. They searched every room, but they found no one. Just a bare wooden cross leaning against a wall and a linen leg cloth draped across its base

Chapter 4

Days passed into weeks and the undercurrent of tension within Jerusalem seethed with praise of the risen Christ on one hand, charges and denials on the other. Peter and John and others preached and taught about Jesus the Messiah. And the numbers who believed in *Him* grew.

After they healed a sick man, Peter and John were seized by the Council. Aware the Apostles were uneducated and untrained, the Council marveled at their confidence. Seeing the healed man standing among those with the Apostles, knowing he was over forty years old, the members of the Council hesitated. Knowledge of the miracle was spreading. Fearful that denying the healing took place would make them look foolish, the elders of the Temple and the members of the Sanhedrin released Peter and John with commands and warnings not to speak or teach in the Nazarene's name.

But Peter and John answered them. "Whether it is right in the sight of God to give heed to you rather than to God, you be the judge, for we cannot stop speaking what we have seen and heard."

Finding no basis on which to charge them, the elders released the two. Reuben was among those who saw and heard the story and rejoiced with Jesus' followers.

But the unrest continued. Word came from the Faceless Men that Reuben's old teacher reminded the Council of other Messiah pretenders, Theudas and Judas the Galilean from the days of the census whose claims came to naught.

"He advised those in Council not to execute Peter and the Apostles despite their insistence on publicly preaching about Christ," the agent reported.

"Then he said——" the Faceless Man told them, "'Leave these men alone! Let them go! For if their purpose or activity is of human origin, it will fail. But if it is from God, you will not be able to stop these men; you will only find yourselves fighting against God.'"

Was Saul there to hear Gamaliel? Reuben wondered. He prayed so. Reuben often pondered whether he had done the right thing challenging Saul with the good news——or if it only added fuel to a fire burning out of control.

Reuben asked anxiously, "Did the members of the Council heed Gamaliel's advice?"

"So great was his authority, they listened, then acted affirmatively," the agent acknowledged. "For the moment they will not hinder the Apostles and the preaching of the good news."

During the time of turmoil between the expanding number of Christ-followers and the resistant Jewish leadership, Josephus, Joseph's son in Rome, wrote that demands for refined lead ingots had increased dramatically. Building projects both in the capital and along the Roman boot called for great quantities of lead piping, and the demand severely depleted the inventory of lead Arimathea maintained in its mainland warehouses.

Reuben quickly dispatched a fast mule rider to Joppa, urging Gwydion to send their newly completed reserve fleet of five new ocean-going ore ships to Rome with the existing lead inventory Joppa had on hand. Once in Rome, the fleet would reprovision and continue on to Britannia for new cargoes of lead ingots.

After he wrote the order and dispatched the rider, new fears plagued Reuben. Commissioning new ships meant more men must be found and trained to crew them. That carried its own host of problems. He questioned placing men of untried loyalty aboard the new Arimathea vessels. In his heart he feared the secrets of their fast ships would be betrayed to others. Realistically, it was only a matter of time before that occurred. Yet with increased market demands, he saw no other option. In the final analysis, he could only trust Gwydion's judgment in selecting the needed crewmen. So far his shipsmaster showed an uncanny talent in selecting reliable men.

Intent on his worries, Reuben missed the subtle sounds of sandals whispering across stone tiles that normally alerted him that someone approached. A voice from the doorway shocked him, but he recovered quickly. Joseph took a childish delight in catching him woolgathering.

"The Twelve summoned the congregation of the disciples," the Pharisee proclaimed, "and they have named the seven men who will minister to the widows."

When Reuben looked up from his reports, the Pharisee was almost breathless with excitement. "They chose Stephen, a man full of faith and of the Holy Spirit," he continued, "and with him, Philip, Prochorus, Nicanor, Timon, Parmenass, and Nicolas, a proselyte from Antioch."

Reuben knew of Stephen. The man was full of grace and already performing great signs and wonders among the people. In faith, Arimathea's minister rejoiced, but he knew from the Faceless Men, the Council no longer heeded Gamaliel's advice about the Apostles and the increasing numbers of Christ's disciples. He knew, too, from the reports that Saul was growing more animated in his attacks against Jesus' followers, urging swift retribution.

Have I fanned the ember that will spark a raging fire against us? he agonized. But hindsight offered no more warning or consolation than before.

He shrugged. *What is done is done,* he affirmed, and he prayed earnestly for Christ's wisdom before he acted rashly in the future as he had done with Saul.

"Boy, are you listening?" Joseph prodded. "Have you learned so much that you turn deaf ears to me?"

Reuben exhaled, focused on Joseph. "No, Master." He shook his head. "If I live to be as old as you, I will never be that knowledgeable."

Joseph crossed his arms in a semblance of pout, picked up a

rolled-up scroll, tapped it repeatedly against his palm. "Do I go away, or do you wish to hear what I remember of the Apostles' words to the congregation?"

Reuben put a sly smile on his face. "Does that mean you actually give me a choice?"

With a sharp exhale, Joseph swung the cylinder like a sword. Reuben blinked and ducked quickly, but the roll still caught his *mitre* and knocked it harmlessly from his head. It slid across the table and toppled to the floor.

"Young ingrate," Joseph growled. "Find out for yourself from others if you want to know so badly."

At the door the Pharisee turned, a wily grin stretching his lips wide. "I surprised you," he challenged. "You did not expect an old man to react so fast. Next time be wiser; stand farther away if you choose to be insolent."

Damhan Mawr left Judea with the fleet Gwydion sent to Rome and Britannia rather than wait for a return trip with the tin ore ships. Reuben found he deeply missed the Dumnonii's quick wit and ready smile.

More and more he realized how much he longed to return to that barbaric northern isle. Britannia's harsh rocky southern shoreline, its precipitous crags and sudden hills, its verdant dappled greens all had an unfinished quality, as if God Almighty paused in His labors and had not yet returned to finish them.

Reuben chuckled as a stray thought whispered through his mind. *When we landed in Britannia I hated the strange odors, the moist pungent smells so foreign to our dryer Judean climate. But they grew on me.*

More and more he was drawn to Joseph's garden, where the fresh earthiness of the carefully tended mounds, the fragrance of the flowers, reminded him of other times. *Almost another life,* he mused.

Judea would always be home, he knew that. But in a way he could not explain, so would Britannia. Joseph would go before him, he accepted that. But he would follow.

"Whither thou goest, I will go," he murmured softly. He thought of the Scriptures, of Ruth and Naomi. Joseph had found him, unwanted and a cripple outcast, and given him everything. Without Joseph of Arimathea he would never have known Gwyr, Gamaliel and the Law, or Jesus ben Joseph who gave him healed legs and the gift of salvation. If Joseph had not come and claimed him, he would have died in the gutter where he begged alms——a Jew without God, forever lost for he would not have known the Christ, been healed, or witnessed for Him.

"Where you go, I will go," he told the absent Joseph. "Where you lodge, I will lodge. Your people shall be my people, and your God, my God."

Reuben rose, walked to the window, an act he still found a miracle. Looking across the estate, he quoted more of Ruth's words to Naomi and made each one a promise to Joseph. "'Where you die, I will die, and there I will be buried. Thus may the Lord do to me, and worse, if anything but death parts you and me.'"

When disaster struck, it came swiftly. Incited by opponents of Stephen, the elders and the scribes had their men seize him, drag him before the Council where they falsely charged the outspoken follower of Christ with speaking blasphemous words against Moses and God.

A runner from the Faceless Men found Reuben preparing to leave for Joppa where he planned to join Joseph and Broch Gorm of Thule at the Arimathea shipyard north of the city. All thoughts of the journey gone, Reuben sent the runner back to the Brotherhood asking that a number of their men join him near the building where the Sanhedrin met.

Quickly he changed into more humble clothing, and fearing Saul of Tarsus would recognize him, he added a pilgrim's *mitre* and head shawl. Then he was away, hurrying through the streets with no thought of what he could accomplish when he reached the place where they held Stephen.

I am relieved Joseph is away, he thought as he threaded his way between people on the street. Had his master been in Jerusalem, he would have intervened in Stephen's behalf, and they both would be arrested.

To Reuben's horror, he came in time to see a frenzied mob driving Stephen through the streets. They were not going to imprison the Christ-follower; they intended to stone him! Before he could act, the Faceless Men joined him, but they refused to attack the crowd, intervene and try to rescue Stephen.

"This is not a battle we can win," they told him. When he ignored them, hands restrained him, kept him from hurling himself against the Jews. "They go to execute him," the Faceless Men argued desperately. "Would you have them stone you and us as well?"

Even when they reached the place chosen for execution, the Faceless Men still held Reuben's arms, fearful he was determined to throw his life away. But he did not struggle.

Reuben watched when the witnesses laid their robes at the feet of a young Pharisee. The young man's head turned, and Reuben knew it was Saul of Tarsus.

Stones flew, a few then a barrage. Cuts appeared on Stephen's face as he lifted his arms, called upon the Lord. "Lord Jesus, receive my spirit!"

A stone, larger than the rest, struck his forehead. Drove him to his knees. Even then he raised his hands, cried out in a loud voice, "Lord, do not hold this sin against them!"

More stones struck him. Reuben clinched his fists in horror as he watched. Then his eyes widened. Stones still struck, but a radiant smile transformed Stephen's face into a vision of wonder. As if an inner light could no longer be contained within his flesh and must be freed.

Stones rained down harder. He reached out with blooded hands, lowered himself to the earth, drew his legs up to his chest, and fell asleep. Incited by his lack of fear, his quiet acceptance of his fate, the Jews continued their stoning long after death had come.

They did not take his life, Reuben marveled. *Stephen gave it up willingly.* His eyes widened. *Like the Christ*!

Hands that held him through the execution hurried him away along alleys and backstreets while the mob dispersed. Reuben did not resist. His mind had seized on two images, and they remained etched in his memory for all time. One was the glare of anticipation twisting Saul's countenance when he awaited Stephen's death. The other, the steadfast faith and grace transforming the martyr's face into an ethereal beauty that blood and suffering could not mar.

CHAPTER 5

A fist hammered at a barred door in lower Jerusalem. When no one came to open it, Saul stepped back, ordered the Temple guards, "Break it down."

Putting their shoulders behind the axe blows, the guards quickly split the planks, splintered the locking bar, and three of Saul's retainers stormed inside. A woman's strident scream greeted their invasion. Then came muted impacts of fists striking flesh. Moments later, two guards hauled out a bruised and battered husband. Another dragged the half-conscious wife from the house by her hair.

Saul studied their faces without compassion. He knew them. They were on his list of known disciples of the Nazarene.

"Rope them together," he ordered the guards. He pointed across the alley. "We still have many more to arrest before dusk."

Will they find disciples in the next house? Saul wondered. After Stephen's death, when the Temple-authorized persecutions began, many of Jesus ben Joseph's followers had scattered into the towns and hills of Judea, Galilee, and Samaria. Saul knew the Apostles remained in the city, but they were elusive. Finding them was proving much more difficult than he anticipated.

Worse, the Council grew increasingly irate as the exiles preached and spread their lies about their Messiah wherever they found refuge. Worried it was becoming an epidemic, the Council and the Temple elders pressured him to set it all aright.

Joseph had returned to Jerusalem and was with the Apostles when word came that Samaria was a field ripe for harvest. Accordingly, the Apostles chose Peter and John to take the good news to Samaria. Joseph and Reuben were with them that night, meeting in secret to avoid Saul's guards.

When all that needed to be said was said, and they departed, made their way back to the estate, Reuben spoke his concerns. His master nodded.

"You need not fear," Joseph said. "God has called me to Britannia. And I shall heed His call. I lingered here only long enough to be with the Apostles and His followers through this persecution, to help where I could."

Reuben did not chide his master. It would do little good. The Pharisee's mind was set. But day and night Reuben worried that Saul would descend on the Arimathea estate and drag them all to prison.

"I have made no secret of my calling," the Pharisee said. "Some wish to go with me. With this persecution, there will be others. I will take all who desire to go."

Relief flooded Reuben. His master would be away and safe. He could ask no more.

"In spite of the responsibilities I have given you," Joseph began, "I know you will follow me." He smiled. "Do what God calls you to do, my Son. In all things you carry my hopes and prayers for you——and my blessing."

Joseph's words hit him like a blow. He could not breathe. Staring at his master, tears welled in his eyes. How could he doubt Joseph would not have guessed his intentions?

"First you must go where I send you," Joseph told him. "When you return, you can set Arimathea affairs in order and follow me. I know you have trained Daniel and others for that express purpose."

Sighing, Reuben nodded. He should have guessed Joseph would suspect that phase of his plans. He sighed. "Where do you send me, master?"

"To Damascus."

Reuben's throat constructed. Raw fear ripped at his heart like a wild beast. "Damascus, Master?" he echoed in a hollow voice. "You send me to Damascus?"

Joseph looked at Reuben strangely. "There are matters there that must be handled before you can follow me. Either I must go, or you go in my stead."

Time seemed to slow around Reuben, but the pace of his thoughts did not. On his table lay an urgent missive from the Faceless Men. Saul of Tarsus had gone to the high priest, requesting letters to the synagogues in Damascus. He desired the high priest's authorization to allow him to seize the followers of Jesus who fled to Damascus and drag them back to Jerusalem.

In his mind Joseph's request carried a death sentence. But the Pharisee's intent was plain. *Either I must go, or you go in my stead.*

Reuben sighed. Time flowed normally again, and Joseph watched him. He bowed his head in submission. "I will go."

Refusing to yield to the dread haunting his thoughts, Reuben prepared for his journey to Damascus. Unlike previous journeys, he planned to go overland on white mules, crossing the Jordan River and going north by way of Pella, routes that he knew. Reuben charged the Faceless Men, who served him, with the selection of his bodyguards. He asked only that their choices be trained warriors and not squeamish if they must fight Jews.

On the day before they would depart, Luke of Arimathea strode boldly into Reuben's bedchamber. His hair was longer, tied at the nape of his neck, graying at the temples and the chin of the short beard he wore. But there was no mistaking the carriage of his shoulders. He may somewhat resemble the Jews he lived among, but beneath the skin he was Tribune Quintus Lucius Carus of the Roman Army.

"Did you think to go without me?" he demanded, his tone and eyes accusing. "Because I follow the Christ does not mean I have forgotten how to use a sword."

Reuben looked down. "I could not ask that of you."

"You did not ask," Luke retorted. "Joseph did. He did not understand your hesitation until he learned the chief priest was sending Saul to Damascus."

Reuben's shoulders slumped. He felt fissures sunder the inner dam he had raised against his guilt and his fear for Joseph more than for himself. Suddenly he felt lost, adrift, the man he thought he was——lay in ruins.

Luke watched the young man he had come to love wilt before his eyes. In heartbeats he crossed the room, gathered Reuben to him in a sheltering embrace, and simply held him.

"Did you think you were Atlas?" the Roman chided softly. "Even the strongest and bravest men are beset by fears. You must face those fears, accept them for what they are and what they are not. Let them flow past you like water curling past the bow of a ship. The sea is stronger than a ship, but a ship sails the sea."

"I caused the persecution," Reuben choked out. "I brought Saul to me, witnessed to him——" The tale came out, all of it, including his fears for Joseph and the pressures he faced as Minister of Arimathea.

Luke listened, amazed that one so young shouldered so much. He truly *was* a young Atlas.

"You witnessing to Saul did not make him the religious fanatic that he is," Luke told him honestly. "And the persecutions of Jesus' followers would have come whether you confronted him or not. In purest terms, the Temple leaders and the elders could not condone losing control over so many people. It threatened their rule."

He exhaled sharply. "What surprises me is that Annas and Caiaphas delayed launching the persecutions. No battlefield commander would have waited. Indecision before the enemy shows weakness."

Reuben rested his forehead against Luke's shoulder. "In facing my fears, I must accept that I am a coward——"

Luke pushed him forcefully to arm's length, shook him. "*Coward?*" he blustered. "How can you think that?"

"I quail at facing Saul," Reuben answered dejectedly. "Of falling into his hands."

"Any sane man would," Luke countered. "But you made a choice. In spite of your fears, you go to Damascus, a substitute for Joseph so he will not be seized. That you go says much. Did not our own Master tell us, '*Greater love hath no man than to lay down his life for a friend?*'"

Reuben frowned. He thought longingly of Gwyr, who fought and died so he and Joseph might live. Beside that sacrifice, he was nothing. "You make me sound childish."

Luke stared at him. "I have not lied to you," he said levelly. "I do not lie now. You may doubt yourself, but you are a stronger, braver man than any I know."

He dropped his hands. "Now gather your sundries. We face a long dusty road to Damascus."

Reuben found riding astride his white mule a new and unsettling experience. He no longer perched atop the mule's back in a padded pannier, his twisted legs strapped to one side, a wicker backrest supporting him. Now, with no ties to hold his legs to the saddle, he struggled to gain a new sense of balance to the mule's gait.

Luke laughed at his efforts, and judging how he looked, Reuben laughed with him. But he persevered and adjusted. Aside from aching thighs, Reuben decided he liked riding astride better than enduring the pannier.

After the first day's gentle ride for Reuben's sake, Luke pushed the pace. By best estimates, Saul was days ahead, but the Pharisee was spurred only by his zeal. A sense of urgency, of danger drove them to greater efforts. To their advantage, the Temple kept no compounds along the Damascus road where messengers would obtain fresh mules.

Reuben smiled, his master's words whispering through his mind. *Speed brings greater profits.* Joseph established and maintained his commercial empire on that foundation: remount stations, faster, more seaworthy ships, superior intelligence. *And Saul has no reason to suspect I chase closely at his heels.*

Their escort, ten Faceless Men, made no complaints at the pace. Instead, they embraced the hardship, almost seemed to welcome it. They were hard men who wore their weapons openly on the road. Men who knew how to use them, had used them, and would again without the slightest provocation.

Each eve, even when they sheltered in roadside inns, the Faceless Men rotated guards outside the chamber Reuben shared with Luke. When he chided them for it, they informed him tersely he was under the protection of the Brotherhood. Before they dishonored their Order and let him be taken, they would die in his defense. Afterward, he slept soundly.

Under Luke's watchful eye, they rode in Roman cavalry formation, two scouts a league ahead of the main column. The lead pair would spur ahead, assess the trail and at intervals one would report back. While he rested his mount with the slower companions, another would spur ahead and join the point rider.

From Jerusalem's high arid plateau, they descended to the green fertile fields of Jericho, forded the river near Bethabara called Bethany-on-the-Jordan, then rode along its eastern bank northward toward Pella. They passed near where John the Baptist witnessed to multitudes who came to hear him preach. John was dead, beheaded at the command of Herod to please Herodias. Reuben realized that was only three years ago; it seemed a lifetime.

Along the Jordan's banks, the dense growth showed a verdant green, and wild oleander which grew thick along the winding course. It bathed the valley in brilliant color, and its fragrance was almost overpowering.

Midway between Bethabara and Pella, the Jabbok River barred their path. It was the dry season; the river was low. When they arrived, the scouts had already located the ford, and they passed on.

On the Jordan's west bank lay Mount Tabor. Reuben suspected Saul came north through Samaria, then turned east below Scythopolis, descended the hills, and crossed the Jordan before swinging north through the Decapolis.

When they reached the Baqaa Valley, Luke pointed ahead. "These slopes are the source for grain for the surrounding Roman provinces all the way to the sea," he explained. "At the northern end shepherds tend their flocks on the less fertile soil."

He turned in the saddle to Reuben. "We must carry our water when we descend into the trackless waste between the mountains and Damascus. We will find no water there."

They passed two nights in the Baqaa Valley before they climbed over the mountains. At dawn they crested the high pass and began the descent down the stark eastern slopes. In the distance, the Syrian desert sun was rising.

Reuben stared at the rock-strewn slopes with some surprise. Even in the early morn, there were no animal cries, no bird calls. Except for the sounds of their mules' hooves against the trail, there was only silence. He stared ahead. They must cross forty leagues of hot barren waste and sand. He knew also when the sun sank below the mountains, they would face one cold night encampment.

Late on the second day in the barrens, they rode east of a range of low, terra cotta-colored hills. To the far west lay the soaring snow-capped peak of Mount Hermon. Ahead to the northwest lay Damascus.

"Master, it is about six leagues away," the Brotherhood guide told Reuben. "Too far for tired mules. With your permission, we will make camp soon."

Reuben nodded. He was bone-weary. That night there was no fuel for a fire; they chewed smoked lamb before bedding down. When Reuben slept, he did not dream.

By mid-morn, Damascus was still two leagues distant, when the lead rider, one of the Faceless Men, hissed a warning, held up his hand, pointed toward the city.

"A rider," he called softly, "coming swiftly." Others of the Brotherhood quickly fanned into a defensive wall ahead of Reuben and Luke before the point man signaled all was well and shouted, "One of our own rides toward us."

He came fast, the Damascus rider, sliding his mule to a halt before them in a cascade of small rocks. Surveying the column, his eyes quickly fixed on Reuben, and he guided his mount through the group.

"Young Master——" he began, "my elders sent me to warn you Saul of Tarsus has already reached the city."

Reuben suppressed a shudder, nodded. But something in the man's expression, his manner tweaked Reuben's curiosity. "Have you more news for me?"

"Yes, young Master," the man responded. "Saul of Tarsus is blind!"

CHAPTER 6

Reuben slept fitfully. Finally he left his pallet, stood at the window, looked from the Arimathea compound out over night-shrouded Damascus. Even in this pre-dawn time, the murmur of '*the city that never sleeps*' reached him as a blended cacophony, the heartbeat of a large and thriving commercial center. Its veins were the streets and the bazaars, its trade lifeblood.

Like Pella, Damascus belonged to the Decapolis, a league of ten self-governing cities in the Roman province of Syria and the area east of the River Jordan. Annexed by Rome ninety years ago, Damascus was a caravan city, a crossroads of converging trade routes linking the Roman empire and the House of Arimathea with southern Arabia, Palmyra, Petra, and the silk market roads of the Far East.

Eight hard days in the saddle had toughened Reuben's thighs and the Syrian sun had baked his skin. Yet he found no solace in reaching Damascus. His fears of seizure and prison dissolved with the Faceless Man's breathless report that Saul of Tarsus was blind. Yet a strange disquiet manifested to fill the void. It gave him no peace.

Finally the eastern horizon began to gray, and soon Damascus' rooftops were gilded red-gold by the rising sun.

"How long have you been up?" Luke asked behind Reuben.

Shrugging dejectedly, he answered, "Much of the night."

Luke rose, stretched, came to stand at Reuben's shoulder, staring out at the city. "What troubles you?"

"I know it is not wise," Reuben began, "but I must go to see Saul."

A stern hand on his shoulder forced Reuben to turn and face his companion. "In God's name, why?"

"If I knew," Reuben retorted sharper than he intended, "I would not have lost a night's slumber." He sighed. "Something will not let me rest until I do."

Luke exhaled sharply. "This is madness, and foolhardy as well. But if it is to be done, I will not let you go alone. You know that."

Reuben nodded, met the older man's eyes with a sheepish smile. "You are my blessing and my curse."

A chuckle answered him. "And you best remember that."

Not long after, when they departed the Arimathea compound, the Faceless Men shepherded them through the warren of bazaars and winding narrow backstreets. On a street called '*Straight*,' the Brotherhood guide brought them to its western end, to the house of a man called Judas.

"The man you seek is inside," his guide told Reuben. "It is said he has sent his guards away."

"How long has he been blind?"

"Two days, young Master, so we are told," the Faceless man answered. "Shall we enter with you?"

Reuben shook his head. "I will take only Luke inside with me. Wait in the street. I will call if I have need."

"As you say," the man bowed, "so it shall be."

At the door Reuben rapped gently on the wood, and moments later it swung open. A man in Jewish linens stood within, his eyes questioning.

"I seek——" Reuben said quickly, "Saul of Tarsus."

The man bowed respectfully. "He is inside. Come." He led Reuben and Luke to a back room, gestured within. "You will find him there."

From a nest of cushions Saul of Tarsus turned sightless eyes toward the footsteps. "Who is there?"

He was garbed simply in unbleached linen. No Pharisee shawl or *talis* draped his head or neck, and his hair was unkept, tangled. In spite of all the persecutions, Reuben found he pitied the young Pharisee.

"I warned you," Reuben said in sudden inspiration, "I would not be in the house when you returned."

Saul cocked his head perplexedly, then he brightened. "I know that voice! The Lame Student——who is no longer lame." He exhaled deeply. "You were right. Our Master Gamaliel would not give you up."

Reuben stepped into the room, and Luke followed.

"I hear two sets of footsteps," Saul announced. "Someone comes with you."

"You hear true," Reuben confirmed. "I did not venture here alone."

"With all I have been, and all I have done, I do not fault you your caution," the Pharisee said. "But I would do you no harm even if I could see."

Saul rested his hands on his thighs. "Do you remember your last words to me?" he asked. "I recall every one, '*Verily, verily, I say to you, the day will come when you, Saul of Tarsus, will no longer deny Him before men.*'"

Reuben nodded. "I remember."

"Then hear me," Saul answered. "Jesus ben Joseph is the Chosen One, the Messiah, the Christ!"

"Do you mock me?" Reuben protested. "I——"

"May it never be!" Saul broke in anxiously. "No, hear me! I affirm for all time that Jesus ben Joseph is indeed the Chosen One, the Messiah, the Christ!"

From the corner where he stationed himself to guard Reuben, Luke demanded, "Tell us why you do this."

Saul tracked him by his voice. "You speak Aramaic like a Roman," he said, "but I mean that as no rebuke." Turning his head back and forth to address them both, he answered, "Why do I now proclaim Jesus is the Christ? Because I have *seen* the living Christ. He appeared to me on the road outside Damascus. It is because of *Him* that I am blind."

Reuben let out his breath in a rush. He had not realized he had been holding it. Glancing at Luke, he saw the Roman shrug, his eyes full of questions.

"We could just see Damascus from the hilltop," Saul hurried on, "when a light brighter than the sun flashed about me. I fell to the ground, and a voice said in Aramaic—— *'Saul, Saul, why do you persecute Me?'*"

Saul paused, caught his breath. "The men with me saw the light and heard the sound, but understood nothing of the words. I knew without doubt it was the Almighty One who spoke for the voice named me twice, *'Saul, Saul——'* as He did with Abraham, Jacob, and Moses."

Wringing his hands, he continued. "You must understand I did not see myself as persecuting God. I believed with all my being that I served God, that I was defending His way. I called out, 'Who are you, Lord?' and He answered, *'I am Jesus whom you are persecuting——'*"

In a strangled voice, Saul admitted, "I knew then that by persecuting Jesus' followers, I was rejecting the Messiah *Himself,* that those I persecuted were the body of which Jesus is the head. That I had been blinded by all I believed, and in truth the risen Messiah stood before me."

Shocked silence greeted the Pharisee's revelation. But Saul was not through. "*He told me, 'Rise, and enter the city, and it shall be told you what you must do.'*"

Saul tilted his sightless eyes upward. "When I got up, my eyes were open, but then as now I see nothing. I had to be led into the city." Again his face moved between the men. "Have you come to tell me what I must do?"

"I am not the one who will be sent," Reuben said. He glanced at Luke, who shook his head. "Nor is my companion."

"How long must I wait?" Saul asked, and Reuben heard the anxiety in his tone. "Is this blindness my eternal punishment for persecuting *Him*?"

"You press questions we cannot answer," Reuben replied for both himself and Luke.

"Then I must expect another?" Saul waited but neither of his visitors answered. "If you did not come to tell me what to do, why did you come?"

Reuben hesitated. How did he ask if his confrontation and witness caused Saul to persecute Jesus' followers? Yet he could not voice the question.

"My companion is burdened," Luke began. "He would know if his witness to you about the Christ drove you to seize and persecute those who follow *Him*?"

Saul's shoulders slumped. "You believed you brought this grief?" He shook his head agitatedly. "No, No, rest your heart. Your witness was not the cause."

He spread his hands wide in a gesture of regret. "Your words greatly confused me," Saul told him. "But my life, my studies with Gamaliel and the Temple leaders, forged and tempered my zeal to defend what I had been taught and understood from Scripture against what I believed were confused heretics. When the high priest laid this task on me, I wanted to be faithful, to be a Gideon, a Joshua, a David."

Saul grimaced, bowed his head. "If anything, your witness delayed the beginning of that persecution."

A great weight lifted from Reuben. He felt a rush of compassion for the tortured man before him. "You have taken the sword out of my heart," he told Saul. "I wish I could ease the grief I feel in you."

A smile softened Saul's pained countenance. "I believe you, but I would not ask another to shoulder what by rights I now must carry. I fast and pray, asking for guidance on what He has assigned for me to do."

Reuben rose, and with him, Luke. "Then we shall leave you to your meditations."

"May peace be with you," Saul said in parting. "May *His* blessing be upon you——and God grant we meet again."

"His peace to you as well," Reuben answered. "And as sure as the sun rises, we will meet again."

Outside, Luke stopped Reuben. "As surely as I breathe, his blindness is no sham. Saul of Tarsus has indeed been touched by the Christ." Then he frowned. "But after all that he has done, will the Apostles accept him? And what of the others, those he persecuted?"

"Thankfully that is not for us to decide," Reuben answered. From the shadows they gathered the Faceless Men about them and went to do Joseph's bidding.

After Reuben carefully rolled and sealed in oiled-skin parchment against their departure, Luke joined him.

"It is the talk of Damascus!" the Roman exclaimed. At Reuben's blank look, he quickly added, "Saul of Tarsus has regained his sight. In the synagogues he proclaims Jesus the Christ is the Son of God."

Reuben stared open-mouthed at Luke. He did not doubt the Roman's words. Considering the news, he chuckled at the shock reverberating through the Damascus Jews.

"Luke, I must——"

"See him," the Roman finished for him. He too laughed. "I anticipated your thoughts. The Faceless Men await us."

They found Saul where the Brotherhood directed them, outside a synagogue, preaching and reasoning with a group of Jews. The Faceless Men left them, seemed to melt into those thronging the nearby bazaars, unobtrusive but nearby.

Soon Saul broke away from the Jews, came directly to them. "I recognized you," he told Reuben when he joined them. "And you, my Roman friend, I think I would have known you by your military bearing."

It was obvious Saul once again could see so Reuben forebear mentioning it. "You are much revived," he said instead, "and true to your word."

"A day after you, another came," Saul said. "His name is Ananias, a Jewish believer. He had a vision which directed him to Judas' house, to find a man who was praying. He was afraid to come, because I persecuted the Christ's own, but Ananias said the Lord told him— —'*Go, for he is a chosen instrument of Mine, to bear My name before the Gentiles and kings and the sons of Israel.*'"

Saul frowned, but strangely Reuben saw joy in the expression. "He told Ananias to tell me also, '*For I will show him how much he must suffer for My name's sake.*'"

When the crowd thickened, Saul motioned them to the side. "Ananias came and laid his hands on me, saying, 'Brother Saul, the Lord Jesus, who appeared to you on the road by which you were coming, has sent me so that you may regain your sight, and be filled with the Holy Spirit.'

"And immediately there fell from my eyes something like scales, and I regained my sight. I rose, was baptized in the manner of the Christ, took food, and was strengthened."

This time Saul smiled, and it transformed his face. "Rejoice with me, my friends. *He* has given me my calling!"

Chapter 7

For many days Saul preached in Damascus, increasing in strength and confounding the Jews who lived in the city by proving that Jesus is the Christ. But Reuben and Luke were not among them. The day after meeting with Saul near the synagogue, they departed the city for Jerusalem.

With remounts drawn from the Arimathea stations, they made an uneventful eleven-day journey to Jerusalem. But when they reached Bethabara, Bethany-on-the-Jordan, a Faceless Man awaited them.

"The School of *Shammai* has coerced the Council to expel all non-Hebrew Jews from Jerusalem," he informed Reuben. "As a result, many of the Christ's followers also have left the city. Your master has directed you to avoid Jerusalem and go to his estate outside the city walls, where he has transferred all the records for the House of Arimathea."

Reuben knew the *Shamma*i history. Gamaliel had spoken of it often. *Shammai*, a rabbi, founded his school before the birth of Jesus ben Joseph. Strictest of the rabbinic schools, it was composed of extreme fundamentalists, and stressed obsessive devotion to obeying hosts of man-made traditions and commandments. Believing Hebrew descendants of Abraham were the only people beloved of God, they taught no other people were of value in His sight. The *Shammaiites* would not welcome Gentile converts to Judaism, because in their belief, salvation was available only to Jews.

Judging Luke, a Roman, a former army officer, would be exempt from the *Shammai* ruling, Reuben still complied with his master's wish and swung wide around the city walls. Late on the second day after receiving Joseph's message, they approached the estate. Reuben slumped in the saddle. He was weary. They had been away almost a month.

Their master knew of their coming and met them at the gate. "Jerusalem is on a knife's edge," he told them as servants washed their feet. "The Governor has placed the garrison on alert." Then he urged them inside.

"Because his threats hold Annas and Caiaphas in check, Pilate grows more bold," Joseph told them. "There is more. Our ears in Fortress Antonia and in the Council tells us more unrest brews. So I have determined it is time to transfer most of our house functions beyond Judea."

Reuben found other followers of the Christ at the estate. Lazarus, whom Jesus loved and raised from the dead, along with his sisters Mary and Martha, and their maid Marcella, and others had taken refuge with Joseph.

"After the chief priests took council that they would put Lazarus to death, I took and hid him and his sisters," Joseph told Reuben. "There are others whom you know here as well. My niece, Mary, the mother of the Christ, and Mary Magdalene as well. Given the ire of the chief priests, none of them are safe in Judea. Surely that danger will grow worse once I depart. I have taken council with each one, and they all will go with me when I leave for Britannia."

Having just returned, Reuben was both relieved and saddened. More and more he feared for his master. "Have you decided when you go?"

"Soon," his master replied. "It must be soon. The persecutions make life here uncertain for His believers. With the strife between Pontius Pilate and the high priest, I fear open warfare may erupt in the streets, and Rome will not tolerate another major revolt here. That is certain."

"What of the Apostles?" Reuben asked. "Will they remain in Jerusalem."

"I have counseled them against it," the Pharisee said, "but I cannot sway them from their course. For the moment Peter and John remain in Samaria with Philip. The other nine are in the city, preaching and teaching at their peril. The *Shammai* edict does not affect the Sons of Abraham, but I fear the chief priests soon will charge and arrest them."

Concerned, Reuben pressed his master. "When we leave Judea, where will we establish the House of Arimathea? In Rome perhaps?"

"The Port of Ostia, possibly," Joseph mused. "Yet the foot of the Roman boot is much too near the Emperor and his jealous eye for my comfort. We are a vastly wealthy commercial house, far wealthier than the House of Quintus Marcellus Gota, which Tiberius destroyed after he seized its wealth and properties to fund the continued construction of his monuments and temples."

"You must choose soon," Reuben reminded him. "We need time to notify our overseas factors and secure new lines of communication. Also, we have ships in transit that follow old courses and procedures. All that must be altered. Since our holdings are so vast, it will not happen quickly."

"What do you advise, my Son?" the Pharisee asked.

"Colonia Julia Carthago," Reuben said immediately. "It is the center of the Roman province of Africa Nova, the second largest city in the western half of the Roman Empire, and a major breadbasket of the Empire. It boasts a fine port for our ships, shoreline for Broch Gorm to establish his new shipbuilding yard, and we already have extensive properties within and without the city."

Joseph nodded. "Well thought. I shall consider it."

So it was pondered; so it was planned; so it was done.

With the assistance of Broch Gorm and Gwydion, and the fast ships crafted by the Thulean, the House of Arimathea moved its heart from Judea to Carthago. A half-league south of the city, on a suitable shore Broch Gorm established his new shipbuilding site. Joseph still retained the estate within Jerusalem and the larger one beyond the walls, but most of the buildings became cargo storage for the Judean and Damascus markets.

Knowing they faced an uncertain future, Reuben made arrangements for chosen ones of the Faceless Men to accompany him, men of great talent and ability who masqueraded as new house servants. Secretly they trained him in their arts. In time, through Reuben's witness, they too followed the Christ, and the Minister of Arimathea purchased their life-long services from the Brotherhood at great price so they became loyal to him alone.

Months passed while Reuben, Daniel, and the Arimathea scribes plunged into restructuring the House trade and supply routes. When they disembarked, Rome was still rebuilding Carthago according to the emperor's grand design. Housing blocks were separated on a grid of straight clay streets twelve cubits wide. On the top of Bursa Hill, the Romans built the forum, with the hippodrome and amphitheater to the southwest.

Arimathea ships began supplying building materials needed from distant ports. From the Celtiberians, Gauls, and Celts, they also obtained amber, tin, silver, and furs. Roman Sardinia and Kyrnos produced gold and silver, and Latin settlements on islands such as Melita and the Mallorca and its sister isles crafted luxuries highly prized from Ostia to Rome. From Carthago, Arimathea ships carried pottery and ornaments in gold as well as silver, iron weapons, and tin ingots to ports all along the Known Sea and traded in goods of every kind including spices from Arabia, Africa and India.

House caravans drove deep into the African interior and into Persia. Arimathea factors traded finished goods and grains to the coastal and interior peoples of Africa for a wealth of salt, gold, timber, ivory, ebony, apes, peacocks, skins, and hides.

Slavers also routed their human wares through Carthago, and many came to its markets to buy slaves. But Reuben and the other scribes did not. They honored Joseph's mandate and refused to buy, sell, or transport slaves in any of its ships or caravans.

In time Joseph and those who looked toward Britannia became restless, and Reuben knew their patience would soon end. He had already alerted Gwydion to prepare a ship to sail northward when he received a message from Judea. Leaving his work, he sought his master, found him with Lazarus and his sisters in the solarium.

Joseph stared at him from the moment he entered. "Out with it, boy," he encouraged. "What has happened?"

"A Samaritan prophet who claimed to be Moses reincarnate gathered an armed following," Reuben told him. "Pilate chose to intervene immediately with a thousand soldiers, dispersed the crowd, then had the prophet and the ringleaders executed as he did with Jesus."

He grimaced. "Believing Pilate's violence was excessive, the Samaritans appealed to Lucius Vitellius, the Syrian Governor. As a result Pilate has been relieved as procurator and is recalled to Rome. Vitellius then appointed a man named Marcellus to replace Pilate."

For a moment, no one spoke. Then Joseph sighed. "I expected more turmoil in Judea," he said. "Pilate was a man of inflexible, stubborn and cruel disposition. But he was predictable. We could anticipate his actions."

He sighed. "But Marcellus' character is unknown. He easily could be Vitellius' puppet. What is worse, no one knows how he will react." The Pharisee sadly shook his head. "Now that we are established here, the House of Arimathea will not suffer unduly, but I greatly fear for Jerusalem and Judea in the days to come...."

When the appointed day for departure approached, Joseph called Reuben to him. "We knew this time would come, my Son," the Pharisee said heavily, regret in his voice. "Without it being said, we both knew I would go ahead to Britannia, and you would follow when the Lord intended. But that does not make this parting any easier."

"When I started making my plans," Reuben answered, "I did not expect or understand I must first put our house in order before I followed in your steps."

Joseph smiled. "I cannot say how much it warms my heart to hear you claim it as *our* house."

"Your house is all the home I have ever known," Reuben answered. "I did not begin to live until you claimed me."

The Pharisee dropped his eyes, ran a rough-veined hand over his face to hide misting eyes. His heart ached; rather than speak of it, he said instead, "I leave Gwydion and *Judah's Hope* here to do your bidding. Use him as you need."

Reuben nodded. "As you have said before."

Joseph looked away. "I am too old to start over in Britannia," he complained. "I have begun my sixth decade, and it is time for a warm fire and a rug to cover my legs."

"For another perhaps, not for you," Reuben answered plainly. "When you had your stroke and Jesus healed you, He told me He had given you the strength of Joshua and Caleb when they entered the Promised Land." Reuben grinned. "After forty years in the wilderness, they were old men——older even than you."

The Pharisee shook a fist at Reuben's jibe. "You best be careful mocking me," he warned. "Remember the last time you were insolent."

Reuben opened his mouth to bait Joseph, tweak his ire, but chose instead to be more tactful. "I will have to send someone aboard ship to keep you nimble."

"And I shall toss him overboard," Joseph warned. "One of you is enough!" Then he put aside his banter. "I shall watch for your coming, my Son, with a new cloak and a fatted calf ready for a feast."

"I will delay only as long as the Lord intends, my Master," Reuben assured him. "And then I shall come swiftly."

Joseph sailed the following day aboard *Judah's Tears*. With him as planned went Lazarus, his sisters, Martha and Mary, their maid Marcella, and the disciple Maximin. In secret, the Pharisee carried the treasure Peter and John brought him by night, the olive wood box that contained the cup. Reuben stood on the quay long after the ship had passed from sight. The words, his promise to Joseph, came unbidden to his lips——

"'Where you go, I will go,'" he repeated. "'Where you lodge, I will lodge. Your people shall be my people, and your God, my God.'"

Reuben whispered where only God and the Christ could hear, but he meant every word. "Where you die, I will die, and there I will be buried. Thus may the Lord do to me, and worse, if anything but death parts you and me."

Chapter 8

The emperor is dead; long live the Emperor.

Dawn came like the day previous. But there the similarity ended. Rome's political foundations shook as word of Tiberius Caesar's death reached the provinces. The monumental shift in power reverberated across the empire with world-changing results. Old alliances were dead; new ones hastily formed, and the world waited with bated breath.

Tiberius drew his final breath in Misenum, a port city on the Roman Coast in the Jewish month of Iyar, forty or so days after Passover. Some time afterward Reuben learned that Caligula, the emperor's adopted grandson and Praetorian Prefect Quintus Naevius Sutorius Macro smothered the out-of-favor emperor, whom Pliny the Elder called "the gloomiest of men." In his will, the emperor left power jointly to his true-born son, Tiberius Gemellus, and Gaius Julius Caesar Augustus Germanicus, his adopted grandson, who was better known by his agnomen, his nickname——'Caligula,' meaning 'Little Soldier's Boot,' earned when he accompanied his father on military campaigns.

On becoming *Princeps*, Caligula quickly assumed power, voided Tiberius' will, and executed his foster-brother, Tiberius Gemellus. Tiberius, one of the greatest Roman generals, was cremated, his ashes quietly laid to rest in the Mausoleum of Augustus.

In the wave of swiftly changing alliances, Reuben knew Josephus, his master's son, would not be threatened. Before his departure for Britannia, Joseph resigned his position, and had Josephus confirmed in his place as *Nobilis Decurio*. Named Minister of the Roman mines in Britannia, he managed the lead and tin mining regions in southern and western Britannia, which was vital to the Roman economy. His position also carried provincial Roman senator status.

Word also had come from Judea as well that Saul would soon be coming to Jerusalem to confer with the other Apostles. Reuben learned as well that Peter and John had rejoined their brethren. In spite of the chief priests and the Sanhedrin's prohibition about preaching and teaching Jesus' name, they persevered. More, in spite of the persecution, the Jerusalem church continued to grow.

Daniel, under Joseph's and Reuben's tutelage, fulfilled his early promise and had become an able administrator after they reached Carthago. Reuben turned his responsibility and duties over to his second and sailed to Joppa under Gwydion aboard *Judah's Hope*. Refusing to be left behind, Luke journeyed with him.

With Gwydion's skill, they quickly made the voyage to Judea, and on to Jerusalem. At the estate, Reuben studied commercial accounts. Luke did not stay. Instead he entered the city and renewed old friendships in Fortress Antonia.

Late one eve he returned, sought Reuben. "Pontius Pilate is dead," he told his young friend. "Word came that he was out of favor with Tiberius for his treatment of Herod Agrippa. Then his supporters and his friends deserted him."

Luke shook his head. "No one here in Judea knows for certain if he fell on his sword or took poison, but I find either tale hard to believe. He may have been in desperate straits, but Pontius Pilate was not the sort to take his own life. In his mind, committing suicide would concede victory to his enemies, and that he would not do."

His jaw hardened. "Pilate warned Caiaphas he had hired assassins to avenge him if he was removed or killed. Not long after Pilate's death, Caiaphas was found dead."

Reuben nodded. He suspected assassins in both cases, but short of resurrection, they would never know the truth.

"The Apostles are coming to the Master's estate here in Jerusalem," he told Luke. "I have been in contact with Barnabas. Saul has been trying to make contact with Peter and the other Apostles, but they are much in fear of him because of the past and the death of Stephen. They do not believe he is a disciple."

"That will change when they meet him and hear his testimony," Luke answered. Then, abandoning his normal stoic posture, he pressed, "When are they expected?"

"Dusk tomorrow," Reuben replied, then his face clouded. "We barely have enough servants to receive them."

"God will take it in hand," Luke assured him, and Reuben marveled at the Roman's steadfast faith, his commitment to the Christ.

When dusk approached, so did the Apostles, and Saul with Barnabas. Luke stood aside with Reuben in a corner of the common room, listening while the Apostles questioned Saul at length.

Saul showed no apprehension or dismay. He freely answered all that was asked of him. Describing how he had seen the Lord on the road. How Jesus had called to him. His face radiated truth as he told of his realization that Jesus was indeed the Christ, how his eyes were blinded until Ananias came to give him back his sight.

"Since that day I have spoken out boldly in the name of Jesus," Saul insisted, "as any who have heard me will affirm."

His eyes centered on Reuben and Luke beside him, and he pointed at them. "These two, standing within this room, heard me outside a Damascus synagogue, proclaiming the living Christ and teaching in His name. Speak, my brothers. Tell them what you heard."

"It is as he said," Luke said boldly. "He was preaching and teaching about the living Christ."

"What say you, Reuben?" Peter demanded. "I do not doubt Brother Luke's words, but I would hear from you."

With a firm nod, Reuben began, "I heard Saul's story from his own lips when he was yet blind. He told it boldly, not knowing to whom he spoke, and there was no shading of the truth in that telling."

He saw Saul's expression when Peter called him by name. It was just as well. He had intended to reveal his identity to Saul in any event before the night was through.

"There is more if you will hear it," Reuben told them. He watched faces turn, regard him intently. Even Saul's.

"I have had Saul closely watched," he reported. "All his actions give evidence that what he tells you is no tapestry of lies. Test him however you must, but I tell you truly, the *Holy Spirit* lives in him."

They brought Saul to the center, laid hands on him, and prayed. Watching them, Reuben's throat constructed. He knew he viewed something holy. Something memorable. Something that would galvanize the spreading of the good news in new and far reaching ways. When the thought ran through his mind, he felt humbled beyond measure for he knew he had played a minor part.

A whisper from his mind brought tears flooding his eyes. A voice he knew, a voice he loved and hungered to hear, spoke plainly in his thoughts.

When you were a beggar in the streets I knew you, Jesus said. *Because you believed in Me and in Him who sent Me, you were healed to be My witness. You shall indeed be My witness, and stand for the truth both in Judea and beyond.*

Caught in the moment, Reuben turned away from Luke, from the others. He knew after Pentecost, the *Holy Spirit* came to dwell in believers, but it still almost overpowered him when that *Spirit* manifested within him.

A gentle hand on his shoulder brought him back to the moment. "You are Reuben ben Ezra," Saul said from behind him, "Minister to the House of Arimathea."

When Reuben turned to face the Apostle, he nodded. "Peter told me who you were," Saul acknowledged. "It is no wonder then that you trained under Gamaliel."

"It remains a wonder to me," Reuben answered. "I was born Thomas the Lame to a harlot in the Jerusalem streets. A cripple with no future. If not for Joseph of Arimathea and the goodness of his heart, I would have died there. He made me what I am."

Saul stared at him intently, wonderingly. "Your words do your Master honor, and deservedly so, because he provided you with every opportunity to succeed. But your will, your drive, and your intelligence made you succeed. And, my brother——" He reached out and once more grasped Reuben's shoulder. "Those attributes are God-given. Father God had a plan for you, and He sent you to point me to the Christ."

He shook his head. "No, Reuben ben Ezra, in every way you answered *His* call and prepared yourself, before you even knew *He* was calling. We share that in common."

Drawing him into a tight embrace, Saul held him. A deep sense of comfort flooded Reuben. In some small ways the two of them were much alike. Like two coins. But Reuben suffered no illusions. He knew he was cheap bronze where Saul was gold.

"God keep us both," he murmured, knowing Saul would hear and understand. "God keep us both."

"He will," Saul reassured him. "He told me He would show me how much I must suffer for *His* name's sake. Something tells me we both will...."

Great winds racked the upper sky, herding huge dappled masses of charcoal gray clouds from the south. At random, blinding silver curtains of rain swept across the white-capped sea. *Judah's Tears* wallowed uncertainly in the high swells. Sail and mast and rack of oars had been torn away by gale force winds that swept out from Africa with little warning beyond a stiffening breeze. Wounded and barely seaworthy, *Judah's Tears* was slave to wind and currents.

Joseph grieved for the men who had been lost. Five crewmen who fought to save the ship had been swept overboard along with Maelgeyn, Broch Gorm's youngest son and *Judah's Tears'* captain. The refugees from the high priests' persecution had been spared because they had been ordered beneath the forward covered deck to escape the storm's fury.

Bracing himself against the pitching ship, the Pharisee tried to concentrate on Elvan the Quiet's words.

"Your friends must work with us to bail water from our bilge or we shall surely sink," Elvan shouted to make him understand against the howling wind. "There are too few crewmen left. The women must work alongside the men."

Slowly Joseph nodded. *We are not promised tomorrow,* he thought morosely, *but Lord, You make it doubly hard for those who only seek to do Your will.*

He sighed and turned his thoughts to the crewmen and their plight. "Where are we?"

"Until I can take star readings, I do not know," Elvan answered honestly. "The storm must have blown us off course, but how far? Until I see the stars, I cannot say."

Most of those beneath the deck were ill. Judeans all, they had never been to sea and the storm-sired seasickness had left them heaving.

How I escaped that plight, I cannot say? Joseph pondered. Perhaps it had been his experience at sea, but he had never endured anything like this storm. *A lesser boat than Broch Gorm's would not have survived that gale.*

With six men lost, they had sufficient food and water to last weeks. Joseph knew Maelgeyn had been running north and west to position *Judah's Tears* for a northern run through the Pillars of Hercules. Spawned from the desert region below Abyla, the storm's wind-wave had a distinct northeasterly bearing. Joseph tried to picture the sea chart. Hispania lay due west. The western shores of the Iberian boot were to the east, and to the north, Transalpine Gaul and the port city of Massilia.

Would the storm have carried the ship that far north? he wondered. But the howling winds gave no answer.

Another rain squall swept over the wounded vessel, and Joseph ducked beneath the bow decking to escape the downpour. First he roused his friend, the Roman Quintus Marcellus Gota. Then, one by one, he woke the weary folk: Lazarus, Maximin, Trophimus, and the rest on the men. Then came Mary and Martha, their maid Marcella, Salome, and Mary Magdalene. His niece Mary he chose not to wake.

With all she had suffered, the voyage already had been a trial for her, so he let her get what sleep she could.

Throughout the long afternoon, with hand bailers, buckets, pots, anything with a bottom, they scooped up the accumulated water, passed it to others who tossed it over the side. With approaching darkness Elvan waved them from their duty with heartfelt thanks. He sent them off to eat what their sick stomachs could hold down. Exhausted, they slept where they found room.

Elvan fought back a weary yawn. He could not sleep. Not yet. Not until he studied the stars and determined their position. He yawned again, fought the lure of sleep.

"Rise quickly," he called to the guiding stars. "For the love of Christ, rise quickly."

CHAPTER 9

Reuben woke in the night, sweat drenched. Desperation laced his dream, lingered into wakefulness. He came to full consciousness with his dagger clutched in his fist. Fearful someone had invaded his chamber, he searched every corner, every shadow. But he found nothing.

He shook his head, struggling to dispel the clawing remnants of the dream. But the tension, the disquiet, refused to fade into unreality like most dreams. This terrible feeling would not leave, would not ease. He knew then something was dreadfully wrong!

Again and again his thoughts flew to Joseph, to *Judah's Tears*, to Broch Gorm's youngest son, Maelgeyn, who captained the new vessel. Maelgeyn was a veteran of many Britannia crossings, a fine seaman and gifted navigator, but this voyage was his first as captain.

Reuben closed his eyes, pictured Maelgeyn's ready smile. But the horrifying image that lanced unbidden into his mind was a man adrift, struggling to breathe amid stormy waves. As if he battled for his life, Reuben sensed the water's deep chill, the instinctive dread of the dark depths below him, his tiring limbs as he struggled against the cresting waves, the yawning troughs between them.

Suddenly Reuben was himself again, all thoughts of waves and water vanished. But a deep grieving sadness remained. Reality swept over him. Shook him. Left him breathless. *Maelgeyn drowned. Broch Gorm's boy is dead.*

He did not question how he knew. He wished he did not. Worse, how could he explain what he experienced to Broch Gorm when he returned to Carthago?

How can I say to my friend——your son Maelgeyn drowned? Reuben agonized. *I will sound like a fool when I tell him I dreamed it. He will ask for proof, and I have none.*

If Maelgeyn drowned, did his ship go down? What of Joseph and the others? But his clawing dread centered only on Maelgeyn. *Does that mean the others are alive,* he wondered. Then his focus hardened. *Why should I even trust this cursed nightmare?*

Perhaps a quarter of the night remained before dawn. His sundry things were already packed for the journey to Joppa. He had little to occupy his mind, and he would not dwell on the dream. Slipping to his knees, he closed his eyes, folded his hands in prayer. "Blessed Jesus," he whispered, "be my strength and refuge...."

Lost at sea without sail or oars, the ship could make no headway. So the rudder was useless. They were flotsam, slave to the wind which blew from the southwest and the sea current that bore *Judah's Tears* steadily north northeast.

"The eastern borders of Gaul lie somewhere in that broad arc," Elvan told Joseph, extending his arms to show the Pharisee. "Early in the night the current ran almost due east. Now it has shifted more northerly. I believe the current bends around the upper reaches of the Roman boot and soon will flow east northeast."

Joseph nodded his understanding. "Will the current bring us near to landfall?"

"I will not lie or offer false hope," Elvan replied. "It may or may not. I cannot say. The routes to Britannia I know. Here in these waters, I have no experience, and we lost the charts when we lost Maelgeyn."

Joseph grimaced. The gale had struck so suddenly. A terrible wind wave swept from the southeast across the surface of the sea before the upper sky blackened. There was no time to lower the spar and furl the sail. Sweeping across the stern, the storm's force was so fierce the straining sail ripped away the rigging stays and tore the mast free of its keel mounting. When the mast broke free, the mounting careened into the overhead racks where the oars were tied, snapping the uprights timbers. Like a mighty hand, the savage wind raked both racks and mast along the decks, carrying crewmen and captain into the raging sea. Along with the captain went the oil-skin cylinder with the sea charts Maelgeyn carried strapped across his back, held in place by a wide leather baldric.

Elvan knew Joseph's thoughts. "If that wind had caught us amidships instead of from the stern, *Judah's Tears* would have capsized and rolled. Everyone would have been lost. We are alive only by God's grace."

Dawn was still a grayness along the horizon when Reuben and the others mounted the white mules and began the long descent from Jerusalem to the coastal shores and Joppa. Luke rode beside Reuben, his face grim, mirroring that of the young man who rode beside him. With experience born of a lifetime of warfare with the Roman army, he believed he understood men.

But Reuben remained a complex mix: young in many senses of the word; old in other ways where no young man should be old. He kept the Faceless Men around him now, but they were like shadows, not companions. With just a nod, without needing to say a word, he seemed able to give them orders with gestures or expressions. They obeyed him without question, without objection. They needed no reminders of what they should do. Seemingly the Faceless Men accepted they were his to command, obedient even unto death.

While they journeyed east Luke pondered what he saw as they rode. *I never reckoned him possessing such a commanding nature,* Luke marveled, *yet I see it happening before my eyes. He displays a thoughtful confidence that borders on bravado, yet it is not. What are you becoming, lad, you who are barely twenty?*

At the Roman's side, Reuben's mind spun. His dream still dogged him, poisoned his thoughts. He was clearly out of his depth. A stab of something akin to sorrow lanced through him, forced him to break his silence.

"When you fought on battlefields," he met Luke's eyes, "did you ever know things had happened far off, even though you were too far away to see it? Somehow you knew things occurred as if you were there the moment it happened?"

"You ask——" Luke evaded, "strange questions."

Reuben set his jaw stubbornly. "Do you intend to answer my question?"

"And if I said I would not?" the Roman countered. "What would you say then?"

"That I had my answer," Reuben conceded. "Even if it did not satisfy me."

Luke sighed. "That Britannia native who came to see you in Jerusalem. What was his name?"

"Damhan Mawr," Reuben answered. "Damhan Mawr of the Dumnonii. Why do you ask?"

"He would call what you described a '*Sight Gift*' or '*Second Sight*,'" Luke explained, groping for words to describe it. "Someone with '*Second Sight*' is said to be able to see things that cannot normally be seen. Many times it involves things that have not yet happened."

"What makes you think——" Reuben challenged, "Damhan would know about this '*Second Sight*?'"

"The Dumnonii are Celtic tribemen," Luke answered. "And it is said the '*Sight Gift*' is not uncommon among Celts." He stared hard at Reuben. "Now come clean, lad. Something is clearly gnawing at you?"

"Broch Gorm's youngest son, Maelgeyn——" Reuben confessed. "Before dawn today, I sensed him drown."

Luke stiffened in his saddle. He had expected almost anything curious from Reuben. But he had not expected that. "You want anything more out of me, you best tell it all."

Reuben tried, as much as he understood.

Luke listened, his mouth showing his discomfort. Like a cat's paw brushing bare skin, a sudden tremor worked its way up the Roman's spine. From his compost of memories, any use of magic filled him with dread. He clung to things man understood and left alone what was outside the physical plane, things man could not control——like oracles who communicated with the dead, primitive people invoking spirits to vanquish their enemies, and strange abilities like the *Sight Gift*.

When a man died, he died. No gray Elysian Fields. In his life he had given little devotion to the gods of his people. His personal gods had been more practical. He had served the *gladius*, *pilum*, and *scutum*, the Roman short sword, throwing spear and shield. He held no reverence for gods——until he came face to face with the Christ....

That changed everything! Reuben had taken Tribune Quintus Lucius Carus north into Galilee to meet the Christ before His ascension. At Jesus' urging, the Roman had touched raw wounds which no longer bled, put his hand into the torn side and found—— the heart of God!

Upon his return to Fortress Antonia, Carus resigned his commission. Pontius Pilate, who had been his patron, flew into a tirade, railed at him, but the former tribune would not change his mind. Carus had discovered within himself a new calling, one that did not lie with Rome. With no regret, he turned his back on what had been home and family for more than half-a-lifetime. He also took a new name; instead of Lucius, he chose Luke of Arimathea to honor men he respected. He chose Luke to honor a Greek physician who inspired him; Arimathea, from his new patron, Joseph of Arimathea.

When Reuben ran out of words, Luke answered him with a quick headshake. "Lad, you ask a man who has never been down this trail to describe the lay of the land. I can only follow your lead, go where you go." His face wrinkled in deep thought. "But it seems to me God would not give you that vision without a reason, without a purpose. We simply have to discover what it is."

Reaching Joppa, Reuben conferred with Kadmos of Byblos, Arimathea's factor at the port, concerning cargo waiting to be shipped from Jerusalem. Luke did not stay with Reuben. Instead he went into the city, searched out Gwydion, Arimathea's shipsmaster. Gwydion who was captain of *Judah's Hope*——and Maelgeyn's older brother.

"I am blunt, a soldier," Luke began. "I never learned to be a diplomat, but I have something you must know."

He told it all, what he knew about the *Sight Gift*, then everything Reuben had confided in him, everything he knew the lad could not bring himself to tell his friend.

The shipsmaster listened intently. His face changed when he understood why Luke had come. He had the look of a man faced with the inconceivable, yet wholly accepting it.

Pain and grief filled the shipsmaster's eyes. He extended his wrist, a silent offering of friendship to the Roman. Luke seized it, clasped wrist to wrist, felt Gwydion's fingers tighten on his flesh.

"You have been a friend to me and mine," he told Luke. "I tell you this, call on me when you have need. Blood to blood. Life to life. I will answer."

Gwydion managed a deep, shaky breath. "Now I must go to ready the ship. With the changing of the tide we set sail for Carthago. Perhaps by the time we make port, I shall discover how best to tell my father what you have shared with me."

Luke watched him turn, stride down the street that led to the quay and *Judah's Hope*. He half-hated himself for bringing a shadow into Gwydion's world, but now that it had been said, Reuben could speak of it with less hesitation. More, he felt certain the shipsmaster would want to hear the true telling from Reuben's own lips.

He glanced at the sky. To the east the blue dome was already darkening with approaching night, but the west was gilded with the setting sun. Luke grimaced. He did not relish setting sail at night. Reuben may pay no mind to it, but Luke doubted if he would ever grow comfortable with the thought of all that dark water beneath the hull. Dark water waiting to swallow them all. Like it had Maelgeyn....

Chapter 10

Spring had come late this year to all of Britannia. Winter's grip had been harsh and long, but now new color spread over moor and field.

Beyond the fringe of thickets lay ancient oaks, the old forest, dark and gloomy. There the only hint of season's change was warmer days.

Damhan stopped. No, that was not true. Spring was a scent in the air that permeated everything. He studied the towering oaks. They were old, massive, the nearby beeches as well. He savored the deep silence. It called to his tribesman's heart. Bow in hand, he walked softly, intent on preserving the silence.

In Judea he had seen Herod's Temple. Restricted to the Court of the Gentiles, Damhan had not been allowed to penetrate its depths. If he could have, he would not. That great pile of stone and wood and tile so important to the Jews held nothing for him. Here in this shadow world he drew closer to the gods than anywhere he knew. Except for the *tor, Ynys Wydryn, 'the Isle of Glass.'*

In the deep twilight where the sun's rays never penetrated, in the heart of the forest, he paused. A twig snapped somewhere near. He settled into the stillness, wrapped it about him like a cloak.

Breathing shallowly, Damhan ignored the tiny daggers of cold sweat prickling his forehead under the woolen cowl. He felt the sudden hackling of the short hairs on his neck, the animal awareness that screamed he was not alone.

Who watches me? he wondered. Here in the gloom he was a shadow among shadows. His gray cloak was its own shadow. Among trees not so old, the greens and leather browns of his tunic and leggings hid him in the colors of the forest.

He felt eyes boring into him. Under that scrutiny, with each heartbeat he grew more and more uncomfortable. Forcing resisting muscles to obey his will, he slowly turned his head, studied every shadowed nook around him. When his dread blossomed into raw fear, he could not say, only that it did.

No longer held at bay, terror tore at his heart. He wanted to turn and bolt from the dark, abandon this twilight. His rational mind screamed nothing stalked him.

But it was a lie. Nothing human stalked him!

Unbidden, his eyes bulged. His mind blazed bright with terror. A silent shadow rose from the ground in front of him. Close enough to touch. Bigger than any man——

Damhan did not remember bolting. But he did. For the first time in his life he fled mindlessly. Legs churning, feet slipping and sliding on rotting leaves and mold, he ran for the light.

When he broke free of the forest gloom, he whirled about, glared back into the dark forest. Nothing charged at his heels. Nothing!

Slumping over, Damhan braced hands on knees. His lungs pumped like a blacksmith's bellows, a harsh sound in his throat. Slowly his breath came back, his heart slowed, his fear took a more somber hue. He glanced down, focused on his left fist resting on his knee. His fingers still gripped the yew bow. With his right hand, he touched the mouth of his quiver. It was empty. He had lost every shaft he possessed in his mad dash.

"I never thought to draw and loose an arrow," he whispered to himself, an indictment he found galling. What was worse, he could not force himself to retrace his path into the gloom and find the lost arrows.

Damhan never thought himself a coward, had never admitted he might be one. Like most tribesmen he had faced battle and death, killed men with the knowledge that any moment he might be cut down.

The worst is always the waiting for the battles to begin, when you know your next breath could be your last, he acknowledged. *When bravery and courage become just words. A man embraces that fear. Does what he must.*

But that was war. He had often heard tales of forest phantoms, tales he had not believed. In his lifetime he had never encountered one. He swallowed hard. Until this day! What he faced in the shadows turned his bones to water, and he had run. Damhan knew when he ran he had lost more than just arrows beneath those ancient boles. He had lost his confidence and self-respect as well.

Weary beyond words, Damhan turned toward the *tor*. He had to find the priestess, confess his cowardice, and tell Arawn Doelguss of the forest phantom that stalked the ancient wood. Nodding vigorously, he made his way toward Avalon. Aye, the Lady of the Lake must be first to know——then Bran the Blessed so the Arch Druid could warn his students not to venture into the deep forest.

Elvan studied the direction of the sun and the current. Slowly he nodded. Even a rank novice could deduce the current had veered to the northwest——toward Gaul——and carried *Judah's Tears* in its grip like a useless piece of driftwood. He had never felt so helpless.

In that moment he resolved never to go to sea again without a spare mast and sail. He knew it was a miracle that the keel remained intact when the mast mooring had been ripped away and took the overhead oar rack with it. After the storm, they had caulked minor leaks. That was normal routine aboard ships.

With the cargo they carried, water would become a problem long before their food ran out. Knowing that, with Joseph's blessing, he started rationing water the moment he assumed command. For the moment, they had ample stores, but the supplies must last. There was grumbling among the passengers, but it passed. At least for now....

Elvan sighed. In a world reduced to the length and breadth of the ship, enforced idleness was the worst. Something they must endure. Shading his eyes with his hand, he scanned the northern horizon.

Lord—— he prayed silently, *You who are our refuge and our strength, rescue us from our peril. Bear us quickly and safely to Gaul....*

True to his word, Gwydion sailed with the turning of the tide. When the sun rose, Joppa already lay far behind them. With wind and current aiding their passage, *Judah's Hope* almost gathered wings and flew over the waves.

With the shipsmaster and Reuben absorbed in their own thoughts, Luke prayed the voyage would be agreeably short. Like a caged lion he paced the waist of the ship.

"Will you perch somewhere?" Reuben protested. "You make a body tired just watching you."

"I am restless," Luke protested. "Naught to do and my bones are stiff." He cocked his head. "Perhaps one of your Faceless Men would spar with me?"

"Perhaps," Reuben agreed. "And perhaps I would."

Luke stiffened, stared at him open mouthed. "You——?"

"Of course *me*, you lout," Reuben quipped in a grieved tone. Then he added in peevish humor, "Better yet, I shall duel you with my reed pen." He forced a grin. "Have you not heard, '*the pen is mightier than the sword?*'"

Ignoring the jibe, Luke demanded, "When did you learn the sword? Who taught you?" His eyes widened in sudden revelation. "You trained with the Faceless Men."

Reuben crossed his arms, stared back at the Roman. "I was told that in Britannia all men carry swords, and I am bound for Britannia." The young face hardened. "Are you saying in your eyes, I am not a man?"

"Do not put words in my mouth I did not say," Luke retorted heatedly. "Words I most assuredly do not intend."

Reuben squared his shoulders. "Then are you saying it would not demean your stilted Roman honor to practice with a poor, humble scribe?"

"I will show you stilted," Luke responded in a tight voice. "Bring it on, *boy*. Let us see if you fight as well as you infuriate."

With blunted *gladius*, practice swords from the Faceless Men's kit, edges and dull points chalked in red to show strikes, they faced each other amidships just aft of the mast. Luke wore soldier's garb, while Reuben changed into a short Greek tunic. With his legs healed, Reuben and Luke were matched in height. For the first time the Roman noted the lad's width of shoulders, the breadth of muscles the Jewish garb artfully concealed. How had he overlooked them?

Luke launched a standard low-line attack, the first tactic any Roman recruit was taught. Reuben beat it aside easily, sidestepping away out of reach and resetting.

"You are quick, I will grant you that," Luke admitted. "But it takes more than quickness to win bouts."

"Should I be scared of an aging Roman——" Reuben countered with a smirk, "who is long past his prime? Or perhaps I should yield to you now to avoid offending the Tribune's dignity?"

"Boy, it is never wise to wave a red flag in front of an old bull," Luke fired back. "He may be slower than he used to be, but his horns are still deadly."

Luke attacked again, faster this time, but Reuben blocked and parried, launched a counterattack of his own which forced Luke to leap back. Sidestepping, his footwork perfect, honed from long experience, Luke attacked again, faking a high strike, then swinging and dropping his elbow left for a cut across Reuben's torso.

Reuben blocked it easily, stepped away, nodding to his cherished opponent. "Did you believe me such easy prey?"

A rare smile creased the Roman's lips. "Boy, I have only just begun." He feinted left and low, sidestepped again, drawing his sword up to the right, a finesse move.

Matching the move, parrying the sword before it could strike flesh, Reuben moved away and reset, sword ready. His mouth was dry, his knuckles white around the sword hilt. He forced himself to relax. That time he had been slower reacting to Luke's blade, and they both knew it.

Luke lunged, sword positioned for a killing strike. Reuben swayed to the right, his blade tracing a short red chalk line on the Roman's hip. It would have been a shallow slash, a minor wound, but it was *first blood*. And the score was Reuben's!

Instead of dancing away from Luke's next attack, Reuben closed with the Roman. Their blades clanged and clashed, and then they separated. Luke's smile widened. Reuben realized so far it had only been a contest of skill and ability. But the older man was warming to the fight, relaxing, employing a lifetime of experience and fighting techniques with grim and deadly efficiency.

While each man probed the other's defense for weaknesses, the fight became more measured. Luke blocked a sudden lunge, and his counterstrike left a red line on Reuben's shoulder that would have left an irritating minor wound had it been sharpened steel.

Reuben circled warily. Again he leaped in, this time hacking and slashing, blocking and dancing. Luke met every attack, launched his own as he parried, forcing Reuben to sidestep instead of retreat. His plan foiled, Luke recovered quickly and pressed Reuben.

His skill unwavering, the older man's reflexes were still surprising. In his heart, Reuben sensed had the fight been with sharpened *gladius*, he would have been slain. Exercises with the Faceless Men had given him both stamina and endurance, but he knew those alone were not enough. With each move his appreciation for Luke's ability soared. For a man of his age, Luke was a marvel. Perhaps even a superior swordsman than Quintus Marcellus Gota, who had begun Gwyr's training on their first voyage to Britannia.

But Reuben knew he was tiring. He attacked furiously, closed with Luke. It became a test of strength which the Roman won. Too soon the point of Luke's *gladius* came up and stopped beneath Reuben's chin.

"Got you, boy," the Roman said, nose to nose with him.

Reuben could not move. Through gritted teeth, he told Luke, "Look down——"

Slowly the older man's chin dipped. Reuben watched the Roman's eyes widen perceptively when he found the point of Reuben's *gladius* poised at his abdomen.

"By the gods——" Luke's old ingrained exclamation from a lifetime of Roman service burst unbidden from his lips. "You slipped it in," he admitted in genuine surprise. "We both would die, you quickly while I suffered a lingering death in great pain, cursing you to my last breath."

"You are a gifted swordsman," Reuben told Luke, awe in his voice. Then he thought of Gamaliel's words, *Let the student find a teacher.* "I wish to learn more," he said sincerely. "Will you teach me...?"

Chapter II

arthago reared its broad acres above the sea across the bow of *Judah's Hope*, and Reuben felt joy, relief and sadness all in one. Joy and relief that he was done with Judea, that he could set his sights toward Britannia. And sadness——for Broch Gorm must learn that his youngest son would not be sailing home.

Reuben wondered why he accepted his vision as truth. But he did. And so had Gwydion. Perhaps it is the way of men who went to sea, he did not know. He only knew that it hurt his heart to the bearer of such sad news.

Broch Gorm took the tidings with admirable grace, Reuben supposed, though the older man's shoulders seemed to sag somewhat. His expression did not change, but Reuben felt unspoken grief radiating from him.

Then the old shipwright heaved a long sigh. "Each time my boys set sail, I live with fear they will face misfortune and not return," he admitted in a strangled voice. "Now it has come, but the One God has given me many happy homecomings to balance against this unexpected loss. I must dwell on those——"

In time Reuben stood with Gwydion on a stretch of Carthago beach some distance from the burning bier offered to the night in Maelgeyn's honor. It was an old custom, brought to the African coast from Thule.

"What if I am wrong?" Reuben asked, intruding on his friend's thoughts. "What if tomorrow or the day after Maelgeyn sails into the bay?"

"Then we shall rejoice and kill the fatted calf Joseph so often speaks about," Gwydion replied. "It would be a homecoming like no other, but——" He shook his head. "It will not happen. I think I also felt him die, but I would not accept it until I heard it from Luke and you."

Up, up the fire climbed, level after level, a magnificent beacon any ship captain lost at sea would see and follow home. Soon the flames reach the bier's crown. So high it seemed to toast the stars themselves.

One by one, those who knew Maelgeyn spoke.

All too soon the beacon collapsed, fell in a shower of burning wood and glowing embers. Saddened, those who gathered for the tribute departed quietly, turned for home.

Reuben waited until the last, then went to Gwydion. "Will you send out ships to search?"

"To what end?" the shipsmaster asked. "The sea is wide and harsh. It does not give up its dead easily. A hundred ships could search a hundred lifetimes and never find a trace. That is the price the kindred pay, those who wait upon the shore for those who go to sea."

Reuben wondered, thinking of Britannia and his need for a captain. "Now that Maelgeyn has gone, will you stay in Carthago with your father?"

Gwydion shook his head. "The sea calls me, and I must answer. My two brothers just older than Maelgeyn stay to work with Da and learn the trade. That way Arimathea will have its needed shipwrights."

"When will we sail?" Reuben asked. "We have sufficient cargo for *Judah's Hope* in our warehouses."

"Then make your plans, young Master," the shipsmaster stated. "On the day you name, we will sail with the tide."

A dark line appeared along the northern horizon. It was there at first light, grew darker through the morn. Too long for an island. It could only be the Gaulish mainland. Elvan reached for it with his heart, as if by desire alone he could drive *Judah's Tears* toward the shore or drag it to the ship.

Time and again he wet a finger, lifted it to the wind. It maintained its northwesterly heading. If it held, given the westerly current, the wind would push the ship the remaining league or so to the shore.

Joseph joined Elvan at the bow. "I had hoped——" the Pharisee began, "the nearer we came to Massilia, the more chance we would be seen by a passing ship. But I have seen no sails."

Elvan quickly shook his head. "I would as willingly see no sails." Seeing Joseph's surprise, he added quickly, "Nine of ten sea captains would see profit in taking your cargo, throwing the lot of us over the side to drown or taking us as slaves, then sinking *Judah's Hope*. On the high seas, who is there to hold them accountable?"

"I had not considered such," Joseph admitted contritely. He chewed his lip thoughtfully. "Since Massilia is a port, there is a high probability we will see sails. Though we are few, let us prepare to receive boarders if their intentions prove less than honorable."

"Well put," Elvan conceded. "Before we call the others, tell me of Massilia. I have often heard of the city but know nothing about it."

"Arimathea maintains a factor and compound there," Joseph told him. "I have visited Massilia many times as well. The city is a '*poleils*,' a Greek city, and does not fall under the jurisdiction of a Roman governor. For my house, this status proves a boon for some goods, a bane for others." At Elvan's glance, the Pharisee shrugged. "A merchant always looks for profits."

Elvan nodded his understanding. Turning, he called all men on deck. Of sixteen crewmen in the crew, they had eleven remaining, not counting the passengers. Joseph studied the cargo manifest as Elvan determined the fighting abilities of the men. They had eight bows with a dozen bundles of fifty arrows. Their remaining men could be armed with *gladius* and *scutum*. Quintus Marcellus Gota had his own sword and the training to muster a staunch defense.

"Determine how much rope is left aboard," Elvan ordered two crewmen, then turned to Joseph. "What type of shoreline does Gaul have if we approach from the east?"

"Almost all the mainland shore is rock with few or no beaches," the Pharisee said. "As I recall, there are several sizeable islands south of the mainland, some of whom have marginal or sparse beaches."

Seeing Elvan's men dragging coils of rope on deck, Joseph asked, "You have a plan?"

"We must break free of the current, or it could dash us to pieces against the rocks or eventually sweep us back out to sea," Elvan answered. "I intend to tie our coils of rope end to end. At the first opportunity, I will have two men swim ashore with one end and tie off the rope to rocks. When the line goes taut, it should temporarily moor the ship. It is a great risk, but I see no other alternative."

"A fine plan," Joseph agreed. "Make it so."

Later in the day they saw the first weatherworn island to *laddebord*. Around its high craggy cliffs the sea foamed white and boasted no rocky shingle that suited their purpose. No sooner than it slipped behind, another small island showed itself, this one closer to the ship.

"Into the water," Elvan ordered. "Swim quickly. Find a rock to moor us."

With rope ends in their teeth, the men dove into the surf, swam strongly for the shore, angling with the current to give them more chance to find a suitable rock and set the ropes. Joseph watched as the first man reached the shore, scrambled behind an outcrop, and secured his line.

Ever so slowly the rope grew taut, then it ripped upward from the waves, vibrating with tension holding the ship against the westbound current. Suddenly the hemp rope went slack, pulling loose from its anchor point. Then the second rope whipped taut, slowing the ship before it could regain sufficient momentum to snatch the second rope free from its mooring.

Without regard to his own safety, the first crewman launched himself back into the surf, caught the trailing rope and swam for the shore beyond the ship. He clamored up the granite lip and hastily wound his end around an up-thrust rock shaped like a cow.

With tether secured, he waved and crewmen on board *Judah's Tears* slowly, painstakingly, hand over hand, began to drag the ship clear of the main current. One man hauled the sideboard rudder hard to *steorbord*, and the current rushing past its angled plane helped force the ship into less turbulent water behind a small headland.

"Well done!" Elvan yelled through cupped hands to the men ashore. "Well done indeed!"

From the long rope drawn on deck, the crewmen made other lines, lashed them to the ship and threw the ends to the men ashore, mooring *Judah's Tears* to the lea side of the headland. With the ship out of danger, other crewmen scrambled ashore and started exploring their rocky berth.

Not long after, a lone man swung back down to the ship's deck. "Hit haint large," he said quickly in broken Aramaic, waving at the island. "Mere two thousand cubits by five hundred. No trees bigger'in shrubs growing topland, but there be a wrecked ship wedged on the high water rocks to the south. With work, we thinks its mast and some of the timbers can be salvaged." He grinned. "Not much else, but there do be five unbroken oars which seem sound enough."

He pointed southwest around the headland. "And there be a spate of sandy beach maybe twice the ship's length. If you think it be worth the haul, could be we relax the first mooring rope, swing her around like we done before, and slowly work her past the rocky headland?"

By nightfall, *Judah's Tears* was gently grounded on a sandy-gravel beach in the headland's backwater, well away from the current. Using broken and scavenged timbers from the derelict, the crewmen built a beach fire——to light the night, for deliverance from an uncertain future, and more important, hot food.

Near the dancing flames Elvan sat with Joseph, sharing a cup of wine and explaining his plans. "With first light we will mount the mast from the wrecked ship to our keel as best we can. Once the salvaged timber is braced, we will run up a spar with a storm sail. Catching the wind, *Judah's Tears* can make some headway, even if slowly." He sighed heavily. "But it should be sufficient headway for our vessel to run with the wind, hug the coast at a safe distance, and reach Massilia where we can purchase what we need to make proper repairs."

With a wry expression, the Pharisee said softly, "Our passengers are not sailors. After what they have undergone, I have grave doubts if they will want to continue on by sea once we arrive at Massilia. If that is so——" He paused. "Once repairs are made to your satisfaction and sufficient crewmen are found to replace those who were lost, I will continue on to Britannia as planned aboard *Judah's Tears.*" He smiled wryly. "With you as my captain."

Elvan's eyes widened. "But I am not qual——?"

Joseph lifted a restraining hand, silencing Elvan. "When your captain was lost, you maintained order, and you held ship and crew together. You saw us through crisis after crisis. I believe you have earned your captaincy."

"As you wish, Master," Elvan acquiesced. He lifted his cup in a toast. "To Massilia. To Massilia and beyond...."

Gwydion stood beside the helmsman, staring at the open sea cascading across *Judah's Hope's* bow. A decent wind filled the big square sail. Ahead lay a long stretch of water, then they would steer southwest along the rugged coast of Ptolemy's Mauretanian Kingdom to the port of Abyla, his master's first destination.

Reuben stood at the bow, willing his thoughts ahead to the port city, to the fighting school run by Titus Antonius Silvanus. He had not seen the Roman fighting master in almost four years, since Gwyr practiced against gladiators in the school's fighting grounds.

When he last saw Silvanus, Reuben's legs were crippled, twisted and useless. Gwyr had been his legs. To his knowledge, the Roman had not learned of the miracle performed by Jesus the Christ on the road to Calvary, how He had healed Reuben's legs. Although their mutual friend, Quintus Marcellus Gota, had written the fighting master about Gwyr's death, he had sent no subsequent missive about Reuben's healing.

He pictured the Roman's shock when they did meet and grinned. Then he sobered. *How will he react to my request?* Reuben wondered. *Will he honor it?*

CHAPTER 12

Judah's Tears snail-crept into Massilia's harbor. Makeshift repairs and the storm sail afforded just enough headway to break free of the running current near the mainland's craggy headland and steer northward along the coast to the port. Within the harbor's breakwater, what wind there was died. Crewman manned four of the five salvaged oars and slowly brought the vessel to the dock.

Large storehouses ringed the quay. Beyond the port districts, muddy streets thronged with hurrying people and rambling carts, noisy with shouts and curses, streets that wound their way through weathered and dilapidated frame buildings. A thousand smells abounded, particularly strong in the alleys and back passages. All manner of rotting filth littered the alleyways and gutters.

Above the poor district, the streets widened, the gutters less cluttered with debris and waste. Bakeries and taverns grew more frequent. Fragrant smells wafting through open doorways made mouths water and throats tighten. Escorted by ten armed crewmen, Joseph led his passengers through Massilia's streets to the Arimathea compound. Elvan remained at the quay, making inquiries for needed craftsmen and shipwrights to repair the ship.

Quintus Marcellus Gota studied the city's inhabitants when he followed the Pharisee through the streets. Most of them he guessed were Romanized Greek, though in the mix he saw a smattering of obvious Roman middle-class: artisans, shop owners and lesser merchants.

Guards lounging at the Arimathea gate challenged them. Bored expressions quickly vanished as Joseph identified himself, and a runner dashed to alert the factor of his master's arrival. Beyond its gateway, the compound was typical of Arimathea enclosures in other ports. Frame storehouses and out-buildings flanked a spacious well-kept house, built with cunning craftsmanship in stone and timberwork, two-storied with ample cellars and kitchen.

David ben Seth dashed from the house, his robes flapping, and warmly greeted the Pharisee. "I did not know to expect you, Master," he exclaimed. Thinning salt-and-pepper hair and matching beard framed the factor's deeply lined features. Slim despite his middle years, he spoke from obvious friendship, without being overly demonstrative.

"I did not expect to visit Massilia," Joseph responded honestly. "Our ship suffered damage in a gale, and we barely limped into port. Even now my captain makes inquiries about the necessary repairs."

David nodded. "I shall send my assistant to aid him." He eyed the men and women with the Pharisee. "And I shall have chambers prepared for your guests." Turning, he gestured through the doorway. "Come. Servants already prepare food and drink to refresh you."

Abyla had changed little in four years. Nestled behind Abyla's low promontory, the Southern Pillar of Hercules, Ptolemy's city displayed its wealth in fine buildings typical of Roman architecture. Educated in Rome, Ptolemy sought to bring Rome's grandeur to the Mauretanian port.

Reuben led Luke to the Arimathea compound, where the factor, Joel ben Heman, welcomed them. When time permitted, Arimathea's minister freed himself from his scribal duties. Both he and Luke donned red Roman soldiers' tunics, slipped baldrics over their shoulders to carry their *gladius*, then Reuben led his companion across Abyla to the edge of the city where another Roman, Titus Antonius Silvanus, maintained his compound and fighting school.

He watched Luke's slow smile when they approached the guards at the gate. In spite of the sultry heat, all six wore Roman armor, the *lorica hamata,* coats of chain mail armor, bronze *conus* helmets, which narrowed from the temples into a bowl with cheek flaps tied by a thong below the chin, and greaves for the legs. Hard men with stone faces, they were discharged veterans from the legions, scourged and cashiered from the ranks for various offenses. But they handled *gladius* and *pilum,* the short throwing spear favored by Roman legionnaires, and *scutums,* the curved shield with a handgrip in the center, with the ease of long use.

"What is your business here?" the guard captain challenged in Latin, then repeated it in Greek and added, "There are no bouts scheduled for today."

"Kindly inform your Master Reuben ben Ezra of the House of Arimathea stands at his gate," Reuben told him, his tone neutral, controlled. "The man with me is the former Tribune Quintus Lucius Carus, who attended the Judean Governor."

Eyes widened at the mention of Carus' name, and the captain quickly dispatched one of his five to alert the school's master. Around barbarians Reuben knew in public, it was judged unseemly for Romans to show haste, but Silvanus covered the ground from the inner court to the gate in long quick strides. His keen eye assessed and passed over the two Romans standing with his guards, seeking—— seeking and not finding a familiar figure with twisted limbs or a burly man who carried him.

Vexed, the school master glowered at his captain, challenged him harshly. "You sent word Reuben ben Ezra was at my gate. Where is he?"

Disquiet shadowed the squad leader's eyes. "Why, he stands there——" the captain countered. "Behind you."

Turning, Silvanus centered his gaze on the Romans in their red garb, his countenance openly perplexed. Reuben knew four years had changed his face, the fleshiness of a cripple honed lean and hard through strenuous sword drills and exercise. Silvanus did not look beneath the obvious.

"How blind are those," Reuben chided, "who do not see."

Silvanus froze. His school master's composure was an iron lid clamped tight over a mix of emotions that burned like wildfire through his awareness: bewilderment, shock, then recognition! He knew that voice!

"Reuben——?" His disbelief began as a question, became as a statement riddled with disbelief, and ended in a joyful cry. "Reuben. By the gods, *REUBEN!*"

Moving like the gladiators he instructed, Silvanus closed the distance between them in a heartbeat, swept Arimathea's minister up in a crushing embrace. Then he thrust the younger man to arm's length, and demanded, "What magic is this? I carried you. I know your limbs were twisted. That you were crippled. Now you are *whole!*" His grin lit his face like a lantern. "This is beyond belief!"

"All you say is true," Reuben acknowledged. "I was healed by Jesus the Christ on His way to His execution."

Silvanus' gaze darkened. "The Judean rebel?"

Reuben shook his head. "*He* was no rebel, my friend, not in the way you think. *He* is the Christ, the Son of the Living God. *He* came and bled and died and rose again from the dead. I stand before you whole of body as *His* witness."

"This boggles my mind," the school master admitted. "Come, I must know all." He half-turned, stared hard at Luke. "You are the Tribune," he said matter-of-factly, "Quintus Lucius Carus of the Legio VI Ferrata."

Luke returned his open assessment without evasion, then slowly nodded. "I served the legion in that capacity."

Silvanus smiled. "Before the Legio VI Ferrata, you were the centurion from the Rhineland in Germania who was highly decorated for bravery and valor in the face of the enemy. You rallied your routing troops into a counterattack that saved your legion from defeat."

Surprised, Reuben cast an aside glance at his friend. Luke had never mentioned his war service in Germania. Or bragged about his exploits.

Arching his brow in an attempt to look unconcerned, Luke

answered, "I did what any centurion would do." He eyed Silvanus. "What *you* would have done in such a situation."

Eyes widening, Silvanus's expression contradicted Luke's humility. "Your superiors emphatically disagreed. Reports of your heroism circulated throughout the Empire, even reaching this backwater post, citing your leadership in the face of the enemy as an example to others."

Silvanus shook his head. "It is not often a Centurion is elevated to the rank of Tribune. Word is that in Judea you caught the eye of the Governor, that you became Pontius Pilate's favorite. It also spread that you were being groomed for great things."

Luke took the praise with good grace, then shook his head. "Perhaps, but not now. I have resigned from the army to follow another calling."

Silvanus smiled, and that smile lent a gentleness to his gravely-chiseled gladiator's face. "I sense you both have more to tell than these accounts encompass. Come, share what refreshments my poor training school can offer and tell me more. I would know all."

Silvanus sat silent and wondering, staring into the throat of his goblet, not seeing the wine within. He knew Pilate, had served with him before the rogue became governor of Judea. The school master knew any Jew who unsettled the procurator, who influenced him to resist and defy the high priests as Luke described, was indeed no common man.

"And you truly believe he could have raised all Palestine against Rome?" the school master pressed Luke. "This man who was just a simple carpenter?"

"Recall the slave Spartacus," Luke countered, "a simple Thracian of Nomadic stock, trained to be a gladiator. A hundred years ago he broke free with seventy others, and under his leadership, they defied the might of the Republic, and threatened Rome itself."

Luke linked his fingers together. "Spartacus was taken and

crucified, his body thrown to the dogs." He stared intently at Silvanus. "Signs and wonders heralded Jesus' birth, which fulfilled hundreds of years of Messianic prophecy. If *He* had proclaimed *Himself* Messiah and challenged Rome, all Palestine would have followed Him."

Bracing an elbow on the chair arm, he leaned forward, intent. "But Jesus would not. *He* told Pilate in my hearing, '*You say rightly I am a king, but My kingdom is not of this world.*' And *He* was crucified. I certified His death. I myself placed the seal of Rome on the rock rolled across the entrance to the tomb where they laid *Him*."

Luke's eyes ignited. "After *His* resurrection, I also met *Him* face to face in Galilee. *He* lives! And I know it is the same man I certified as dead, because *His* resurrected body still carries the wounds inflicted by the nails and the whips, and the mark of the spear that pierced *His* side."

"Jesus *is* the Son of God," Reuben proclaimed. "How else could *He* have done miracles? How else could *His* blood have healed my legs, limbs you well know were twisted, crippled. Because of *Him*, I walk. Others like me walk or see or hear because of *His* compassion and *His* grace."

"He healed them all?" Silvanus pressed. He turned to Luke, "You know this?"

"I do know this," the Roman answered firmly, "with my eyes and with my heart." Luke braved Silvanus' demanding stare. "And I am no man's fool. The evidence was most compelling for me to willfully turn my back on a future with the legions of Rome. You would do well to consider my testimony."

Silvanus sat back, raised the goblet to his lips, and drank deep. When he lowered the cup, he told them, "I shall think on all you both have said."

For long moments, no one spoke. When he could no longer stand the tension, Reuben said to the unsettled school master, "You have not asked about Gwyr——"

Silvanus hesitated, did not answer quickly, his opaque eyes deeply shadowed. "Quintus Marcellus Gota sent me word Gwyr died saving you and Joseph." He paused, sadly shook his head. "Gota also wrote you were incoherent for months. I did not want to cause you more grief."

"My friend, there is much you must know," Reuben said. "It was as Gota wrote; Gwyr died saving us. A Dumnonii chieftain, Damhan Mawr, brought me the tale the *bardds* sing of Gwyr. Because he killed silently, they branded him a scion of the underworld. He slew every one of the armored attackers, then turned on the archers. They put three arrows in him, yet, one by one, he still ran down those who faced him. What few who remained alive fled the *tor* in a single boat. When last they saw him, he still roamed the shore wildly waving his swords."

When Silvanus started to speak, Reuben lifted a restraining hand. "There is more. When they went back, Gwyr was not among the dead. His swords were on the *tor's* summit." Reuben's voice grew hoarse with emotion. "His body was never found. Tales spread that Gwyr is sleeping, recovering from his wounds, regaining his strength. That one day he will return when the Dumnonii and the other Tribes most need him."

Silvanus pushed to his feet, poured himself more wine. "He was the most remarkable fighter I ever had the fortune to see," the school master admitted when he sat with them once more. "And Gota agreed. So it does not surprise me that tales and legends grow around him. Thank you for coming and sharing them with me."

Reuben smiled. "Sharing what Damhan told me was not my sole reason for coming."

Intrigued, the school master leaned forward, cocked his head. "What more could there be?"

Glancing aside at Luke before he addressed Silvanus' question, Reuben answered softly, "A student must find a master. I come to learn the fighting arts...."

Chapter 13

A bright blue sky dappled with fleecy white clouds allowed the harsh Mauretanian sun to invade the ten-foot high tan brick walls encompassing the fighting school. Luke stood with Titus Antonius Silvanus in the tall iron-picketed enclosure the school master reserved for visiting patrons, watching combatants practice on the sandy inner court open to the elements. A roofed passageway surrounded the court, opening into small whitewashed cells, each one housing a single gladiator.

"He is no Gwyr," Silvanus told Luke as they watched Reuben barely sidestep a thrust, twist away and reset for his opponent's next attack. "He lacks the height or body mass for an arena gladiator, but he has good moves, good instincts, and is deceptively quick. Good as he is, in time he will be a fine swordsman."

The schoolmaster glanced aside at the Roman, his eyes questioning. "You trained him?"

Luke shook his head. "I only sparred with him on the voyage here. His training was at the hands of the Faceless Men, a brotherhood of a lower order in Jerusalem."

"I know of them," Silvanus answered. "Their Order is more widespread than you know. It reaches even to Abyla." He turned away from the combatants, faced Luke. "Why does Reuben fight? Under Joseph of Arimathea he was raised for a gentler life."

A frown twisted the schoolmaster's lips. "More, from what I know of this savior of yours, does he not teach peace and love in place of war and violence?"

"*He* has told us," Luke answered, "'*the foremost and greatest commandment is——you shall love the Lord your GOD with all your heart, with all your soul, and with all your mind, and the second is like it, you shall love your neighbors as yourself.*'" Then the Roman paused. "But *He* also told us, '*Greater love has no one than this, that he lay down his life for his friends.*'"

Comprehension widened the old veteran's eyes. "The way Gwyr did," his voice barely above a whisper. "If needs be, our Reuben makes himself ready to buy the lives of others with his own."

Luke nodded. "Schoolmaster, did you not tell Gwyr that in Britannia every *man* carries a sword?" he countered. "Reuben listened. When our Lord healed his legs, *He* also healed the lad's self-image."

Breaking the bridge of eyes, Luke focused on Reuben as the young man evaded another attack. "Like Joseph, he feels he is called to witness for the Christ in Britannia, and yes, he makes himself ready for whatever that calling demands." He sighed heavily. "As they say Gwyr did. I have no doubt Reuben will do just that. And I go to guard his back and witness in any way the Lord bids me."

Reuben suddenly lunged, parried his challenger's blade aside. Then he whipped his blunted sword with its chalked edge across the man's bicep with bruising force, continued the blow. Left a stark red line across both arm and chest.

Silvanus nodded approvingly. Both he and Luke knew in the stark life-or-death drama of the arena Reuben's attack would have left his opponent disarmed and probably would have killed him. "Never take small men for granted," the schoolmaster said with resignation. "Especially one like him: brave, quick, and agile."

Two days after their arrival in Massilia, rain descended, making repairs to *Judah's Tears* almost impossible. Beyond the Arimathea portico, curtains of rain swept across the paving stones in the courtyard. Joseph watched the capricious winds bring the rain in waves, and he shivered when the chill and dampness washed over him.

"Storm weather, this," Joseph commented aloud although no one was near to hear. The sullen downpour of the past week swept away his plans and left him frustrated.

Despite the chill, inclement weather, Elvan persevered in his search for seasoned timbers to replace the main mast and sail spar, and locate adequate material for the big square sail. Elvan knew his craft's needs better than the Pharisee, and Joseph had not interfered with his captain.

To his surprise, his passengers chose not to remain in Massilia but would sail on to Britannia aboard *Judah's Tears*. Although the rain hampered many facets of their plans, it could not stop their witness of the Christ, both in the synagogues and wherever Greeks would stop and listen. Although some Jews opposed them, others listened intently, and the number of Christ-followers increased in the city.

David ben Seth, Joseph's factor, was one of the first to accept the Christ and receive the *Holy Spirit*. Energetic and charismatic, he arranged many opportunities for the new arrivals to spread their testimonies among the people.

Joseph stared out at the rain without seeing it. Instead, he pictured southern Britannia, its moors and fields awash in color this time of year, the verdant greens of its ancient forests. He loved his homeland and the Jewish people, but the tribesmen, with their liveliness and their energy, held a special place in his heart. He felt his calling keenly; an ache that never eased....

A drenched and dripping David ben Seth found Quintus Marcellus Gota in his chamber away from Joseph. From the man's manner the Roman knew something was amiss. Something coursed through the factor, shaped his anxiety on the anvil of personal loyalty. "Whatever brought you here——" Gota pressed him. "Out with it."

David drew a deep breath, his decision made long before he approached the Roman. "A merchant, a leader in the synagogue, threatens to have Joseph seized and stoned. Many listen to him. I fear for the master."

Gota nodded. Because of the damp, he wore the red Roman fighting tunic, and under it, brown woolen pants, favored by Roman legionnaires, and a thin woolen shirt. Scooping up a thick woolen cloak and his scabbarded *gladius*, he told David, "Take me to this merchant."

When they left the house, the storm's worst had blown through, and the light was almost gone. Only a slight drizzle continued to fall when David led Gota through the Massilia streets to a large storefront shop filled with sundry wares. While they watched, several well-dressed patrons left, Jews by their dress.

"What is the name of this merchant?" Gota asked pointedly. "And how will I know him."

"Mordecai ben Nathan," David answered. "He is tall, a robust man of middle age, who favors a long black beard in spite of the Greek penchant in Massilia for no beards."

Gota nodded. "Stay here," he ordered. "I will not have you drawn into this——"

Turning on his heel, Gota entered the shop. Deeper than it was wide, wares displayed on tables and shelves opening on a center aisle, the stall was organized, orderly. Before he walked a dozen paces, a man, clearly a bodyguard, opposed him. "Leave," he confronted Gota. "My master closes his shop. Come back tomorrow."

Taking advantage of appearing old, the Roman did not slow. Twisting his hip to put his bodyweight behind the punch, Gota hit the man solidly on the jaw. With a sudden catch of breath, the guard's head snapped back, his eyes glazed, and he slumped to the floor unconscious.

Nearby a second guard, a Gaul, attired like the first but stouter, saw his companion fall. When the bodyguard drew his sword, Gota advanced on him, saw uncertainty waver in the Gaul's eyes. Then the man attempted an overhand slash. Sidestepping the obvious attack, the Roman smashed his left fist against the guard's torso just below the ribcage. Breath hammered from the Gaul's lungs. When the bodyguard collapsed over Gota's fist, the Roman struck him hard behind the ear, shoved him carelessly aside.

A dozen strides away, Mordecai froze, his wide, shocked eyes met Gota's. In heartbeats he had witnessed both of his veteran guards fall to one empty-handed, white-haired old man. "What——?" the merchant blurted. "What have you done to them?"

When the intruder continued his slow advance without answering, Mordecai hastily scuttled backward. His voice rose, strident and fearful. "What do you want?"

Dodging behind a table, the Jew tried to flee, but Gota cut him off. Muscles honed by a life in empire service and kept hard through a disciplined regime of exercise, Gota slapped aside the frantic hands the Jew raised against him. Gripping the merchant's throat with iron fingers, the Roman shoved him hard against a wall. With his off hand, he drew the *gladius*, brought it near Mordecai's fleshy face.

"Scripture tells us that '*All men sin and fall short of the glory of God*,'" Gota said softly, his tone belying the threat. "Though I am a Christ-follower, Romans are known to be back-sliders. You have seen what I can do with my hands." He brandished the sword edge closer to Mordecai's cheek, let the light reflecting from the steel flash into the Jew's eyes. "Think what I could do with this sword——"

"What do——you want?" Mordecai whimpered. "If you want money, ransom——?"

"I want nothing you own!" Gota snarled. "You have threatened Joseph of Arimathea with harm." In a harsh voice colder than the winds of winter, he promised, "If you or any of your conspirators harm him in any way, or threaten him with more harm publicly or privately, I will return and teach you just how good I am with a blade."

Gota squeezed Mordecai's neck, almost strangling him. "Have we reached an accord?"

"Ye—Yes!" the merchant sputtered. "But—how do I control—stop what others do?"

"Find ways," Gota demanded. "Or I will return and make good my pledge."

Careful to strike with only the *gladius*' ball-like pommel, the

Roman drove the round bronze against the Jew's ample gut. With an astonished gasp, Mordecai doubled over, and Gota left him gagging in the shop floor.

Sheathing his sword, he surveyed his carnage. Then he turned and strode without haste toward the street. Gota found David watching from the doorway.

"Would you have killed him?" Joseph's factor asked the Roman when they made their way through wet streets back to the Arimathea compound. "Will you do what you pledged if Mordecai continues to make trouble?"

Gota smiled, but there was little humor in the expression. "Perhaps we should both pray your merchant does not put me to the test."

Overhead, the stormy sky still hung oppressively low and retained its dull leaden hue. But surprisingly, the rain no longer fell. Gota hoped in some small way, he could take that as God's answer....

With insistent probing thumbs Silvanus examined Reuben's bruised jaw. "You will be sore for a time, but it is not broken." With a headshake, the schoolmaster added with a lopsided grin, "But perhaps that bruise taught you a timely lesson. It is not wise to allow your opponent's offhand fist to come so near your jaw. If he tries to close with you, punish him. Make him respect you enough to maintain his distance."

Again the Roman probed, and Reuben grimaced.

"You must accept——" Silvanus continued. "Because you discipline yourself to fight under your own code of honor, that does not compel your opponent to adopt that same code. If anything, he will use it as a weakness against you."

Silvanus rubbed his hands vigorously on a linen cloth. "My man fought to win against you, as my gladiators must. You adhering to your code of honor gave him the win. In the arena doing so would have sealed your death."

When Reuben still did not speak, the schoolmaster plunged on.

"When you step beyond these walls, there will be no blunted weapons, no red chalk on edges and points. Out there war and combat seldom offer second chances. The victorious walk away; those who lose, die. Or they are crippled, maimed for the rest of their lives. Something you should understand far better than most men."

Reuben's chin lifted. "I do not wish to kill."

"Neither did Gwyr," Silvanus countered. "Until he had to choose between yours and Joseph's lives or those attacking you. He made his choice; because of it, you live. Now you must make yours. Wearing a sword means accepting and living with the consequences that one day or many days you may *have* to kill."

Silvanus flung the cloth away. "If you cannot accept the consequences, lay down the sword. Turn and walk away. Never pick it up again. Whatever you decide ultimately is between you and your God."

At dawn in the main room of the Arimathea compound, Joseph met with the men who journeyed with him, fasting and silently praying their mission to Britannia would honor their Lord and Savior Jesus Christ, and that the good news they carried would be well received. With the noon hour, they paused, continued to fast, and spoke among themselves, sharing with one another the promptings of the *Spirit.*

While they conversed, a man entered the chamber. Attired in Jewish robes, he strode boldly toward them. Joseph felt a sudden jolt of recognition. Philip! Philip of Bethsaida. The Apostle Philip! One of the Twelve——

"Ah, Joseph," Philip said in a relieved tone, "I found you before you departed."

They embraced warmly. The Apostle was little changed. Hair and beard worn in typical Judean fashion, he was tall for a Jew, with fair skin and grey eyes from a distant Greek ancestor. Philip's gaze was steady and direct and filled with joy at his reunion with Joseph.

"I did not expect to see you here in Massilia," the Pharisee exclaimed. "I understood you would concentrate your ministry from the Roman boot eastward to Greece."

Philip nodded. "For several months I have divided my time between Massilia's Greek-speaking community and outlying villages. However, very soon I will leave Gaul. From here I travel east toward Greece, Syria, and Phrygia with my sister Mariamne and Bartolomew, preaching as I go."

"When the rain ends, I head for Britannia," Joseph told him. "We hope to establish a church there to aid in the spread of the good news."

"It is for that reason I have come," Philip responded. "Our Lord has laid it on my heart that the Christ's messenger who will carry the good news to Britannia be consecrated an Apostle to the Celts. My intention is to enlist one of your company for that role."

Joseph nodded. "Who will you name?"

"That is the Lord's decision," Philip answered. "We shall cast lots the way we did to replace Judas."

David ben Seth quickly provided small pieces of unfired potsherd, all cut to equal size and a container to hold them. He also brought reed pens and ink. When Joseph called forth each of his companions, Philip wrote the man's name on one of the sherds. Once the chore had been accomplished, they prayed at length over the pieces, consigning them to God and His plans.

"Somehow I feel it is fitting there are twelve," Philip said softly. With slow, sure fingers, he collected the sherds, placed them in the cylinder, and covered its open mouth with a palm. Gently he shook them, mixing the pieces. Then he sat down and gave the cylinder to David. "I shall pray, then slowly upend the container into the lap of my robe and let the pieces fall as God intends."

David nodded solemnly. Philip raised his hands in supplication. "Thou, Lord, who knowest the hearts of all these men, show which one of these twelve *Thou* has chosen."

Leaning forward, David tipped the container. A single sherd fell from the cylinder before the others. Philip's right hand captured it a heartbeat before the cascade began. When the remainder tumbled, they produced muted, almost musical, tinkling sounds. Unmindful of the other eleven in his lap, Philip stared at his clinched fist. Within him the *Spirit* surged, and before he opened his hand, he knew beyond doubt the name inscribed there.

But the others did not. Slowly Philip relaxed his fingers. The sherd lay revealed in his open palm, inked side down. With a fingertip, he turned it over so the inscribed name could be read.

"The Lord has spoken," Philip announced to them all. "*He* has chosen His Apostle to Britannia and its people." His excited eyes and rapt expression held them speechless. His soft voice carried to them all. "He has chosen Brother Joseph of Arimathea."

A shout of exaltation rang through the hall, all eyes focused on Joseph. Hands clasped before him, the Pharisee stood humbly, head bowed, tears upon his cheeks.

"Come, Brother Joseph, stand before me," Philip urged. "I ask all in this hall to stand around him, touch him. If you cannot reach him, touch one who touches him so there is an unbroken link between him and us."

They came and reached toward Joseph. Those who could not, clasped the shoulder of him standing in front.

Philip lifted his voice heavenward. "The Christ said before *He* left us, '*All authority has been given Me in heaven and on earth. Go therefore and make disciples of all the nations, baptizing them in the name of the Father, and the Son and the Holy Spirit, teaching them to observe all that I commanded you, and lo, I am with you always, even to the end of the age.*'"

Joseph's eyes closed, his chin lifted, a soulful humility mantling him. Philip saw it though other eyes and marveled at the moment of intense clarity.

Drawing a deep breath, Philip continued. "Our Lord also said when *He* sent out the Seventy, '*The harvest is plentiful, but the laborers are few; therefore beseech the Lord of the harvest to send out laborers into His harvest.*'"

All felt it, the *Spirit* moving within them, a silent consecration no man could deny. It flowed inward to Joseph, and the Pharisee's face grew radiant with it.

"Our Lord and Savior said as well," Philip affirmed, "*The one who listens to you listens to Me, and the one who rejects you rejects Me, and he who rejects Me rejects the One who sent Me.*'"

Philip paused. "Brother Joseph, in keeping with the commission our Savior gave us, I recognize and name you an Apostle of Christ. As *He* commissioned us, I also commission you to take the gospel to the shores of Britannia. Will you accept this commission?"

Joseph sighed, lifted his eyes heavenward, almost too overcome to speak. "God help me, I will."

CHAPTER 14

hy does terror often goad men to foolhardiness? Damhan Mawr pondered the thought anew as he stared at the ancient forest beyond the woodland. The *tor* and the water that made it an island half a day stretched high and wide behind him. He kept coming back here, drawn to a place he dreaded and would put behind him, never see again. But he could not.

More and more his nightmares drew the Dumnonii chieftain back to *Ynys Wydryn*, 'the Isle of Glass,' and the enchanted dark woods surrounding it. It became a paradox of rejection and yearning, like striving to forget a snippet of elusive melody that kept doggedly echoing in his thoughts.

He could cite no reason; the drawing grew from a place deep inside where words and reasons had no meaning. A hidden part of his soul he never knew existed. He grimaced. It began when he encountered the forest phantom and fled in abject fear. It was like seepage from a old wound that never fully healed.

"What do you want, Damhan Mawr?"

Startled from his pondering, Damhan spun around. He recognized the voice before his eyes focused on her. Arawn Doelguss. No one else could come upon him so silently.

Arawn stood a dozen steps behind him, a half-smile on her lips. Her eyes were mild and gray-blue, opaque and bright, serene yet cradling deep mysteries——like the waters surrounding the *tor*. Beneath the smile, her mouth was severe but comely; on a gentler woman it might have been beautiful, but on Arawn's face it was a finely chiseled instrument.

Her face framed with dark hair worn long and uncovered, she was stunning, ethereal, and unforgettable. Although she could not be much past girlhood, she seemed never to have been young. More, there was something about her that proclaimed Arawn Doelguss was no man's woman.

Damhan inclined his head in respect to the Lady of the Lake. "Priestess, I did not hear you come."

She nodded, her eyes saying without words that was as it should be. "What truly seeds your fears, Damhan Mawr? The desire to know——or the desire to forget?"

He struggled with her question. It opened an abyss he did not wish to plumb. But she waited for his answer, an imperative in its own way, leaving him with little choice but to stare into that emptiness. Finally he shrugged, answered lamely, "Perhaps I fear I am not man enough or wise enough to embrace the truth once I discover it."

She smiled, and it warmed him like sunlight breaking through darkness. "Mayhap now you begin to frame the proper questions. Your answers are there. Seek them diligently."

Arawn Doelguss tilted her head, her black hair molding to one side of her face, her wise eyes silently reminding Damhan anew she was more than a comely *fey* Celtic maid. She was a priestess——from an ancient line of priestesses.

"I go to speak with Bran the Blessed," she told him. "Perhaps you care to come——?"

There was command and strength in her, even when it was posed as a question. Damhan nodded solemnly. "I would."

Dawn crept slowly over the seven hills of Rome. In the hallways of the palace, knots of servitors and members of the Senate conferred in whispered tones. Emperor Gaius Julius Caesar Augustus Germanicus, known to the people of his empire as Caligula, was gravely ill.

Physicians hovered closely about the emperor. After Caligula took power, his doctors noted a change in his personal habits. He became obsessed with taking numerous warm baths each day. Worse, his carnal appetite for women of all kinds, for great amounts of alcohol, and for lavish meals increased dramatically. Soon he began to complain of weakness in his upper and lower extremities, headaches, and insomnia. Then came the day he could not appear at the Senate or in public because of extreme dizziness, great difficulties in walking, standing, or even sitting.

Loved by many for being the beloved son of the popular Roman general Germanicus, Caligula began his reign favorably. In the first two years he governed nobly and moderately. Renown historian Suetonius, an intimate of Caligula's, wrote that more than one-hundred-sixty-thousand animals were sacrificed during three months of public rejoicing to usher in his reign.

However, the emperor's affliction brought the administration of both Rome and the empire to a standstill. His ambitious construction projects ground to a halt, especially his notoriously luxurious personal dwellings and two new aqueducts for the city of Rome, the *Aqua Claudia* and *Anio Novus*, designed to bring more water to the people.

In one of his more lucid moments, he called for the general of the Praetorian Guard and demanded he bring the generals of his armies to his bedside. When they attended him later in the day, Caligula informed them, "While I have been lying here, the gods came to my bedside and told me it is time to invade Britannia, that the island is ripe for plucking. Go, make the necessary preparations, and return to me when they are done."

Questioning glances passed between the generals. "Invade Britannia, my Emperor?" one more bold than the rest questioned. "Where will we obtain the capital for such a campaign? The Empire treasury is low——?"

"Must I think for you all?" Caligula retorted, his shadowed eyes narrowing dangerously. "Ptolemy of Mauretania has prospered. He grows too rich for my taste. Annex all of Mauretania, if you must, but hear me, I will have Britannia. The gods have given it to me."

His face hardened, "You have your orders. Now get out. You disturb my rest."

Again looks passed. His obvious personality changes rankled the generals, but with the Praetorian Guard at hand, the real power in Rome, they had no choice but to comply.

"As you have said it," they said in unison, "so it shall be...."

Along the northern shores of *Ynys Wydryn*, tribesmen gathered in groups, young scholars from many schools of learning, one in each capital of the forty Tribes, and among them, young scholars from Rome. For twenty years they pursued their studies before they completed all the Druids had to teach, fields such as astronomy, arithmetic, geometry, jurisprudence, medicine, poetry, and oratory. Each day they walked leagues to sit at the feet of the Druids, the high *tor* in the background.

There Arawn Doelguss and Damhan Mawr found the Arch Druid Bran the Blessed watching over his students while his subordinates taught. To Damhan, the Arch Druid was a legend. Bran, son of Llyr, educated in distant Rome during the reign of Augustus Caesar, who returned to Britannia to take up the crown of the Silures. Bran the Blessed who resigned the crown to his son, Caradoc, and became Arch Druid of the Silurians. Bran the Blessed who took to wife the Jewess Anna, daughter of Matthat ben Levi and sister to Joseph of Arimathea.

A tall imposing man with a wild gray beard that climbed his lined cheeks like wild vines, Bran the Blessed stood with one arm at his side, the other outthrust, gripping a carved walking stick almost his height. Bright light brought to sharp relief his strong features, arms without arm rings, hands that in times past wielded both sword and scepter, hands that now guided the finest minds of Britannia's youth.

Bran's head turned as they approached. He nodded respectfully. "I see you, Arawn Doelguss." His eyes focused on the Dumnonii. "And you, Damhan Mawr. Have you come to join my students?"

Before Damhan could shape his denial, Arawn spoke. "The earth turns, the patterns change. We must change with the turning or be swept away." Her face grew radiant, seeing what they could not. "A new center has been forged; a delicate balance once lost has been restored——"

Damhan held his breath. All tribesmen held a deeply-rooted fear of any change that came too suddenly. A century past the Romans invaded Britannia; the after-shocks still reverberated through the land and the Forty Tribes.

"Before autumn's leaves fall," Arawn proclaimed, "the prophet, who is not a prophet, the one the prophet serves, and others with them come to bear witness to the truth. I have *seen* it."

Turning abruptly, the Lady of the Lake walked away from the astonished men, nor did she heed their questions when they hurried after her. When it became plain she would say no more, they halted, let her go her way alone.

"She is infuriating when she does this," Bran said softly. He shook his head perplexedly. "Mysteries within mysteries——?"

A strange irrational calm settled on Damhan, a certainty that all that passed and all that was to be, what Arawn spoke was a puzzle of many pieces waiting to be linked together. He just had to make sense of it all.

When Bran started to speak, the Dumnonii chieftain held up his hand for silence. Then his eyes widened, his thoughts reeled. The prophet who is not a prophet——could that mean the Lame prophet who is no longer lame? Reuben ben Ezra? And the one whom the prophet served——Joseph of Arimathea? Could it be...?

I have always said Reuben would return, Damhan told himself. The more he considered it, the more right it felt.

Bran studied Damhan's expressions. "I think you begin to understand her," he said with conviction. He brandished his staff in empty threat. "Must I beat it out of you?"

Fragments of memory, gleanings of years began to weave together into a tapestry that both excited and mystified the Dumnonii. The more he combined the isolated and contrary strands, the more desperate his quest became. To be sure, he must know more——

He faced the Arch Druid. "Before I do, explain to me the mysteries of the Triad...."

When the south winds finally blew away the rain, Massilia reminded Elvan of a drenched and miserable alley cat, wet fur slick and unsightly. Although the worst refuse from the gutters had washed into the harbor, a soggy, wet stench settled on the city and lingered, slowly eradicated by the baking sun.

Once the rain ended and Elvan found the needed seasoned timbers, Massilia's shipwrights quickly repaired the ship to the captain's direction. Crafting the cloth for the square sail took the weavers another week to finish. Finally, almost a month to the day of their arrival, her passengers aboard, *Judah's Tears* caught the turning of the tide and put out to sea.

At Joseph's direction, Elvan steered southwest toward the Pillars of Hercules. Rather than the northern route through the strait beyond the port of Calpe, the Pharisee directed them toward Abyla and the southern route to the Unknown Sea. Because of the prevailing southern wind, they turned southeast, passing the island where they found the derelict, then turned west again when the wind blew from the right quarter.

Chapter 15

In Carthago, Daniel opened dispatches sent from the factors in from Jerusalem and Judea and smiled broadly. Knowing his reports would chase Joseph and Reuben along the trading routes to Britannia, he prepared several copies, sent them off by different routes on the first available ships heading west.

Missives from the Faceless Men showed the power struggle between the governor and the office of the high priest continued unabated. Almost immediately after Vitellius replaced Pontius Pilate as governor of Judea, he deposed the quarrelsome Caiaphas as high priest. Not long thereafter Caiaphas died by strange means.

Privy to the agreement with Rome that the House of Ananus would retain control of the high priest's office, Vitellius chose the old priest's brother-in-law, Jonathan ben Ananus, to replace Caiaphas. But over the past year Jonathan proved no less quarrelsome, so Vitellius stripped the Jew of his power, supplanting him with another brother, Theophilus ben Ananus.

Word also has come from Christ's followers, Daniel wrote. *The Apostle Peter left Jerusalem for Antioch where he established a church in the Kerateion quarter.*

Located in the southern portion of the city, between the Forum Colonnades of Herod and Mount Tauris, a rocky crag at the foot of Mount Silpios, the Kerateion quarter boasted a large Jewish population.

Not long after Peter founded the church, an earthquake struck the city. Many buildings throughout the city were damaged, but Peter and the new believers escaped harm.

Daniel set aside his pen, flexed his tired fingers. There was trivial detail he could add. Spies from the Faceless Men also learned from Vitellius' scribes in Fortress Antonia that Caligula had dispatched two senators to report on the condition and damage in Antioch, but he chose to omit it from his letters to Joseph and Reuben.

Ah, he considered, *one more item, a posting to Antioch.* Taking up the pen, he directed the dispatch of a young scribe, Titus, to train under the aging head scribe in the Arimathea compound who had requested assistance.

He is a young man of exceptional ability, Daniel wrote, *a cripple, and wholly dedicated to Arimathea. A bond-servant to our House serves as his legs. Treat them well.*

Daniel set aside the pen. He knew of Titus from Reuben ben Ezra and had been told to watch and encourage him. Like the minister of the House of Arimathea, Titus had been a Jerusalem beggar, a cast-off like himself, but few knew the boy's true name, Elias the Penitent. In years to come, Daniel made sure, the name would be completely forgotten.

Reuben paced before the window. Outside the morning heat increased steadily as the sun rose higher. Suddenly impatient with himself for delaying his decision, he called a servant, sent for the Faceless Men.

When they came, he waved them to nearby cushions. Although their faces betrayed little, he knew they wondered at the summons.

"You have attended me faithfully," he told them. "Even obeyed me when I commanded you to remain in the compound, not attend me each day when I went to the fighting school. In this you have my thanks."

They showed so little reaction they may as well have been carved from stone. Of the two, the senior bowed his head respectfully. "How may we serve you, young Master?"

"Soon I will leave for Britannia, which is most distant as you know," Reuben answered. "It is in my mind to release you from your covenant when I leave, allow you to return to Jerusalem if that is your wish."

For the first time since he had recruited them, Reuben saw doubt register on their faces. The younger took a deep breath. "Who will protect the young Master from harm?" His chin dropped, his face clouded, shame clearly etched there. "You have lost faith in us."

"No," Reuben said flatly. "That is not true."

"Then why do you discharge us?"

Reuben strove to help them understand. "I go to Britannia——to witness for the Christ, but in that land, a man should carry a sword to be respected. If he wears a sword, he also is expected to know its use."

He spread his hands toward the Faceless Men. "You were my first teachers. Because of you I can walk among the Britons with my head held high, and they will listen to my words when I testify about the Christ."

With an eloquent shrug, Reuben pressed on, "But if I go with protectors at my shoulders and back, they will judge I place no trust in them. Thus my witness for the Christ will be diminished."

His eyes pleading, the elder stood. "We understand the kindness you offer us. But if we return to our Order with our covenant broken, we face disgrace or worse from the brotherhood." He spread his hands in supplication. "If we indeed have served you well, surely——?"

"Then remain here in Abyla," Reuben compromised. "Serve my interests here. Serve the factor who represents me. Serve the House of Arimathea." He met the elder's eyes, then also faced the younger. "Is this acceptable?"

They both bowed low, touched their foreheads to the floor. "So you have said. So it will be."

Balmy night breezes off the Great Sea often tempered the deep chill radiating from the southern desert wastes once the hash sun slipped below the western horizon. But on the eve prior to *Judah's Hope's* departure for Britannia, the chill's cold fingers crept through Abyla and along the Mauretanian coast. Its clamminess slithered under doors and through cracks, nipping at bare skin like ill-trained dogs.

Reuben woke shivering, but it was not from the cold. Something had jarred him awake, some innate caution that warned not to sail with the tide. He tried to dismiss the feeling, but it persisted into full wakefulness. He tossed and turned, but his premonition clung to his idle mind like wet cloth against the skin.

Finally, his inner tension preventing any return to sleep, he thrust back his coverlet and rose. Breathing shallowly against the chill, he hurriedly dressed, intent on reaching the harbor to alert Gwydion to halt preparations to sail. Slipping the baldric of his *gladius* over his shoulder, he stepped outside his chamber. Like ghosts, his two Faceless Men stepped from the hallway shadows.

Frowning, Reuben gestured impatiently, "Why are you here?" he demanded. "You are no longer in my service. You now serve Arimathea."

"With respect, young Master," the elder said. "Until you sail, you are Arimathea."

Reuben sighed. He understood their ingrained concepts of loyalty; there had been a time when he had welcomed that protection. Now it rubbed against his self-confidence like an ill-fitting shoe. However, arguing would only delay them. "Come, then——" he said with a shrug. "If you must."

Outside, with no moon, a stygian darkness brooded in the streets, and Reuben grudgingly appreciated the light cast by the Faceless Men's torches. Once they reached the harbor, the quays blazed with light as ships' crews readied their vessels for sailing. He found Gwydion where he expected, overseeing the loading of their cargo.

"I did not expect you for at least two more turnings of the

sand glass," the shipsmaster said. "Soon we will have the cargo loaded and——"

Reuben interrupted him, shook his head. "We cannot sail with the tide."

Gwydion frowned. "And the cause——?"

"I can give you no ample reason," Reuben countered. "All I can says is——we must not sail today."

Long ago Gwydion learned to trust Reuben's hunches. Perhaps fate whispered in the minister's ear where others heard nothing? In the old days, before he had come to accept the Christ, the shipsmaster would have said Reuben was touched by the gods. Perhaps in truth he was; the Christ had healed his legs.

"Then we do not put to sea," Gwydion said simply. "However——" he glanced at the ship, "we will finish stowing the cargo in preparation for sailing."

"Do as you think best." Reuben turned to go, then spoke his thoughts. "There will be an east wind today."

Gwydion raised an eyebrow, but said nothing. He did not need to glance overhead to know the harbor pennants still hung limp against their staffs. But if Reuben said the east wind would blow, then it would blow.

Sensing Reuben's hesitation, his uncertainty, Gwydion grinned. "I shall expect the wind. You did warn Damhan Mawr about the sea coming to Ictis."

Reuben's mouth twisted wryly. His eyes locked with Gwydion's. "That Dumnonii talks too much."

Then the minister stalked off toward the Arimathea compound, his Faceless Men silently escorting him.

The morning dragged. Reuben spent the time with his Abyla factor, Joel ben Heman. In spite of the extensive planning already in place against his absence, Reuben discussed additional options regarding lead shipments to Rome. Joel understood his master's tension and accepted the recommendations with good grace.

When Reuben finally left the compound for the harbor, both men privately sighed their relief. In truth, the morning's work accomplished little.

Patience, Reuben inwardly reminded himself. *You were a mother hen with Joel, and you know it.*

At the quay, he glanced at the fluttering pennant. It clearly pointed west, showed a prevailing wind blew strongly from the east. Reuben found that somehow comforting.

"What else will the afternoon bring?" Gwydion said from just behind Reuben. Arimathea's minister shrugged. His presage moments caught him unawares, brief glimmers that, more often than not, made little sense. It was as Scripture said——like seeing through a glass darkly.

"You expect me to know?" Reuben countered. Irked, he quipped, "If I said a great kraken would rise up from the waves and devour us and the city, would you believe me?"

"If your kraken changed into a ship of Arimathea design, I would," the shipsmaster affirmed. He gestured frantically eastward. "Look beyond the harbor."

Reuben squinted, followed Gwydion's extended finger. There it was, a sleek ship, clearly not of Phoenician design, cleaving the waves toward the harbor, big square sail filled. As he watched, the sail spar lowered, and oars were run out. Then, like a giant water bug, it crawled across the channel approach to the harbor.

Beside Reuben, Gwydion's breath caught. "I know that vessel," he exclaimed wide-eyed. "That is *Judah's Tears*, Maelgeyn's ship."

Lord, Reuben prayed silently, *grant that I was wrong. Let Maelgeyn be aboard that craft, alive and well.*

Other crewmen recognized the approaching vessel, ran to join Reuben and Gwydion at quayside. A figure leaped up on the bow rail, one arm wrapped around the high bow stem. A hand lifted, began to wave excitedly, side to side.

With slow, even oar strokes, they entered the harbor, made for the quay. At the last moment, the helmsman cut the tiller hard over, the crewmen drew in the oars, and *Judah's Tears* eased gently against the quay's mortared stones.

Elvan was first ashore. He ran straight to Gwydion, his face anguished. "We lost Maelgeyn and five others at sea," he cried, "in a terrible storm that ripped away our sail and oars and left us derelict."

Grief old and new shadowed the shipsmaster's face. He accepted Elvan's heartfelt embrace. When the man stepped back, Gwydion said quickly, "We knew he was lost. Reuben sensed the moment my brother drowned."

Elvan blinked in surprise, cut his eyes to Reuben in open question. "How is this?"

Reuben did not pause to answer. He demanded instead, "What of Joseph? Was he lost with Maelgeyn?"

Elvan shook his head. "The Master lives, safe and uninjured. He will disembark shortly with the others."

"You must tell us all," Gwydion insisted, his spirits rising. "Come, let us assist the others ashore."

CHAPTER 16

Bran the Blessed led Damhan Mawr to the large wooden hall on the north shore above *Ynys Wydryn*, the *'Isle of Glass.'* North and east of the hall, the surviving trees were hundreds of years old, all second growth, seeded long ago to replace the ancient giants the Celts harvested for timbers to build the communal hall and outbuildings which served as students' dormitories.

They entered the cozy gloom of the large main hall. A welter of scents surrounded them, moldering hay from the thatched roof vying with the mouth-watering aromas of cooking meats. Near the central fire pit, a bluish smear of wood smoke drifted upward to mingle amid huge overhead timbers, blackened by years of hearth fires. Women moved in the ember-lit shadows, preparing and roasting beef, venison and capon for the evening meal along with a dozen varieties of fish.

Bran waved Damhan to a bench, called for goblets of mead. The Dumnonii cradled the wooden cup in his hands, savored the mead, rolled the sweet fermented honey brew over his tongue with evident appreciation, and let it slide down his parched throat.

Lifting his own cup to his lips, the Arch Druid barely tasted it. "I worry about the Atrebates," he told the Dumnonii chieftain, "and their designs on *'the Isle of Glass.'* They no longer spy covertly. Afraid of the forest phantom, they move armed through the woods in large numbers. For now they offer no open threat to us or our students, but I am uneasy on what the future holds."

Damhan squirmed, suddenly uncomfortable. Growing older, Kimbelinus became more desirous of all the land in southern

Britannia. He had virtually reduced the once proud Belgiae to vassal status, until they rebelled and sided with the Dumnonii, the Dobunni, and the Durotriges against him. The Atrebates resisted, but Kimbelinus was relentless.

"The Catuvellauni——" Damhan admitted, "push the Atrebates to expand this way, to '*the Isle of Glass?*'"

"Yes," Bran acknowledged. "That is what I fear."

"That would set the other Tribes against them," Damhan countered. "One against many."

"Tell me when the Atrebates have ever shown caution?" Bran answered. "I warrant you will not soon forget their attack on you and Joseph of Arimathea."

Damhan's eyebrows gathered like storm clouds. "I have not forgotten," he said in a tight tone, "nor will I ever forget. Although my people grumble, for the sake of the peace here, I hold back from making war upon them."

"Old friend," Bran offered, "I know *your* want, how special these forests are to you. But hear my appeal——do not walk these woods again without guards. I would not lose you to your own stubbornness."

Raising his cup to Bran, Damhan nodded. "To your sage words," he toasted. "I will honor them."

Oil lamps flickered in the Arimathea compound, their light casting dancing shadows on the wall of the common room. Dusk had long fallen and still Joseph of Arimathea, Reuben, Quintus Marcellus Gota, and Luke of Arimathea sat together discussing the Pharisee's ordeal. Joseph reclined on plush cushions, sipping refreshments, with the others grouped around him. Time and again, Joseph's gaze strayed to the scabbarded *gladius* Reuben had slipped from his shoulder and set aside.

Reuben regarded Joseph levelly, his gaze older by years than his boyish face. He knew of no way to counter his master's calm judicial gaze except complete honesty. "I watched you eye the sword. Even now your curiosity burns to ask about it? Shall I explain——?"

Joseph smiled ruefully. "I am that obvious?"

Both Gota and Luke chuckled. Reuben would not dare. His expression did not change, but he felt the humor leeched from him by the demand in the Pharisee's eyes.

"You are called to Britannia," Reuben said. "I am called to follow you——"

His eyes strayed to a lamp's dancing flame, then back to Joseph. He had not realized such a simple explanation would prove so difficult.

"When last we were there, I was a crippled youth," Reuben continued. "And as such, I was tolerated because it was beneath the honor of any tribesman to challenge one who could not defend himself. In those days Gwyr served as my champion and where he walked, mute or not, I was accepted because of him."

Reuben's expression sobered. "Through the grace and blood of the Christ, I am a whole man. Now, if a tribesman chooses to challenge me, and I show myself incapable of fighting or refuse to fight, I will be shamed in his eyes. As a result my witness, my testimony for my Lord and Savior Jesus the Christ will be irrevocably tarnished. They would dismiss me out of hand and no longer listen to my words."

He gestured toward Gota and Luke. "These men well understand a Celt's concept of manhood, his code of honor. Ask them if what I say is in error. Ask them——"

Joseph inhaled deeply. "I am not a fighting man, and I have never been ridiculed for that lack of ability."

"No tribesman would," Reuben told him. "They see you as a holy man, to be honored, much like one of their own Druids. As such, they respect you and fear you and hear your words when you speak." He shook his head. "They will not accord me that privilege. I do not have your sanctity."

Joseph opened his mouth to refute Reuben's claim. Instead he looked to Gota and Luke, his eyes questioning.

"What the lad says is true, Joseph," Gota answered. "All of it.

That is why in Britannia every man carries a sword. But you——"
He shook his head. "You are unique. The tribesmen venerate you."

Luke leaned forward. "Reuben understands what he will
encounter when he returns to Britannia. The Faceless Men tutored
him in the fighting arts. Then he came to me, and here in Abyla, he
attended the fighting school. Titus Antonius Silvanus says he would
never make a gladiator, but he praised Reuben's fighting ability. As
do I. In Britannia the Celts will respect him, and they will listen and
honor his witness. You have my word in this."

Joseph slumped back against the cushions. "Keep your sword,
Reuben. I will not gainsay you." The Pharisee sighed. "This has
been a night for revelations," he said musingly. Then his lips twisted
perplexedly, his manner clearly ill at ease. "Venerated, you say, Gota?
I never thought to question the respect they gave me...."

Dawn had yet to gray the eastern rim of the sea when Reuben,
Joseph, and remainder of the travelers boarded the ships. Reuben and
Luke joined Gwydion aboard *Judah's Hope* while Joseph, Quintus
Marcellus Gota, and the remainder of the Christ's followers from
Judea stayed with Elvan on *Judah's Tears*.

Prior to sailing, Gwydion, with Elvan at his shoulder, inspected
the repairs made by Massilia shipwrights for flaws or weaknesses and
pronounced them satisfactory. However, the new Massilia sail had
already been replaced. Its cloth was judged too thin for the turbulent
weather and winds on the Unknown Seas. Gwydion had requisitioned
a replacement from stores in the Arimathea compound within a day
of *Judah's Tears* arrival in Abyla.

They pulled away from the quay under oars with a strong eastern
wind in their faces. Once they cleared the harbor, the ships turned
north, then west into the strait.

"The strong east wind bodes well for us," Gwydion said to Reuben
and Luke from the helmsman's platform. "Even so, we steer a perilous
path. If we stray too far into the strait the great current flowing

inward into the Great Sea will snare us and force our retreat to the east. We will lose all the westward progress we have gained." He turned to Luke. "You can distinguish the inward flow by the water's ripple. It is visible on the surface."

Reuben remembered well the previous voyage. From Abyla they must set a course just far enough out from the southern shore to avoid the shoals and rocks that would rip their hulls to pieces. He recalled Gwydion's stern warning; never attempt this passage in the full or change of the moon because the eastern current ran perilously fast. During that time the western winds formed heavy eddies and dangerous whirls a good distance from the southern shore.

He grinned up at the shipsmaster. "When the sun reaches its zenith, the tide will turn. Before it does, we must be out of its grasp or we will be pushed backward."

Gwydion nodded. "I am pleased you remember. Soon we turn southwestward for the harbor of Tingis," he nodded to Luke, "a Roman colony. There is a sweeping sand beach that leads to the harbor. We will wait there for dawn and the changing of the tide."

Overnighting at the Arimathea compound in Tangis, they sailed due west the following day far out into the Unknown Sea, far enough to cross the eastward flowing current before it rushed headlong through the strait between the northern and southern Pillars of Hercules. Once across the current Gwydion took them ever northward along the Hispanic coast as winds and tides permitted. When the tides turned against them, the two ships broke their voyage at fishing villages or convenient sand beaches.

In time Gwydion guided the ships farther away from the craggy coastline. Reuben told Luke, "The shore curves——" He cupped his hand, laid a straight finger from the bottom of his palm to fingertips. "And we reduce the distance we must traverse by crossing open sea."

Overhearing, the shipsmaster nodded approvingly. "You *did* listen on the trip out. Once we pass the headland west of Lacobriga, we will turn almost due north running near to the shore to use the wind off the land. But, if we venture too far west, prevailing winds will contest us, push us back toward the south."

In the next days, as the helmsman steered north, Reuben and Luke spared on deck to keep their muscles limber. Twice Luke tried to lure him into a fault, only to have Reuben dance away unscathed. "I think you learned too much in that blasted gladiator's school," the older man grumbled when his blade cut only air. "Stand still and fight."

"You told me yourself to use tactics," Reuben retorted, "that I had to think two to three moves ahead. Or is it that you are just getting slow in your final days!"

"I will show you slow!" Luke shot back and launched a series of attacks that only Reuben's agility managed to counter. Dancing back, he blocked blade on blade, adding an extra half-step to be sure. He sucked wind when Luke's thrust missed only by two finger-widths.

"That was almost your undoing," Luke chuckled. "Never relax until you well out of thrust range. Against another opponent you might worry, since I am terribly old and slow."

"Old you may be," Reuben said through gritted teeth, "slow you are not," and he launched attacks of his own.

When Reuben expected the Roman to retreat, Luke suddenly stepped forward, cupped Reuben's chin roughly in his palm and shoved him backward. When he fell, he arched his back into a roll, came up with his blunted *gladius* extended in a stop thrust. Luke sidestepped, also thrust but Reuben was able to catch it with his sword and dance out of range.

"Nicely done," Luke said. "But what if that palm had been my fist, and it knocked you senseless? Expect the unexpected, boy. When you are fighting for your life, there are no second chances. Your opponent will kill you if he gets the chance. Do not make it easy for him. That was one of the lessons Titus Antonius Silvanus tried to teach you."

Luke's rebuke stung. But Reuben knew he deserved it. It made no difference he enjoyed the duel dance. If he lapsed in a fight with sharpened swords, he suffered no illusions. He would die.

"Again," Luke announced and attacked. This time the Roman was relentless. When he parried and sidestepped away, Reuben found himself almost wishing for easier days, like on the last trip out when he studied the tiresome Latin tongue under Gota's tutelage.

By day they stayed within safe maneuvering distance; by night, a storm lantern affixed to the tops of the masts kept them together.

"If I recall properly, we are nearing the lands the Romans call Gallaecia," Reuben told Luke. "On the trip out, Gwydion identified a bad stretch of coast where unwary captains run their ships aground or tear them apart on the offshore rocks. It is called the '*Coast of Death*.'" It will not be long before he takes us more to seaward, and we sail only by day."

For two days lookouts searched for safe havens along the rugged shoreline, often losing afternoon hours with good winds rather than having night fall with no accessible beach nearby. Finally the vessels rounded a last promontory and the craggy headlands curved eastward.

Gwydion gestured. "Open water lies northward."

"This is the northern part of Gaul," Luke said. "Our name for this large body of water is *Sinus Cantabrorum*."

Reuben nodded. "It means '*Bay of the Cantabri*,' named for a wild Tribe your legions conquered over a century ago." At Luke's surprised look, he grinned. "Gota told me."

Making a lazy arc, the Arimathea ships swung seaward to catch the prevailing offshore sea winds and to avoid the large fog banks that frequent the southwestern half of the Bay of the Cantabri.

"Late spring is the worst time," Gwydion said. "Fog banks often stretch for leagues. With no true heading, unable to see the sun's direction by day or the stars by night, a helmsman could easily reverse course and sail right into the '*Coast of Death*.'"

He pointed north northeast. "Open water lies ahead. From here on we need not worry about beaching each night. With this good wind at our backs, ahead lies Albion. That is the old name for Britannia. Now, Roman," he gestured toward Luke and held up a gold coin. "You will see just how swift Broch Gorm's ships truly are. In his writings, Pliny described Albion as six days sail from Gaul. If the wind holds, I will do better." He bounced the coin on his palm. "I say four days. Any takers?"

Chapter 17

For two days high winds sired in the southwest vastness of the Unknown Ocean lashed *Judah's Hope* and *Judah's Tears*. Broch Gorm's ships responded like fleet racehorses with whips laid upon their flanks. They ran before the gales that sent rain squalls whipping across the open decks, their bows cleaving the high waves and gracefully sliding down the deep troughs.

On the fourth day of their trek across the *Sinus Cantabrorum*, the day dawned fair. Wisely no one wagered against Gwydion's prediction of a four-day crossing. Two fingers past noon, they sighted the towering red-gray cliffs that marked Britannia's southern promontories. They began like shadows along the northern horizon and grew into heroic crags that soared many times the height of the ships' masts.

White froth wreathed the headland's ankles where waves battered ceaselessly against the rock. Gulls ringed the ships, riding the winds, calling raucously to one another.

Reuben stood with Luke near the bow. "Britannia," he said simply, waving at the cliffs. Those high, foreboding ramparts still left him breathless. He had not realized how much he missed the savage land. How much he longed for the scents and smells so alien to dry Judea.

Somewhere ahead, on the inner elbow of the arm of land reaching into the 'Bay of the Cantabri' lay the Roman port of Ictis. When last Reuben had seen 'Karrek Loos y'n Koos,' it had been 'the gray rock in the wood,' leagues from the true shore. But if Damhan was to be believed, the land had sunk, and the invading sea made 'Karrek Loos *y'n Koos'* an island for part of the day where once it had simply been a tall hill that dominated the thick forest surrounding its rocky base.

"We must choose our course wisely," Gwydion said as he joined them. "Salt water has killed the forest around Ictis, but rotting trunks remain hazards to incoming and outgoing ships. They are massive enough to impale hulls."

Overhead, the sun moved another two fingers toward evening before Reuben saw *'Karrek Loos y'n Koos.'* Damhan Mawr had spoken faithfully; the incoming tide had indeed rendered the gray rock an island. A Dumnonii hill fort still crested its summit. A vivid image of the *tor* on the *'Isle of Glass'* flashed through Reuben's thoughts, and squat *'Karrek Loos y'n Koos'* paled beside that memory.

Much like it had been before the sea invaded, the port had no stone docks. Whole tree trucks had been hewn and wedged into the sand, then earth backfilled behind them to form dirt platforms, earthen quays that ran along the new beach. Deeper draft trading ships moored there. Vessels with less draft nosed their bows high on the beach, their goods offloaded over the rails by crewmen. Arimathea ships, their masts raised again to vertical, grounded on the beach alongside the other craft. Thatched-roofed storehouses had been rebuilt along the new shore, all but one in timber, surrounded by a long wooden palisade.

Gwydion stood with Reuben, Luke, and Quintus Marcellus Gota, preparing to go ashore. Around them, Arimathea crewmen sorted cargo to offload into the thatched-roofed storehouses Joseph indicated or to haul into the village. On *Judah's Tears*, Elvan planned to stay behind, seeing Joseph and his passengers safely disembarked and escorted to the Arimathea compound, their gear to be brought later.

"For reasons I do not understand, the Dumnonii resist building in stone," Gwydion said dryly. "They have never fully adopted Roman culture, like permanent stone buildings. When timber structures rot, they simply rebuild."

Reuben nodded. "Most of the Dumnonii tribesmen live in small timbered farmsteads," he told Luke, "protected by a wooden palisade like the one here."

Luke nodded at Gota, then casually motioned toward the tribesmen standing guard at the fortified timber gates. "Someone expecting trouble?"

Gota nodded. "Always."

When Reuben dropped from the ships' rail to the shore, he eyed the armed guards. When he first came to Britannia, his twisted limbs forced him to look to others for protection. Gwyr had carried him everywhere, a big Iceni with a pair of swords. Now, in the eyes of the Celts, with healed legs and feet and a *gladius* riding his hip, he was no longer beneath the tribesmen's notice. He could be challenged like any other man. In that sobering knowledge, Reuben walked with studied caution.

Before they approached the larger palisade encircling the town, Luke said, "Romans call the port *Ictis*. What is it in the Celtic language?"

Reuben chuckled. "*Marazon*, but it is better known as *Margas Jew*. Both market and the town bare the same name. Once the Celts called the village *Marghas Yow*, or 'Thursday Market.' But as the Jewish population increased, drawn to Britannia by the tin trade, when the village became a town, disgruntled tribesmen twisted the name to *Margas Jew*, 'the Jew Market.' In time, however, the name stuck."

"What was once meant as a slur against the Jews," Gwydion added, "has become a source of pride. '*The Jew Market*' has brought great wealth to the surrounding lands and many Tribes. Today many Celts proudly refer to the town as '*Zion by the Sea*.'"

Higher than the walls that surrounded the storage houses on the beach, *Margas Jew* offered relative safety for townsfolk, traders, Jews, and slaves who sheltered within its walls and for crews from the merchant ships. Manned guard towers had been raised every seventy cubits with strong gates that could be barred against brigands.

In place of cobbled or flagstone Roman roads, muddy rutted paths slippery from the last rain meandered between storehouses and tall, round houses, so different from the flat-topped Judean dwellings or stone and brick structures in the port cities along the Inner Sea.

Gray-thatched roofs were everywhere, supported by rough-hewn planks or irregular white-washed facades.

Once Reuben would have wrinkled his nose at the moldering scents, the damp odor clunging to the mud, so unlike the dry Judean air. But no longer. Now they brought a sense of homecoming. In *Margas Jew*, the air itself felt damp, like moist sea air, and the odors lingered as the waste moldered.

Reuben noticed Luke's unconcealed discomfort. "Gota once told me every land has its own smells," the little Jew said. "In time you will get used to Britannia's."

To maintain open land within the walls for future storehouses, settlers in *Margas Jew* built their dwellings close together. Streets were little more than rutted dirt alleys, and merchants' dwellings, shops, and a few inns crowded along the unpaved tracks.

Shops selling produce, fish, and wine had been near the main gate. Reuben saw other workrooms and shops he recognized, a smith at his forge, a tanner's apprentice hawking wares from his master's tannery, potters at their wheels, and weavers at their looms. There also were others he did not.

While they walked, Reuben pointed out the springs within the walls that supplied the town with ample water and the stables for pack horses and cart shelters so necessary to transport goods and cargo from the harbor storehouses.

Luke stopped, studied a round Dumnonii house. Short upright walls of brownish material formed the dwelling's outer perimeter, supporting high peaked rafters, and a roof of straw or heather packed with mud placed on top to retain the warmth. A center hole at the top allowed the smoke from a central fire pit to escape.

Abruptly, the Roman blinked, his eyes questioning. "They have doors," he blurted with open surprise, "but no windows——"

"And many tribesmen keep their animals inside the houses with them at night," Reuben added. "Until traders came, the Celts had no use for the long structures now used for storing wares and cargo. Away from *Margas Jew*, the Dumnonii seldom build such buildings."

"Barbaric," Luke mouthed softly. Although he admitted his

bias, he accepted what realities he found with a patient tolerance. A lifetime in Roman service taught him that every foreign land had its oddities. Soldiers who could not adapt to strange ways had no future in the army.

Before they reached the Arimathea compound, a voice hailed them from behind in fluent Latin. "Reuben ben Ezra, I see you."

Reuben turned and grinned. He recognized that hail. "And I see you, Damhan Mawr of the Dumnonii."

They clasped wrists as brothers. "I also see things have changed. Indeed some things have much changed," Damhan marveled. "You wear a sword at your side."

"As every man should," Reuben retorted. "Or so a good friend, Damhan Mawr, once told me."

"I am honored that you remember," the Dumnonii chieftain answered. He turned, inclined his head to Reuben's companions, the Arimathea shipsmaster whom he knew well, and the two Romans in turn. "I see you," he greeted them ritually. "Welcome to Britannia."

Gesturing his own companion forward, Damhan presented him. "At my side walks Beli Fawr, Chieftain of the Belgiae, and a friend of many years. He has come far to be on hand when you arrived."

Then Damhan waved to each in turn. "Beli, you remember Reuben, Gwydion, and Quintus Marcellus Gota. This other Roman is Tribune Quintus Lucius Carus, late of the Roman army, who chooses to be called Luke of Arimathea."

"I see you," Beli nodded in ritual recognition. "And I echo Damhan's greeting. Welcome to Britannia." His eyes sought Reuben. "Especially you, who came as *the Lame Prophet* and warned us about the whims of gods and the sea."

Reuben flushed, then glanced from Beli back to Damhan. His face reflected his puzzlement. "How is it that you knew we were soon to arrive? That Beli knew to be on hand?"

Both Damhan and Beli grinned. "Arawn Doelguss foretold you would soon make landfall, and the Lady of the Lake is seldom wrong."

Flames leaped high in the great hearth, shadows dancing merrily on the walls. But among the benches in the hall, men guarded their voices, kept them low. Kimbelinus on the high dais, brooding over his mead cup, was in a foul mood.

He was a tall man. His once hard frame sagged with excess fat, but there was still a strength in him that humbled lesser men, and he unleashed it at his whim.

But tonight his mead had small effect on the irritating pains radiating from his lower back and left shoulder. He had ruled his people, the Catuevellauni, more than thirty years. Brought up in the courts of Augustus Caesar, trained by the best military minds in Rome, he had consolidated his power and become the most powerful monarch in Britain. Even the emperor honored him, the Roman historian Suetonius styling him as '*Britannorum rex*,' king of the Britons.

"Bah!" Kimbelinus muttered into his cup. No syrups distilled from honors and vanity could combat the pains old age brought. His mouth twisted wryly. He had labored a lifetime to carve out a kingdom in Belerion. He had fathered four warrior sons: Amminius, Togodurunus, Arviragus, and Caratacus. Sadly, none were his equal. He doubted if any of the four could hold his kingdom together when he went to his gods.

"Caratacus," he bellowed in the gloom. "Where have you perched?"

"Here, Father," Caratacus answered, stepping away from the hearth, climbing the dais. It galled him, but he kept his face neutral. No other Tribal chieftain had the audacity to mount his chair higher than his retainers. But his father was '*Britannorum rex*' and a legend, if only unto himself. "How may I serve you?"

"Tell me again of the Atrebates," Kimbelinus insisted, "and what they agreed."

Caratacus sighed. He had already told it many times. What was once more——? "They welcomed your proposal to stop Catuevellauni incursions into their lands for a year and a day in exchange for allowing the Atrebates to raid Tribal lands belonging to the Dumnonii, the

Dobunni, the Durotrigues, and the Belgiae and all their interests around the '*Isle of Glass*.'"

"But you cautioned them to leave the Druids alone," Kimbelinus pressed, "and also the university students?"

"Aye, Father," Caratacus insisted. "As you ordered."

Kimbelinus stared hard at his son. Eyes gray as woodsmoke and flecked with gold returned the king's gaze. Caratacus was dark-haired, well-muscled and taller than most Britons. He had wide-set eyes, a high fair brow, and lips thin but finely curved. His mother's Silure blood ran strong in him.

Misgivings stirred in Kimbelinus. He knew his son. There was something Caratacus was not saying. The king sensed it. "Spit it out, boy. Do not leave me guessing."

"The Atrebates begin to grumble at the bargain," Caratacus confessed. "They steadily lose men in the forest. Some of their best warriors."

"Which of those cursed Tribes bleeds the Atrebates?" Kimbelinus demanded. "Find out. Then hire mercenaries, renegades and outcasts that cannot be traced back to the Catuevellauni. Send them against the offenders."

Despite misgivings, Caratacus stood his ground. "It is not that simple."

"Why——?" Kimbelinus demanded, his voice low, dangerous. "Tell me why?"

To his credit Caratacus did not wilt under his father's vexed scrutiny. Gray eyes burning with stubborn fire challenged the king's ice-blue stare when he answered, "Because the bodies of the slain are never found. Oh, there is blood aplenty where they die. You can be sure of that. But there are no clues to show which Tribe does the deed. None! It is as if the Ancient Forest surrounding the '*Isle of Glass*' swallows them up."

"*Impossible!*" Kimbelinus thundered. Ignoring his pain, he surged to his feet, stretched to his great height. A single finger stabbed toward Caratacus. "Shall I set you aside and send another in your place to sort the truth?"

Too angry to speak, Caratacus turned, made for the wide hall door. Before he reached the portal, Kimbelinus stopped him with one word. "Son——?"

Caratacus halted. His face burned. He had been shamed before all those in the hall. Come what may, he would not face his father. "What?"

"Show me I raised a true son."

Somehow Caratacus managed to force air past the rage and hate constricting his throat. When he could breathe again, he strode through the open doorway. Until that moment he had never wished his father dead. He did now——

CHAPTER 18

D usk shrouded *Margas Jew*, a smothering blackness with no moonrise to soften the night. Within the Arimathea compound candles burned where rush lights normally sufficed. Damhan Mawr of the Dumnonii and Beli Fawr of the Belgiae sat with the far travelers, Joseph of Arimathea, Reuben ben Ezra, Quintus Marcellus Gota, and the Roman who wished to be called Luke of Arimathea. Others from Joseph's ship, with Gwydion and Elvan, sat in the shadows listening.

"You must hasten to *Ynys Wydryn*, 'the Isle of Glass,'" the Dumnonii chieftain urged. "After all, the land was gifted to the House of Arimathea and is yours to claim. More, the land needs its Master."

Joseph chewed his lip thoughtfully. Then he sighed, choosing the only course the *Spirit* left him. He must answer with the truth. "I gained that gift of land through cunning, pitting the desires of your Tribes to have my house's chief trading center in Britannia in your lands against the ambitions of Kimbelinus."

Joseph alternated glances between the chieftains. "While that may yet come to pass, my aims have changed. I have been sent to Britannia to establish a religious center, a church, from which those among us——" He gestured to include the people about them. "Where we can share our good news across the breadth of Balerion, with the rest of the Tribes, and beyond these shores."

Damhan deferred to Beli who spread his hands wide. "Joseph of Arimathea, of all those assembled here you should know the depths of our Celtic hearts. Circumstance may change a thousand-fold, but what is given, is given. All the land is yours to do with as you will." He flashed a wide grin. "And even the least child among us knew you would rather share borders with us instead of that pompous pig of a Catuevellauni, Kimbelinus."

"We may seem simple to your cultured eyes," Damhan said, his gaze resting first on Joseph, then Gota and Luke, before gesturing to include all those assembled. "But we are more than we seem. Our people choose to live simply, but we view it as a strength, not a weakness."

Silence answered Damhan. Beli broke it. "Arawn Doelguss, whom we call our priestess, has told us our peoples, yours and mine, are not so different. She has bade us bring you quickly to *Ynys Wydryn*."

"Overland would be quickest," Damhan added, "but only for a select few who can endure the hard ride. You, Joseph, and the rest of your company should take ship along the coast route to '*the Isle of Glass*.'"

Joseph rubbed the bridge of his nose thoughtfully. "And your select few——?"

Damhan did not mince words. "I would take Reuben and the Roman called Luke."

With the dawn Reuben and Luke rode northeast with the Dumnonii on strong Roman horses, the descendants of mounts brought to Britannia by Julius Caesar for his cavalry a century ago. Joseph and the other immigrants returned to *Judah's Hope* and *Judah's Tears* for the voyage around the Lands End headland, then north, following the coast as it curved to *Ynys Wydryn*. With Gwydion and Elvan, Damhan sent tribesmen who knew the winds, the tides, safe beaches where they could overnight, and the sheltering villages that would welcome them along the way.

Away from the coast, the land rose in an west-east ridge, with granite intrusions, outcrops, tors, and clitter slopes, rich in minerals such as tin, silver and lead, much prized by Rome. While they rode,

Damhan pointed out deep depressions, great holes hundreds of cubits in circumference and half as deep, their irregular bottom littered with rock flakings, sheared from vertical sides, sculpted by the wind, rain, droughts and frosts of millennia.

"You wonder why my people do not work in stone the way Romans or your Judeans do," the Dumnonii chieftain commented. He pointed at granite flakes, bigger than a man. "There is little harder in nature than granite, so why should we waste our labor when timber is easier to cut and mill?"

"But you mine tin, silver and lead from the granite outcroppings?" Reuben protested. "Surely——?"

"Merchants pay us for what we mine," Damhan countered with a half-smile. "Why waste time building stone houses. No one pays us to build them."

Reuben cast a quick side glance at Luke who chuckled at the insight. "He makes a strong point."

Occasionally they passed smaller dimples in the broad landscape, some filled with water and tall weeds. When they approached, a flock of broad-winged birds with black plumage and brightly colored legs, feet, and bills took flight, twisting and turning in the air, screaming at the intruders who disturbed their peace.

"They are *choughs*, like your Roman *monedula*," he told Luke. "They nest in caves and crevices in the granite."

Leagues later, the granite outcroppings, spattered pink and white with the miniature stars of stonecrop plants, grew less frequent, giving way to a treeless desolation of short grass. But even here, it remained a restless land, with rocks of great size and shape creeping at random through the grassy blanket. The moor ran before them in broad waves and troughs like a suspended tan-green sea——as if it were holding its breath. Overhead clouds created a patchwork effect of sun and shadow, knitted together by grass and heather. Purple blossoms lingered on some of the plants, swaying in the breeze.

Intrigued with the color, Reuben asked, "What are those bright blossoms?"

"They are called foxglove," Beli said. "Its showy flowers range in color from purples to whites, with variable marks and spotting. When they are in bloom, the land is awash in color. Our wise women make medicines from them."

Where the moor grew more verdant, standing stones appeared. They marched across the landscape like immobile warriors in patient formation.

Damhan followed Reuben's gaze, waved at the irregular, upended rocks. "These were old before my people came to this land," he admitted. "There are many such, and stone circles, stone rows, and cairns as well. My people believe they are tributes to old gods and the dead. We consider them unlucky and avoid them."

After the standing stones, small copses of trees surrounded by moor heather appeared, small isolated islands of tall growth in broad arid tracts of wasteland where before only heather and low shrubs found root in the rocky soil.

In a thicker growth of heather, thrush-like birds with a gray back, buff breast, and white rump shot skyward in a sudden flurry of wings, spooking the horses. Reuben reined hard, fighting to control his mount, thankful he had learned to handle Joseph's white mules. Beli's cackle announced several tribesmen in their escort had been unhorsed, unlike Luke who clung stubbornly to his mare's saddle band.

"I should have warned you to expect *wheatears* in the deep heather," Damhan said, fighting to suppress his own grin. "But I see you fared better than my own men."

Soon the groundcover took on a deeper healthy green, and tall trees appeared, sheltering a rill that watered the desolate landscape. Verdant green grass lined the stream banks, and ancient oak and ash followed the irregular water course like guardians. Gnarled roots clung to the old soil, anchoring the silent sentinels that proclaimed mankind was still young in Belerion. Their broad canopies shaded a winding blue-water stream, rippling through moss-covered rocks in a series of shallow waterfalls.

"We will rest and water the horses here," Damhan told them. "We still have far to go before nightfall."

Beyond the rill, the moor continued a broad sweep toward the woodlands, but its grip on the land was weakening. More and more island copses appeared until they slowly fanned out into the beginnings of a true forest.

Damhan did not enter the trees; instead, he led them north. By the time dusk darkened the sky into the beginnings of night, the silhouette of a hill fort appeared on a broad hill rising on the far side of a deep and marshy valley. Stubby points of perhaps a dozen round houses showed above the palisade.

"Our shelter for the night," the Dumnonii chieftain said over his shoulder. "There will be a heavy dew tonight. I feel it in the air."

Reuben dismounted, bent to knead his tight and aching thighs. He had been too long away from a saddle, and his muscles protested the abuse. But the soreness would pass. Tribesmen appeared to take the horses, and Damhan and Beli led them to the central round house, waved them inside.

"Rest yourselves by the fire," Damhan urged. "Beli and I will join you shortly. Our women will bring food and prepare your resting pallets for the night." Regret showed on his face as he shook his head. "I know these poor accommodations are less than your want, but——?"

"They are more than ample," Luke said quickly. "I have had less on countless campaigns." He gestured around the interior. "We have shelter and fire, and pallets and the company of fine companions. What more can a man ask?"

Damhan nodded, warming to the Roman's good-naturedness. "What we have is yours," he returned. "You have but to ask."

When the Dumnonii left, Luke said softly to Reuben, "I would trust that man to guard my back."

Luke's admission caught Reuben by surprise; the former tribune gave his trust sparingly. He had often counseled Reuben——*Keep your enemies close, and your friends closer.* Something in Damhan had struck a deep chord with Luke.

Jaws clinched in distaste, Caratacus picked and chose what sundaries he would take with him west. His father's stiff rebuff had angered him. Yet the anger ebbed quickly; a coldness replacing it that would not thaw.

"My brother," a gravelly voice said from the doorway. "I see you."

Caratacus turned, recognizing the speaker. "And I see you, Amminius. Enter, my brother."

Much like his younger brother, Amminius was cut from the same mold as Kimbelinus, tall and fair like most of the Catuevellauni. Older by four years than Caratacus, three years senior to Togodurunus, and two years over Arviragus, Amminius was deeply jealous of Caratacus' sunny nature and the favor their father showered on the last of his sons. But he hid his spite around Caratacus and pretended familial affection and friendship which he openly denied Togodurunus and Arviragus.

"I understand you are being sent west," Amminius offered in a sympathetic tone. "I offered to go in your place," he lied, "but our father would not hear of it. He would send none but you."

"What is done, is done," Caratacus quipped, stowing the last of his articles. "A faithful dog answers his master."

"I would not have you go without my well wishes," Amminius protested. "Here, I have fetched a tray with two goblets and an amphora of fine Greek wine to toast your going and herald your swift return. Drink with me?"

Caratacus glanced up, heartened at his elder brother's favor. "You honor me. Of course I will drink with you."

Amminius offered his younger brother the choice of goblets, knowing he always reached for the one nearest his right hand, and was not disappointed. Setting the tray down, he filled Caratacus' goblet first, then his own still on the tray.

"To good fortune, my brother," Amminius toasted, "and all the gods have in store for you."

He drank deeply as did Caratacus; he drank confidently, knowing the slow-acting poison was in his brother's goblet, not in his own.

Upending the tall cup to show it was empty, that he had honored the toast, Amminius caught up the amphora. "Another——for the trail?"

"I will," Caratacus said with a delighted smile. "But only one more. Wine is my weakness."

And why would I know that? Amminius hid the thought, smiled as though answering the admission. "I would not have it on my conscience that my wine had you fall drunkenly from the saddle in front of your men."

Caratacus chuckled, finished his second goblet. "Never that. Death first."

Amminius nodded sagely. "Death first."

Embracing his younger brother warmly, for it would be the last time, Amminius gathered cups and amphora and took his leave. Caratacus strapped on his armor and sword, caught up shield and wallet, and left his quarters.

His empty stomach rumbled almost painfully, and he regretted he had been too angry to eat after his exchange with his father. No matter. He would grab some smoked fish and munch on it in the saddle.

When the first mind-numbing pain stabbed through his gut, Caratacus had just strode into the stable. Shield and wallet forgotten, he fell to his knees, spewed wine and bile into the fragrant strewn hay, retched until he had no strength left.

A darkness blacker than the longest winter night swooped down like a raptor and seized his mind. With a strangled breath, he collapsed face-first in his own filth.

CHAPTER 19

Caratacus' retainers discovered their young prince when they came to saddle their horses. Doli, captain of his war band, gently turned Caratacus, wiped his leader's mouth and face with his own cloak, then pressed an ear to the unconscious man's nostrils.

"He lives," Doli cried to the other two. "You!" he stabbed a finger at one man. "Run and summon Kimbelinus." Pointing at the other, Doli ordered, "Fetch the healers. Go now! His life may depend on your speed."

Suddenly alone, he cradled Caratacus in his arms, felt the rise and fall of his master's chest. *Live!* Doli urged Caratacus. *You must live! You are the best of us all.*

Old, Kimbelinus was, and gruff, and seemingly uncaring for the welfare of others, but the '*Britannorum rex*' was the first one to his son's side. "What passed here?" he demanded when he threw himself to his knees, took his son's limp frame from Doli. His eyes blazed promised wrath. "Do you know?"

"I do not, Sire!" Doli answered quickly, for given Kimbelinus' anger, his own life hung by a thread. "We found him as you see him. I sent for you immediately. And sent for the healers. They can be only heartbeats behind you."

"Someone fed him wine," the king snapped. Anger, hot and silvery pulsed through him at the condition of his son. "His waste reeks of it." Kimbelinus' wrathful gaze froze Doli. His eyes promised retribution. "Lean to me," the king demanded. "Breathe in my face."

Doli's heart caught. He knew he had swallowed no hard drink this eve, not when they had to ride, but Kimbelinus' mood was uncertain. Still, he obeyed the command.

With an audible sniff, the king sat back. "It is plain you did not drink with him," Kimbelinus relented gruffly. He returned his attention to Caratacus. "Though he has a weakness for wine, he is my son and drinks like me. At his drunkest, I have never seen him so."

"Nor I, Sire," Doli affirmed. "Never like this!"

"When this is past," Kimbelinus told him, "you shall know my pleasure for this service."

"I ask not," Doli answered quickly, though the king's words eased his dread. "He is my lord."

"And I am the King——" Kimbelinus retorted, ending any protest Doli might press.

Running feet quickly brought two out-of-breath healers and a half-dozen of their apprentices. Though he was clearly loath to do it, Kimbelinus surrendered Caratacus to the healers' ministrations. Slowly the aged king pushed to his feet. His run to the stable had cost him dearly. Knees screaming, he fought a searing catch in his side that almost doubled him over. Staring down at his son, he pressed a knuckle against the pain.

"Well——" he demanded of the healers. "What have you to tell me?"

"It is too early to say," the chief healer said without looking up. "Clearly, Sire, Caratacus will not ride tonight." He swallowed hard and gave his fears voice. "Or any time soon——if he lives."

"I am not blind," Kimbelinus growled. He turned, cast a quick gaze over the throng that had grown in the last moments. "Where is Amminius?"

"Here, father," his older son answered, pushing through the assembled people. He kept his face controlled, but his thoughts were black. Caratacus was to have collapsed on the trail. Not *here* in *Camulodunum*.

"You remember my plans regarding the Atrebates?" Kimbelinus

demanded. When Amminius nodded, "Go and do what your brother was to do."

Amminius bowed. "As you have said it, so it will be. I and mine will be on the road by the second watch."

"Do not fail me," Kimbelinus shouted after his eldest son with no regard to what others overheard. Amminius did not turn or acknowledge the demand.

But he heard his father's tone. Face controlled, Amminius gloated. *In serving you, I serve myself.* He allowed a smile the night hid. *In time I will serve only myself——* His smile broadened. *When I am king....*

At dawn Damhan led them from the hill fort. Away from the moor, night fog still clung to the low places or tangled in the broad limbed canopies above their heads. Damhan guided them along a forest path that angled northeast. White gauzy light illuminated the high reaches of the shadowy forest, a light made almost intangible by the creeping mist overhead, and it lent an eldritch sense of timeliness to the riders below.

Reuben's heart surged, his throat ached. *I love this land*, he acknowledged. *It is not my birth land, but when the Lord calls, my flesh will rest here until resurrection.*

Under Damhan's leadership, they were several days on the road, overnighting in hill forts, and once in the Dumnonii capital, *Isca Dumnoniorum, 'Isca of the Domnones,'* which was situated on a dry ridge of land ending in a spur that overlooked a navigable river. From the capital, they continued north, with the chieftain guiding them across moorland and through ancient forests.

One day, near midmorning, Damhan raised a hand, signaling a halt. He pointed ahead, northward to the upland rising before them.

"We call this land the *Mynydd Hills*," he told Reuben and Luke. "In our tongue it means *'upland moorland.'* Some call it *'Meynduppa,'* which is the joining of two words in our language, "the *meyn*,' drawn from '*the stone pit*,' and the second part, '*dyppa*,' referring to collapsed cave systems in the hills."

He waved in a wide arc. "From these hills comes our lead ore that the Romans prize," Damhan said, nodding to Luke. "The ore is dug from deep grooves that follow the veins near the surface. It is hauled to *Margas Jew*, your port of Ictis, by pack animal and cart."

To the east the grassland hills also embraced stretches of ancient forests. Overhead, motionless wings spread to ride thermals, a large bird paralleled their path, slowly angling away, but returning again and again to shadow them.

"It is a peregrine falcon, a beautiful bird," Beli told Reuben, "a natural predator. They find ample nesting in the inland cliffs. My people capture and train them to take wild game."

When they reached a hill crest, a shower of light rain fell from gray-white clouds scudding from the north, spattering their faces and scattering sparkling droplets through the long grass and heather. Rain left a shimmering haze in the air that quickly burned away, and a fine, crisp afternoon spread over the moor.

In time Damhan signaled a halt, although there was no watering place near. He pointed north northeast. "By this time tomorrow, you will see the *tor* rising above '*the Isle of Glass*,'" he promised them. "There were faster roads we could have taken, but I have brought you by the safest route. Other ways are too accessible; the Atrebates might have staged an ambush."

"Why do they set themselves against my Master?" Reuben pressed him. "If not for Gwyr, you, Joseph, and I would have died that day on the *tor*."

"That day haunts me still," Damhan confessed. He shook himself. "Tonight, in a hill fort, when we break our fast, we will talk. Until then, we must ride...."

In the Catuevellauni capital, shadows danced on the mud-and-daub walls inside the round house, given life by the many flickering candles that surrounded the still form of Caratacus. Healers bathed his face with cool water, but the king's son did not stir.

"He lives," the chief healer said, answering Kimbelinus' oft-pressed question. "Your son clings to life by a thread, how or why I do not know. But he does."

He glanced painfully at the king who knelt on the opposite side of the bed. Kimbelinus must be told. "By what I have seen of his condition, by the wine and bile he retched upon the ground, it is my belief there was strong poison in the wine Caratacus consumed."

Kimbelinus surged to his feet, his pained face white with rage. His hands were angry fists that shook with the need to vent their pent wrath. "*Poison*," he repeated, his words deceptively, dangerously calm, counterpoint to the emotions that wracked him. "You claim some villain in my capital, in *Camulodunum*, dared to raise his hand against *my* youngest son?"

Swallowing his apprehension, the healer shrugged. "If it looks like a hare, hops like a hare, and leaves tracks like a hare, who am I to tell the king otherwise?"

Fighting down impotent rage, Kimbelinus began to pace. His mind raced. There were those among his own council who disagreed with supporting the Atrebates against those around 'the Isle of Glass.' But none who would dare strike against Caratacus. But someone had.

"He could tell me who gave him the wine," Kimbelinus pondered aloud. He glared hard at the healer. "How long until he wakes, you cursed bag of bones?"

"Who can say?" the healer answered with a shrug. "Some poison entered his body. How much, I cannot say? No more than I can say when he will wake. If he wakes—— Caratacus' life is in the hands of the gods."

"Does he know——" the king asked, "that I am here? Can he hear me when I speak to him?"

Again the healer shrugged, his hands spread wide. "Only he can tell us——if he wakes."

Night had fallen and Damhan ordered torches lit against the darkness. Watchers on the wall were careful not to stare at the dancing flames. Instead, they alertly scanned the darkness.

Within the common round house, Reuben and Luke sat with Damhan and Beli, listening to the Belgiae's words.

"Long have the Atrebates distanced themselves from the other Tribes," Beli explained. "Their Celtic name means '*settlers*,' and they believe all the land in southern Britannia is rightly theirs. They are second only to the Catuvellauni in power, but Kimbelinus and Epaticcus, his brother, have culled much of the Atrebates' territory."

"Understand that the Atrebates are a grouping of lesser Tribes under a single dynastic family," Damhan added. "Verica now rules, but he is constantly goaded by Kimbelinus who uses the Atrebates as a whip against the other Tribes. Had your Joseph been content to accept only Kimbelinus' gift of land, the Catuvellauni probably would have been content to pare away only the choicest lands from their chief rival, the Atrebates."

Then he shrugged. "We are as much to blame," he admitted. "We did not believe Kimbelinus would use Joseph of Arimathea as a pawn to stir war among the other Tribes. That Catuvellauni pig taunts Verica who sends his vassal Tribe, the Regni, to plague us at '*the Isle of Glass.*'"

Reuben's brow furrowed. "But the might of your combined Tribes——"

"Cannot be everywhere at once," Damhan finished for him. "They watch us constantly, probing in small groups, then striking where and when we are weakest."

Beli gestured for their attention. "It remained so, until the Regni did something unpardonable and unleashed a *Forest Demon*. Now everything has changed. Regni warriors come only in large groups, and our Tribes do not have the manpower to keep a standing army around the *tor*."

"What is this *Forest Demon* you speak of?" Luke pressed. "I have not heard of such in Britannia."

"Arawn Doelguss says it belongs to the forest," Beli broke in, "conjured by the Old Ones who held the land before the coming of the Celts."

"We believe the Demon has slain the best warriors the Regni send against it," Damhan said. "Even when they send small groups against it, the *Demon* hacks them to pieces. Now they never go into the forest with less than two score."

He hung his head. "Hear my shame. I once sensed the *Demon* rise in the trees behind me. My insides turned to water, and I ran."

He pressed his hands against his chest. "I ran. Who never ran from any fight in my life——except when Gwyr sent me away to save Joseph and you, Reuben. I ran that day and count myself lucky to be alive."

"You must have seen it," Luke insisted. "Describe it."

"I cannot," Damhan groaned. "Can you grasp how hard it is for me to admit I was too scared to look behind me?"

Silence swallowed his outburst.

Then Luke sighed. "It is not so hard to understand shame," he admitted. "In the Rhineland, the Hermundures ambushed our legion, pressed us so hard we could not regroup. My men ran; I ran with them."

Luke's eyes met Damhan's without evasion "My enemies were only tribesmen, bloodthirsty men, it is true. But I ran." He grimaced. "I cannot condemn you. Never have I faced a *Forest Demon*."

"My friend," Damhan said in earnest, "I pray with all my heart you never do...."

CHAPTER 20

Kimbelinus summoned before him the Ard-file, his steward and chief counselor. From his high seat on the dais, the king stared down at his comrade of many years, but this day his eyes held no friendship.

"You will render me an accounting of the wine stores in all of Camulodunum," Kimbelinus demanded. "Then you will match your accounting against the wine manifests of the foreign factors who trade here. Are my wishes understood?"

Linus, the son of Ceretic, stared at his master open-mouthed. "My lord jests?" Linus stammered. "Surely——?"

Leaning forward, Kimbelinus' countenance was a mask of barely controlled anger when he interrupted his Ard-file. "Search my face, Linus," he challenged. "What do you see?"

A valiant warrior gone to seed, Linus was no coward. He also was no fool. "You shall have your accounting."

"Be thorough, old friend, and be quick," Kimbelinus warned. "Someone used wine to poison my son. In my realm where mead is the drink of choice, it should not be difficult to find who imports wine, and who drinks it. Track every amphora, Linus. Every one. I will have my vengeance."

You set an impossible task for me, Linus wanted to protest, but he wisely kept silent. Word had spread quickly of the poisoning. Caratacus lay comatose, unresponsive abed in the healer's hut. Linus fervently prayed the prince would soon wake.

"Go now," Kimbelinus ordered. "No door shall be closed to you——by decree of the king."

Come the dawn, a sweeping mist covered the moor and reduced the reach of the world to perhaps a hundred paces. Damhan and Beli stripped the hill fort of men to augment their escort and rode on.

How does he know which direction to ride? Reuben wondered, but the tribesmen plunged on through the mist as if they knew their destination. On his last trip he and Joseph had come with Damhan by boat from the west. He knew nothing about the approach from the south.

Sounds seem magnified by the mist. From disembodied animal calls and bird screeches his mind conjured mythical beasts, and he jerked anew at every cry. His elbow brushed the hilt of his *gladius* reassuringly. He was a stranger here, and this was the land of Celtic lore, the haunt of the Faery King Gwyn Ap Nudd. Avalon, their destination, was heralded as the meeting-place of the Dead, the point where they passed into another level of existence.

Damhan led them doggedly northward. They passed through stretches of ancient wood, where mighty oaks snared the mist in their canopies, and Reuben thankfully could see some distance ahead.

They entered the moorland and the mist once more. Time held little meaning. The sun's light was defused into an eldritch brightness overhead. Twice the tribesmen paused to let their horses blow. While they rested, the mist seemed to thicken, isolate them from the world around them. Undeterred, Damhan and Beli led them on, proving their Celtic prison indeed had no bars.

Sometime in the late afternoon, the white light overhead took on a golden hue. Damhan waved them to a halt, motioned Reuben and Luke to join him.

"Look," he urged and pointed. "Tell me what you see."

It seemed his words cast a spell. Mist near the ground took on shadow, supporting an ocean of frothy white. In the distance, the *tor's* crown dominated, climbing high and free, an island thrust up from the nameless white sea, and the sky above it, was layered in shades of afternoon golds.

Reuben smothered a choked cry of wonder. Beside him, Luke exhaled sharply.

"And you wonder why the Celts call *Ynys Wydryn* the land of myth," Damhan said in hushed tones. "There is a magic here that is found in no other place on earth."

For long moments they bathed in the land's beauty. Then Damhan led them on. They had safely run the gauntlet of invading Atrebates and come through unscathed. More, they evaded the clutches of the *Forest Demon.*

Reuben found himself wondering what new perils they must conquer to fulfill their purpose here. He had journeyed far to witness, to testify for the Christ. He must not fail....

Amminius led his followers through the night, to the appointed meeting with the Regni sub-chieftain. He was weary to the bone, but the knowledge he had eliminated his chief rival and cost Kimbelinus his favorite son buoyed him through the grueling ordeal.

Fer of the Regni stood with fists on hips glaring when the Catuvellauni contingent drew rein. "You are late, Caratacus," he growled. "I expected you by midnight."

"I am Amminius——" he clarified, "Kimbelinus' eldest. "Caratacus is ill, unable to fork a horse. I have been sent in his stead."

Clearly Fer was not pleased. "Swing down. There is roast boar on the spit. Eat and grab what sleep you can. We ride at first light."

"Why the haste?" Amminius demanded. "I was to gather men who could not be traced to the Catuvellauni."

"Joseph of Arimathea has landed at *Margas Jew*," the Regni retorted. "Even now he is in route along the coast to '*the Isle of Glass*' with a pair of ships. We must attack before his ships' crews swell the defenders around the *tor*. More Dumnonii are said to make their way north overland."

"Let us split our men into raiding groups," Amminius suggested. "Take them from all sides."

"No! We will not split our forces." The Regni's eyes were guarded, adamant. "I will not allow it."

"You will not allow——" Amminius repeated slowly, his eyes hard. "Who are you——"

"I mean no offense, Princeling," Fer said quickly. forestalling the Catuvellauni's rebellion. "The Lady of the Lake has raised a *Forest Demon*. It guards the forest approaches to Avalon. In two years I have sent two-score men in small groups into that wood. What few made it out refuse to return. Their grisly tales of blood and death have unnerved the staunchest of my men. The Regni go in force——or not at all."

Amminius shrugged away his anger. He did not believe Fer's tales, but he lacked the authority to force the Regni to his will. "Then we go in force——" He turned toward the fire. "After I eat and sleep...."

"How is my son?" Kimbelinus asked in a subdued voice as he entered the healer's round house. His eyes quickly adjusted to the gloom. On the pallet beside Caratacus the healer hovered, arms around his ankles, his wrinkled forehead resting against his drawn-up knees.

"Healer——" the king raised his voice. "How is my son?"

Awaking with a start, the old man blinked, then focused on Kimbelinus standing over him. "Forgive me, Sire, I must have dozed."

He drew a deep breath, scratched his graying head. "I believe you asked about your son? Yes, yes, that was it. Caratacus sleeps a natural sleep. In time I believe he will wake. But when, I cannot say."

In spite of protesting joints, the king went to one knee, rested a compassionate hand on the healer's shoulder. "When did you last sleep?"

The old man frowned. "Two——no, three nights ago?" He sadly shook his head. "At this moment I cannot remember. Does it matter?"

"No, Wise One, it does not matter," Kimbelinus said softly, surprised at his own compassion. "Go to your own pallet and rest. I will sit beside my son for a time."

"Thank you graciously, Sire. No more than forty winks." He nestled down on straw-filled bedding. "No more than forty——" His words slurred, replaced by soft snores.

Kimbelinus turned back to Caratacus, and his lined face softened. With the assistance of the king's personal guard, his Ard-file continued to scour *Camulodunum* for the source of the wine that poisoned his son. He knew it was an impossible task when he demanded it, but he had been beside himself with fear and anger. Ordering something, even something impossible, seemed better than doing nothing.

Now I must see it through. Kimbelinus knew he must also be prepared to reward the valiant efforts even if no source of wine was discovered.

Grunting, he pushed to his feet. Strode to the door. Growled at one of his guards. "Fetch me a proper chair. My cursed knees have grown too gnarled for long kneeling."

Damhan and Beli led them to the shore immediately south of the *tor*. A woman in a long black cloak stood at the water's edge staring out across the tidal basin at the *tor*, so still she might have been a shadow.

But Damhan recognized her for who and what she was. Drawing rein, the Dumnonii glanced worriedly at Beli. Something unspoken passed between the men.

"Reuben——" he said defensively. "You must dismount and go to her alone."

"Her?" Reuben repeated, full of questions. He turned, saw the woman for the first time. "Is that——?"

"The Lady of the Lake?" the Dumnonii finished for him. "Aye, she is Arawn Doelguss. A holy one. The priestess who foretold your coming."

He hesitated. "She awaits you, my friend. Go to her. And go with care. She is *holy*."

Ill at ease, Reuben dismounted on stiff legs. While he watched, Damhan, Beli, Luke, and the escort rode around the shore in a soft clatter of hooves. He felt bereft, suddenly and completely alone.

She turned when he approached and any greeting he might have made fled from his mind. Red-gold rays of the setting sun illuminated one side of her face, casting the other in shadow, but he could see her eyes clearly. Gray-blue and mild, opaquely bright. Those eyes——serene yet cradling deep mysteries——like the waters surrounding the *tor* behind her. And those eyes centered on him.

Raven-haired Arawn Doelguss was not beautiful the way some men fancied beauty; yet in the same breath, he could not say she was not unbeautiful. He recalled Damhan's description: stunning, ethereal, and unforgettable. She was all of that——and much, much more.

As if she knew his thoughts, she smiled suddenly.

In that timeless moment, he questioned how he could ever have believed she was not beautiful. *I who have never known a tender kiss or the loving touch of a woman.* Reuben realized then, *I could pass all the remaining years of my life adoring that face....*

"Who is to say, Reuben ben Ezra, *the 'prophet who is and is not,'* that you will not do so?"

His face flushed. Had she truly read his thoughts or simply guessed them from his gawking countenance? He bowed low, trying to quell his overwhelming awkwardness.

She extended a slim white hand. "Come with me out on the lake." Her light tone made a command of the request.

For the first time he saw the slim boat nestled against the bank behind her. Reuben felt her eyes on him, and he met her gaze without evasion. "I would be honored," he answered, and wondered how he accomplished the smoothness of the delivery. "But only if you let me sit at the opposite end and watch you."

She smiled again, and it was as golden as the sunset. "Be careful what you ask for, Reuben ben Ezra."

She waved him to the craft. He slipped aboard, going to the bow. Arawn unhooked her cloak, laid it across the rear bench. Deftly she launched the craft, slipping in at the last moment without wetting her skirt. Taking up a slim, long-bladed paddle, she stroked with the ease of long practice.

"Some years ago," Arawn said in fluent Aramaic, "I knew a young student who came here from Judea." She watched surprise register on his face at the shift in language. "His name was Yahshua ben Joseph——"

Reuben's eyes widened.

She smiled dazzlingly. "Tell me of *Him*. I must see *Him* through your eyes as the Christ...."

Chapter 21

From the north a horn pealed, long and strident. Bran the Blessed stood with Reuben and Luke, Damhan and Beli, speaking of the Atrebates and the peril they posed. Moments later, a lone horseman appeared from the forest shadow and urged his horse across the open ground toward them.

"Ah!" Bran heaved a relieved sigh. "The lead rider for the Silures. Caradoc comes——"

When the tribesman drew reign before them, the man greeted Bran with a respectful nod. "Well met, Arch Druid. My King follows perhaps a league behind me with his host as you requested."

Bran nodded in reply. "Go to the hall. Refresh yourself with venison and mead."

"My thanks," the rider acknowledged. "My throat is dry." Deftly he reined his mount away.

Bran faced his companions. "With Caradoc's host, and Joseph of Arimathea's crewmen when they come, we will not be easy prey for the Atrebates." He glanced aside at Reuben. "You spoke of a warning from Arawn Doelguss."

Reuben nodded. For much of the past two days he had talked with her, responding to her questions about himself, his healing, and the Christ. He found her knowledge and her insight both amazing and disconcerting. "She says in two days the dawn will be heavy and deep with mist. That is when the Atrebates will come, led by a warrior and a fool."

"As she has said it——" Damhan responded in perfect trust, "so it will be. Who among us doubts her prophecies?"

No one spoke. "Then we have two days to marshal our defenses," Damhan concluded. He glanced at Luke. "What would a Roman do?"

Luke chewed his lip, turned and studied the terrain to the east, the way the Atrebates were sure to come. "On open ground your Celtic cavalry is a force unto itself. My council: do not give them that advantage."

He pointed eastward. "Meet them just inside the wood where their massed horsemen will prove useless. Since we know the mist is coming and will be heavy, build and set barricades, barriers with bowmen behind them, to hem in and harry the riders with their shafts."

Meeting their gaze, he raised a fist. "Make your reserve a host of mounted warriors, to meet and crush any Atrebates who break through the defensive line."

Beli offered Luke a formal bow. "There is little wonder you gained the rank of Tribune. Never would I wish to oppose you in battle, my Roman friend."

Amid the chuckles, Damhan raised a hand for silence. "Your face——" he pressed Luke, "tells me you have other words for us——?"

Luke nodded. "Bran, declare a holiday. Your students would provide welcome hands in erecting the barriers."

"Done!" the Arch Druid stated. "These days will weave tales long remembered."

Time flew and waiting for the Silures' arrival proved short. But it was long enough to strain the nerves with many preparations yet to make for the Atrebates' assault. So it was with great relief that the newly appointed defenders of Avalon stood side by side to welcome Caradoc, king of the Silures.

Caradoc rode bare of head, brown hair blowing with the breeze. His gray eyes met each of the men in turn, nodding, before he drew rein and dismounted. "I received your call, Father," he said to the Arch Druid, "and I came at once. More warriors follow when they can."

Luke raised a questioning eyebrow at the greeting, but Reuben was more forthright in his surprise. *"Father?"*

A faint smile creased Caradoc's lips. *"'Prophet who is and is not,'* how did you not know? My father was King of the Silures before he willingly ceded the throne to me so he could serve our combined peoples as Arch Druid."

Reuben's face flushed. He cut his eyes quickly to Damhan who feigned innocence and Beli who grinned impishly. "My prophetic abilities leave much to question, Majesty," he denied. "In spite of wagging tongues who press the case."

Something in the young man touched Reuben deeply. When he bent to kneel, Caradoc caught his arms, drew him up. "You shall not kneel to me," he commanded. "Now or ever."

He drew Reuben into a tight embrace. "Consider me a companion in arms or a kinsman." His gray eyes were riveting, compelling. "But never more than this."

Reuben swallowed hard. "As you wish, Maj——" At the king's sharp glance, he amended with a nod, "Caradoc——"

Turning on his heel, the king faced Luke, extended a welcoming forearm. "And this would be the esteemed Tribune Quintus Lucius Carus, Centurio of Legio VI Ferrata."

Luke gripped Caradoc's arm, wrist to wrist, nodded in greeting. "No offense, Majesty, but Reuben is right," he grumbled. "Someone carries tales...."

In the final two days of march to the *tor*, the combined Regni-Catuevellauni host had grown to a century strong, one hundred mounted warriors.

Grinning openly, the prince pictured the coming attack. Crushing the combined force of tribesmen around *"the Isle of Glass"* would be a sweet victory. He intended to grind the tale of that victory so deeply into Togodurunus' and Arviragus' memories that his beloved brothers would never dare to challenge him.

"Aye," he mouthed. "It will be a sweet indeed."

"You spoke?" Fer questioned, reining his horse closer. "I did not hear——?"

"Just curses that I am ready to have this over and done," he lied. "And you?"

Fer considered the welcomed absence of Amminius' insufferable presence. "I too wish it behind me."

They both rode on in silence, allies by necessity.

"Two sails! Two sails from the west!"

Excited students quickly shouted word of the sighting to other study groups. Soon the Druidic university discipline disintegrated into chaos. Signals from the *tor* summit heralded the ships' arrival. They also summoned armed Celtic horsemen to the shore in the event the ships brought Atrebatian warriors.

Controlling his mount with a strong hand, Luke pulled the sorrel gelding to a sliding halt, pointed at the Arimathean pennants waving from the distant mastheads. "It is *Judah's Hope* and *Judah's Tears*," he cried. "Joseph of Arimathea will be aboard. He has come at last."

Anxious days had passed while they kept watch over the western waters for signs of incoming ships. Damhan and Beli waited for the thirty-odd Arimathea crewmen who would bolster the small defensive force landward of the *tor*, while Reuben and Luke waited for Joseph and the Christ-followers aboard Broch Gorm's longships.

Men standing with the chieftains on the long narrow ridge southwest of the *tor* began to wave frantically, first with their hands, then swinging cloaks. Damhan doubted they would be seen, but when the thought rooted in his mind, both ships quickly altered their courses. The Dumnonii's sharp eyes noted the reduced bow wakes, saw the ships slacken speed. In moments the sail spars dipped, then were lowered to the decks. Crewmen ran oars into the slots, and the sleek vessels began to claw their way shoreward, bypassing 'the Isle of Glass.'

Cheers erupted from the anxious students. Damhan chuckled, assured them, "You will all see them soon enough."

Below, on the shore, at the water's edge, two figures awaited the new arrivals. Damhan sighed, shook his head. He might have known Arawn Doelguss and Reuben would be first to greet the immigrants.

With a hiss of keel sliding up the sandy shore, the Arimathea ships grounded. From *Judah's Tears*, several crewmen swarmed over the side, turned to assist Joseph of Arimathea to firm footing.

Reuben stepped forward eagerly, embraced his master. "At last you have come."

Joseph blinked unashamed tears. "Thanks be to God!"

Reuben drew back. "Master, I would present to you——"

"Someone I know," Joseph finished for him. "I see you, Arawn Doelguss, Lady of the Lake."

Arawn nodded solemnly. "And I see you, Joseph of Arimathea, my cherished friend."

Before Reuben could question the greeting, Caradoc's voice froze the words on Reuben's tongue. "Thrice welcome, revered Uncle," and the king dropped to his knees, bowed his head to the Pharisee. Joseph placed a blessing hand on Caradoc's head. "You do me great honor, Nephew."

Dumbfounded, Reuben gaped like a fish. Joseph knew it and said softly, "I had many secrets long before Reuben ben Ezra was ever born. You have not learned them all."

Caradoc rose. "My Father waits on the hilltop. Will you come up?"

"I will."

Joseph reached a questing hand back toward the ship, and a crewman passed him a tall walking stick. Reuben remembered it, a long gnarled wand of white hawthorn, stout and durable, a gift from the Apostle Peter. With Caradoc at his elbow, and Arawn Doelguss and Reuben following, Joseph of Arimathea climbed the steep hill.

"A hard climb," the Apostle to Belerion acknowledged when they gained the summit. "Though I am most weary, my heart is exceeding glad."

Bran the Blessed quickly stepped forward. Joseph thrust the tip of his walking stick deep into the dark earth and embraced him warmly. "You have come at last, Joseph," the Arch Druid murmured with a wide smile. "I have longed for this day. I only wish my beloved Anna had lived to see and be a part of it."

Catching his breath, Joseph sighed. "Never again shall I leave this land, Bother-in-Law," he promised. "My mission is here in *Belerion*."

Arawn seized Reuben's arm with insistent fingers, whispered in an awed tone, "Reuben——? The staff——!"

Reuben glanced first at the Lady of the Lake, then his eyes followed her pointing fingers to Joseph's staff. Where the tip was imbedded in the dirt, the wood was visibly greening——as if life and sap flowed through it from the earth. While they stared, nodules appeared here and there along its gnarly surface. Nodules that sprouted. Became the beginnings of branches——

Absorbed in their reunion, Bran and Joseph and Caradoc gave no notice. But others did. Damhan and Beli stood rigid, wide-eyed.

Luke, too, was caught up in the unfolding spectacle. Unable to tear his eyes away, he breathed——"Sweet Christ!"

His shocked exclamation seemed to embody both blessing and benediction——for leaves quickly sprouted on the fragile limbs. Buds appeared, opening immediately into dazzling five-lobed white blossoms of great beauty, filling the air with a delicate enticing fragrance.

Of the others, Caradoc noticed first. His eyes widened. He grasped Joseph's shoulder, lightly at first, then more insistent, arresting the Apostle's attention. When Joseph turned, his breath caught. Weary old knees, unable to sustain him, gave way, and he knelt. Clasping his hands in silent prayer, he bowed his head.

Reuben stepped close to Arawn. Whispered for her alone. "Was this *your* doing?" he pressed. "Your miracle?"

"You credit me with powers I do not possess," she answered in a hushed, awed tone, her eyes on the thorn bush. "I am a seer, and skilled in herbs and healing. No more than this, no matter what the Tribes say. You must believe me when I tell you——" she gestured. "This——is not my doing. Nor is it Bran's."

CHAPTER 22

Bran the Blessed walked with Joseph of Arimathea outside the timbered hall where the students assembled for meals. Despite their years apart, their old friendship reasserted itself as if they had only parted yesterday.

Hands caught at his back, the Arch Druid paused, stared out toward the *tor*. The day was half-gone since the ships arrived. "Already it spreads," Bran said wistfully. "Today it is a wondrous tale, and indeed it is. All of that. But today's tale will become tomorrow's legend."

He chuckled. "With you in mind," he cut his eyes chidingly to Joseph, "the students have even named the hill." Mindful that you were most weary after the climb from the ship, they have dubbed it '*Wearyall Hill*.'"

Joseph grimaced. "I fear they laugh at me."

"*Laugh* at you?" Bran echoed with unfeigned surprise. "I should say not! They stand in awe of you, old friend." He placed a reassuring hand on Joseph's shoulder. "Have you not seen the adoring looks, the extreme deference they accord you? And that deference extends beyond the students. I must confess even I share it."

Ill at ease, Joseph wanted to protest. Instead he turned away, said defensively, "I came with a mission——"

Bran sighed. "What better way to begin your mission than with a miracle?" He quickly raised his hand to forestall Joseph's objection. "And we must call it that, because no one here can explain what or why it happened. Not even Arawn Doelguss."

Anxious to turn his thoughts in other paths, Joseph asked, "Will the Atrebates really come with the dawn?"

Bran shrugged. "Arawn Doelguss is seldom wrong."

"I caused this," Joseph confessed, "pressuring the Tribes to match Kimbelinus' gift of land."

"You are not the cause," Bran told him. "If you drop a pebble in still water, ripples spread. Kimbelinus' lust for power was the pebble; all else around it are ripples. Once they run their course, the water will be serene once more."

At the forest's verge, hundred of students worked at Luke's direction. For timbers to erect barriers and obstacles the university's stable had been razed. Ropes from the ships were stretched across open areas accessible to horsemen, high enough to drag advancing riders from their saddles or sufficiently low to trip and send the enemy horse catapulting to the earth. Deadfalls were rigged to swing from stately limbs on taut tether ropes, set to sweep down and smash advancing horsemen who triggered the traps.

Beyond the forest perimeter, at intervals sharpened stakes had been set in the ground to protect archers, and covered bundles of arrows spaced for easy access. Caradoc would hold his mounted tribesmen in reserve. Since they could not be sure where the Atrebates would emerge, the archers had been split into three strong groups to defend as wide an area as possible.

When the students completed their tasks, Damhan and Beli waved them back to the university. Joseph's ships would ferry them to the *tor*, well before nightfall, out of harm's way and safe if the battle turned against the defenders.

Finally Luke was satisfied, and he joined the architects of his defenses, Damhan and Beli, Gwydion and Elvan, Quintus Marcellus Gota and Caradoc. "We have done all we can do, my friends," he told them. "Now the hardest part begins. The long wait before the battle...."

Night came swiftly. Moonlight could not penetrate the forest canopies, and though little underbrush barred their way, the Regni force proceeded slowly, cautiously. Few spoke. Anxious eyes scanned the deep shadows, dreading what they might find there. Frayed nerves conjured every thrashing sound into *forest demons.*

Amminius chafed at the slow advance. Had he been in command——? He stifled the thought. Resolutely, he turned his growing ire inward; the hot anger cooled, steeped into cold fury. It would fuel his sword arm when they struck.

Well before dawn, the wind died and a dense gray-white mist seemed to seep from the earth. Damp and clinging, it gathered in low depressions, then congealed into an ever-deepening sea that swallowed the moor, then the ancient forest and its traps.

From his command post with the center group of archers, Luke could barely see the forest. Then the ancient boles slowly vanished like ill-remembered dreams. He judged his line of sight reduced to a mere ten paces, no more. Even the air felt chill and dense and reeked of wet heather and leaf mold.

Sounds carried strangely. The sight-dampening opaqueness seemed to amplify them. Snapping twigs and the furtive crackle of leaves whispered the Atrebates advance. But Luke knew it for what it was...the waiting playing havoc with their senses.

Dawn would bring no relief, for them or the Atrebates. Dense tree canopies would defuse the rising sun, denying them morning light. In their world of gray-white fog, they would face their enemy only when they blundered upon them.

A tremor worked its way up Luke's spine. He remembered such nights in the Rhineland, in Germania. Nights of fog and the seemingly endless waiting for the barbarians——

Suddenly a blunt crushing sound reverberated loudly through the white fog. Confusion reigned immediately: horses' screams, men's pain-filled cries, and curses.

"It begins at last," Luke whispered to Reuben at his side. "Stay with me." Raising his voice, he shouted, "To the barriers! Archers, at our shoulders!"

Fer cursed his gods when their advance triggered a deadfall. He feared it would be the first of many.

"I should have foreseen this," he agonized. They had lost their element of surprise. Worse, in the fog, they were more prey than predator, and it rankled. "Advance," he yelled in a strident voice. "Kill them!"

More screams answered from different quarters, then all along the line. In the sound-carrying fog, the Regni leader heard the hiss of arrows, but he could see nothing. Then scant feet before his horse's nose, he glimpsed a hastily-erected timber barrier arrayed with sharpened wooden spikes.

When he hastily reined aside, an arrow shot past, just beyond his face. With new curses hot on his tongue, Fer heeled his horse forward toward the barrier, anxious to close with the elusive enemy before another shaft found his range. Vaulting from the saddle, he steadied a foot on the blocking timber and leapt beyond it.

He came down, sword in hand, amid a group of startled defenders. But they recovered quickly. A voice to his right yelled, "He is mine!"

Fer turned in time to catch the first strike with the edge of his broadsword, but an open palm smashing against his nose sent him reeling back half-stunned against the barrier. He tried to recover. But his attacker was a fiend. A Roman *gladius* battered against his frantic parries, and he grunted in shocked surprise when the point of the short sword drove through his iron mail, pierced flesh, and rammed deep in his gut.

Reuben did not pause as he jerked the blade free of the Regni's middle and whipped a slashing edge across the enemy warrior's throat. It was his first kill, but he did not dwell on it. Instead he paid homage to Titus Antonius Silvanus' chiding on fighting honorably. "That kill was for you, Teacher——"

Turning aside, Reuben leaped atop the barrier, gathered himself, jumped forward onto the ground, and sprinted into the fog-shrouded forest.

Sounds of battle raged all around Amminius. Sword in hand, he cursed the white fog. He had lost Fer, lost contact with his own men. Alone, isolated by the mist, his battle frenzy evaporated. Fear replaced it.

"Curse Fer. He caused this." Amminius blamed the Regni for this and more. "If I had been in command——"

His gelding threw up his head, screamed in pain, and toppled. Somehow Amminius freed himself from the saddle, and launched himself from the horse's back before the animal fell. Rolling as he hit, the prince quickly regained his feet, his sword lashing out——

Amminius' blade bit only air when he recoiled backward. A giant black shadow oozed from the bole of an ancient oak, stood towering over him with a silver sword in each hand. In abject fear the Catuvellauni sucked wind, all but wet himself. His mind recoiled in horror. He knew what he faced. Fer's *Forest Demon*——

Against his will, his fingers convulsed, the sword toppling from his grip. Half his awareness screamed he was defenseless. What remained was frozen in terror.

With the speed of a falling leaf, one of the *Demon's* swords whipped out, its point slicing a shallow furrow from cheek to jaw line. Then with blinding speed, the other sword descended, striking the prince's helmet at the temple with the flat of its blade. Pain exploded through Amminius' skull. Darkness claimed him. He was unconscious before his face buried itself in the rank leaf mold beneath the oak.

Turning with almost inhuman speed, the *Demon* rejoined the battle, taking the Regni from the rear. An avenger, the *Demon* cut his way into the Regni's mounted reserve. Horses and men fell to his flying blades. Those who survived the frenzied attack fled before the *Demon's* wrath.

Luke fought with trained ferocity, his *gladius* cutting a path of destruction through the attackers. With Gota beside him, they were a driving wedge that led their men against Atrebates, Regni, and their Catuvellauni allies. All along the defensive line, they surged forward.

Suddenly a wide-eyed attacker ran from the mist. Luke impaled him with his *gladius* before he realized the man carried no sword. When the Roman pulled his blade free, the man whimpered "*Demons* among us——" and died.

Others fled the mist, casting aside their weapons. In abject terror they fell at the defenders' feet. Begged for mercy. For protection against the evil in the wood....

Giving himself to the battle, Reuben pressed on into the forest beyond the barriers. Why——he could not say? He took wounds as he killed, mere scratches compared to the death blows he delivered. Pressing on, finally he reached a wide clearing.

Abruptly the mist thinned. A battle raged beneath the oaks, Regni against——the *Forest Demon* of Damhan's tales. An avenging golem, the dark giant moved like woodsmoke among the attackers. Warriors fell before him. His twin swords left only the dead and dying.

When there were no more to fight, the giant turned. Stood motionless facing Reuben a score paces away. A true shadow, he was black from crown to toe.

A lifetime passed in mere heartbeats. Reuben's sword arm fell limp and hanging at his side. Frozen in his tracks, he stared at the phantom in wide-eyed disbelief.

Then the moment shattered! More screams erupted not far away. Like the eldritch creature he seemed, the giant whirled away with inhuman speed. Vanished into the mist like the wraith——

Reuben turned slowly, all desire for battle evaporating. Slowly he made his way back to the moor. No one challenged him. There he found the mist thinning. Somewhere along the way out, he had wiped his blade free of blood and sheathed it. Where? When? He could not say.

Avalon's defenders had won. Caradoc's men guarded the few attackers left alive. Reuben felt no elation. No sense of victory. He left that in the forest clearing....

CHAPTER 23

I n abject terror, the surviving Regni had fled the forest. Arrows rained down on the enemy tribesmen when they scaled the barriers and decimated their ranks. Many died or fell wounded before the defending archers saw the empty, upraised hands. Heard the cries. Pleas for mercy and protection from the *Forest Demons*.

A goodly number lived. Joseph's crewmen, guarded by Caradoc's Salures, isolated the disorganized Regni, divided them into manageable groups and roped their wrists and necks together. Moving among them, Damhan and Beli quickly learned the Regni were more fearful of the *Demons* attacking their unprotected rear than anything before them.

Luke listened to Damhan's account and nodded. "We were the anvil, and the *Forest Demons*, the hammer." He nodded approvingly. "Considering all, I could not have devised a better strategy."

"We defeated them," Beli said, a touch of pride in his voice. Looking from face to face, he shrugged, voiced the obvious. "What shall we do with our prisoners?"

"Enslave them," Caradoc answered. "Or sell them——"

"No!" Reuben said defiantly. He stepped through the gathered defenders and confronted Beli and Caradoc. "That we will not do. We will not start our mission for the Christ by becoming slavers."

Heads turned, regarded him in open question. He felt the pressure from those eyes, but he would not yield. "We came to Belerion to evangelize the island for the Christ," he said simply. "Would you taint that ministry and our testimony with the sin of slavery?"

Silence answered him.

Beli broke it. "Then what say you in this?"

Reuben did not hesitate. "They fear the *Forest Demon* far more than all the swords and arrows we will ever mount. I say, take their oaths and release them."

He let his gaze range the faces. "Let the survivors carry tales of what happened here back to their Tribes. After this, you will need only a small guard around the *tor* and its lands to maintain order. Only madmen would chance facing enraged *Forest Demons* in order to harass the university or Arimathea interests."

Heartbeat by heartbeat, the tension mounted. "Hear well," Damhan said finally. "So speaks the *'the prophet who is and is not.'*"

Reuben glared at the Dumnonii chieftain, then realized his friend made no jest. His face revealed his sincerity. Quickly Reuben glanced from man to man. Clearly Damhan's words had struck a chord. All who heard were nodding.

"It is a bold strategy," Luke admitted. "But I approve with this addition. Have someone they hold in high regard witness their oaths. I say it should be——Bran the Blessed or——the Lady of the Lake."

Slowly consciousness returned. Amminius sucked in a ragged breath. Everything stank. He lay face down in the muck of decaying leaves. Head pounding, his face burned like the Furies had branded him.

Somehow he got his hands under his chest, pushed to a sitting position. Fumbling with the buckle of his helmet's chinstrap, he finally managed to loosened it. With great care he pulled the dented bronze bowl from his bruised head and flung it aside. He winced as his exploring fingers brushed swollen flesh above his temple. The entire right side of his head throbbed. Fevered skin drum-taut, it obscured vision in that eye.

Amminius did not need eyes to picture the *Forest Demon*. That black nightmarish being was forever etched in his mind. His lips curled in disgust. "I froze," he groused. But with a parched throat, it came out only as a harsh whisper. "I should have died——"

But the *Demon* had not killed. Instead it casually wounded him. Then struck him down. Left him alive. Displayed the depths of contempt for a warrior unable or unwilling to defend himself.

"I should have died——" the prince repeated, mired in self-loathing. But in the same thought, he realized no one alive had witnessed his dishonoring.

Lifting his eyes from his misery, Amminius saw the mist was thinning. All about him, the small glade held death. Horses and their Regni and Catuvellauni riders lay where they fell, vacant eyes staring. Lips frozen in silent screams, they lay grotesquely intertwined, twisted in their death throes.

I could lie with them, Amminius realized, and an ember of hope flickered in his self-serving heart. *I shall live to fight another day.* He grimaced, and the expression brought renewed pain. *But not here——*"

In the far distance, a horn sounded. From its melancholy peal, Amminius knew the skirmish was over. In time tribesmen would come to identify the dead and collect weapons and armor. *I must be away when they come.*

His head swam when he swayed drunkenly erect. Unsteady, he had to crawl over the dead to escape the glade. Only when he got his feet under him, Amminius managed to stagger back the way they had come. Even in the gloom, the churned trail left by many horses was easy to follow.

Slowly he traced the back trail. In time his irregular stride steadied, grew more confident. His head hurt abominably, but he forged on. Some time later, Amminius chanced upon a riderless horse. Frightened by the reek of blood and death, it had bolted.

Away from the battleground, its fear gone, the gelding stood alone and bewildered. Whinnying to him, it trotted close, stopped just out of reach. In spite of his dry throat, he spoke softly to the warhorse. Coaxed it nearer. Earned its confidence.

Amminius found blood on the saddle when he mounted, but filthy as he was, he paid it no mind. At their last camp, he found provisions they left, smoked meat and fish, water, and garb. Carefully he bathed his bruised head and the swollen flesh around it. He washed the filth of the clearing from his body before he donned clean breeks, shirt, and tunic. In a better mood, he chose from among the stores what he needed for his return and abandoned the rest.

With his head pounding, he did not push the horse to a fast pace. Amminius fought back a smile, knowing stretching the hurt cheek would only bring more pain. He did not fear Kimbelinus' wrath over the bungled skirmish. His father's attention was suitably diverted. Amminius doubted his grieving king would take notice of the failed skirmish.

When the council laid its plans, Damhan searched in vain for Reuben. Thinking back, the Dumnonii did not remember him speaking again after taking his stand against slavery so forcefully. Quickly he asked others. But no one had noticed Reuben leave.

Damhan hurriedly sought him among the warriors at the barricades without success. On a hunch, he hunted Gwydion.

"Aye, I have seen him," the shipsmaster admitted. "He took my ship's small skiff and rowed across to the *tor* some time ago. Is there reason to be concerned?"

"Nay," Damhan said quickly. "All is well. I wished his advice is all. Will you lend me the other skiff?"

"Elvan is at the university, but I am certain he will not object. The skiff is yours to use."

Moments later, when he started to shove off, Arawn Doelguss was beside him. He had not seen or heard her come.

"I go with you," she said simply. And she did.

A runner brought the healer's summons. Kimbelinus immediately abandoned his work. Unmindful of his kingly dignity, he would have run, but the catch in his side was growing worse, and just walking left him short of breath.

In my day I fought long and long without pause, he told himself. Was it a trick of memory, or did he grow better and stronger with each retelling? He shoved aside the musing. In those days, none could stand against him in single combat.

"Just when did I grow old?" he murmured to himself alone. Truth was a stinging salve applied to a festering wound. It galled him to face the undeniable fact that time was one battle he could not win. That no matter how much strength remained in his axe arm, death eventually would drag him down.

"Not yet," he vowed. "I still have an heir to name."

Entering the dimly-lit hut, Kimbelinus gestured impatiently at the healer, hoping the gesture would draw attention away from the knuckles he pressed into his side. "How is my son?"

"His eyes have been opening for brief moments before slumber reclaims him," the old man answered. "But judging from the rhythm of his breathing, I believe he soon will wake. I felt certain you wished to be here."

"You judged rightly," Kimbelinus affirmed. Pulling knuckles away from his side, he dragged a chair close to the newly raised pallet. "Leave us," he commanded the healer. "I would be alone with my son."

Mouth open to protest, the old man consider it better not to press and anger the king. "I shall be near. Call out and I will come."

Kimbelinus waved him away, sat brooding, watching the rise and fall of Caratacus' chest. He must have dozed, but he roused when his son called his name.

"I am here," he answered reassuringly. "I am here."

"I am weak as a babe," Caratacus whispered. "And the flesh has wasted from my limbs, my body."

"It was the poison in the wine," Kimbelinus told him. "But I promise you will grow stronger each day, and in time you will be yourself again."

"Poison——in the wine?" Caratacus repeated distantly, then his face hardened. "I was a fool."

Aye, you wer̲e̲, Kimbelinus wanted to agree, but he bit back the accusation. He told himself he would not upbraid Caratacus for being foolishly simple. That could wait until later, when his son was stronger.

"Who brought the wine, boy?" the king pressed. "Who gave it to you?"

Caratacus was visibly tiring. His eyelids flickered closed. Kimbelinus despaired of receiving an answer, but then his son rallied, spoke again. "Amminius," he answered in a fading voice. "Amminius brought the wine."

Damhan's expectation proved true. They found Reuben on the *tor's* summit. He sat with crossed legs, his naked *gladius* laid on the ground before his knees.

Suddenly afraid, Damhan cried, "Reuben, did you take injury in the attack?"

Arawn Doelguss shook her head. "Not to his body," she said knowingly. "But he suffers."

Reuben heard her voice, lifted accusing eyes to hers. His tone challenged her. "You knew."

She nodded.

Damhan looked from face to face, lost. "I do not understand."

Reuben seemed to hear only Arawn. He faced her, demanding, "Why did you not tell me, warn me?"

Her eyes were full of tenderness, but she only shrugged. "Some things are not mine to tell."

Sensing a gulf growing between them, Damhan dropped to his knees, cupped Reuben's cheeks in his palms, turned Reuben's face so their eyes met. Reuben did not resist.

Concern in his eyes, Damhan pleaded, "What has happened?"

"There are no *Forest Demons*," Reuben said distantly. "Not even one. A giant flesh and blood man wields two deadly swords. He is garbed in black. I watched him fight. Gwyr is *alive!*"

Damhan's hand dropped. For a moment he was speechless. Then his eyes found Arawn's. "Is this true?"

Slowly the Lady of the Lake's chin dipped. "What I have done, I have done," she said. "Now that you know, I can speak." She sighed heavily. "I found Gwyr sorely wounded and nursed him to health. He chose this path and bound me to silence."

Reuben was unmoved. "Why?"

"Because he knew this day was coming," she countered. "As surely as I did. He prepared for it, made people believe in and fear *Forest Demons*." She waved eastward. "How many of our lives did he save in so doing?"

"I grieved for him every day," Reuben protested, "a thousand small deaths. I loved him——"

"And love him still," she stated bluntly. "That is why you feel betrayed. Do you think I do not know?" she demanded. "Our lives are entwined more than you know, Reuben ben Ezra. "There is love between us, you and me."

One part of her mind registered Damhan's shock, but she hurried on. "In time I shall bear you a son, Reuben ben Ezra, and you will give me a daughter. He shall be a mighty man for the Christ, and she will be Arawn Doelguss after me, the Lady of the Lake. And Gwyr is there. In tale, legend and myth. Watching over us all."

Chill winds from the lake blow across the lofty *Tor*. But Arawn knew they were far less potent than the winds blowing through three souls.

For Reuben, time seemed to slow. Fear and despair and grief lifted. Floated gently out of him. Left an emptiness he did not want to face. An emptiness he must fill. Every sense he possessed screamed she was right in all she said.

Her prediction of a son and daughter laid a feast before him. Promised a woman's love, contentment, and offspring. Things he had never dreamed were possible.

"Why do you tell me this now?" he asked earnestly. "Why tell me so much now, when before you said little?"

Arawn Doelguss bowed her head, "Because all things come with a price, Reuben ben Ezra."

Time turned upon itself. He saw the Christ on the road to Calvary. Watched His lips frame silent words that changed his life and his future. *Be My Witness——*

Reuben drew breath deep in his lungs and did not falter when he asked her, "What price must I pay?"

CHAPTER 24

Reuben was subdued, silent, when he rowed Arawn Doelguss back across the narrow channel between the *tor* and the mainland. Nor did the Lady of the Lake speak. From this point onward, Reuben ben Ezra must take the lead or all would be lost to them both.

Damhan followed in the other skiff, more perplexed than they. Revelations had fallen hard and fast, and inwardly he reeled from what Arawn had shared. Almost he wished he had not listened. Almost——

They were waiting on the shore: Caradoc and Beli, Gwydion and Elvan, Luke and Quintus Marcellus Gota.

"Fine time to go gallivanting about in a skiff as you please," Luke chided, "when we still have work to be done."

"I do not recall making you captain of my life," Reuben retorted sourly. "When did I take service under you?"

Caught off guard by Reuben's sharp rebuke, the Roman frowned. Worse, he found no humor in Reuben's face. Nor in the lad's eyes. Luke glanced at Arawn, who only shrugged.

Changing tactics, the Roman said, "Joseph meets with Bran the Blessed in the hall. He has requested that you three and the company from Judea join him."

Arawn waited for Damhan to beach the skiff, then gestured up the hill. "We will come."

Caradoc led through the hall to the yard beyond where a curious round table had been set. Cups of honey mead awaited Reuben and

Arawn, Damhan, and those who had come to the beach seeking them. Benches for the Judeans bordered the round table. Students stood nearby with jugs and cups offering mead, the fermented honey for any who asked.

Bran sat beside Joseph. He waved them all to seats. Accustomed to lecturing students, his voice carried easily.

"The time has come," he announced, "for us to speak about your Christ since many of you have come to teach us about Him and spread His gospel."

Bran paused, his eyes ranging the assembled people, meeting the gazes of those about him. "Joseph and I have had such discussions before. Along general principals, our faith and that professed by you Christ-followers are not so different."

Joseph nodded. "Bran's Druidism has much in common with my people's history in the Scriptures up to the Judges period," he explained. "Our Jewish language and the Celtic tongue also share common roots as well: similar sounds, phrasing and meanings. The point we diverge is basically when the codification of our beliefs began after the Babylonian exile. Jews from our distant past may have shared our faith with Bran's ancestors which grew into the faith the tribesmen practice today."

Intrigued despite his melancholy, Reuben listened. Arawn's hand crept into his, and he did not draw away. She had once stressed to him they were not so different.

"We hold certain truths sacred," Bran said, "such as the '*Three duties of every man: worship God; be just to all men, and die for your country*.' One of our core beliefs is '*the Triad*,' very similar to what you Christ-followers believe: the Father, Son, and Holy Spirit. Our world of the Divine is not composed of three separate persons, but one with '*three*' emanations. These are Beli, who was the Creator of the past; Taran, who is providential god of the present; and Yesu, the coming Savior of the future."

No one stirred. Every eye centered on the Arch Druid.

"We have long anticipated the coming of our Yesu, which in your Aramaic tongue is '*Yahshua*.'" Bran looked about, then continued.

"Years ago Joseph brought a young man to Belerion to study with us. Arawn Doelguss remembers Him well. His name was Yahshua ben Joseph."

A quickening ran through the Judeans on the benches.

Bran smiled. "We teach that when our Yesu comes, He will be known as '*All Heal*.'"

His gaze moved to Reuben. Other men and women followed the direction of Bran's gaze, stared at Reuben. "Damhan Mawr states that this young man seated among you was crippled from birth. The esteemed Joseph of Arimathea confirms this. Is this true, Reuben ben Ezra?"

Reuben stood tall. "It is. Until I was healed by Yahshua ben Joseph, who is our Christ, our Messiah. Our Jesus, who was crucified by the Romans, died on the cross, and who on the third day was raised from the dead by *His* Father in heaven, just as *He* promised *His* followers."

Surveying the entire circle, Reuben's gaze came to rest on Damhan, then Caradoc. "I have seen Him alive, saw *His* body which still carried the wounds from *His* crucifixion." He waved his hand about the circle. "So have many of the Judeans who are seated here. Because of *Him*, those who were blind, see, those who were deaf, hear, and like me, who were lame, walk."

He saw guarded skepticism in Caradoc's face; acceptance in Damhan's. *I can only witness*, Reuben mused without excuse. *It is the Christ who brings conviction*—— With a sigh, he settled back into his chair.

"We have so much to learn from one another," Bran concluded. "In days to come we will speak more of this. But I state for all gathered here that I accept and believe that Joseph's and Reuben's Yahshua, their Christ, their Anointed One, is our Yesu, whom we have long sought."

Before he swung onto his horse's back and departed, Caradoc

faced Joseph, embraced him. Reuben stood with Bran and Arawn Doelguss, watching from the side.

"Uncle," he said respectfully, "you and my father are learned men and wise, while I am stubborn and prideful as befits a soldier and a warrior." His face fell. "Your arguments linking your Christ and our Jesu weigh upon me. You almost persuade me. Perhaps in time——?"

Joseph sighed. "The Christ has set it on our hearts to share the good news. His sheep hear His voice and follow Him. Perhaps one day you, too, will harken to His voice, set aside your pride, and be His."

Caradoc shrugged. "I make no promises."

"Who has asked for them?" Joseph answered. "Still, you cannot deny an old man his dreams."

"Who am I——" he countered, "to be so bold as to deny Joseph of Arimathea anything?" He grasped his horse's mane, swung into the saddle. "Blessing be upon you, Uncle."

"And upon you, Sister's Son."

Caradoc wheeled his gelding, waved to his retainers, and they spurred northward, toward the lands of the Silures.

The three joined Joseph and watched the departing warriors disappear into the northern forest.

"I see his mother in him," Joseph said wistfully. "In his eyes and in his stubbornness."

Bran chuckled. "My Anna was a Jewess after all."

"And, as I recall, she made you a fine queen," Joseph reminded him pointedly, "and bore you fine sons."

"That she did," Bran admitted with a smile. "My people adored her."

"Your son is a good king," Arawn said of Caradoc. "In time he will grow to be a great king."

"With the promise of his bloodline," Reuben countered, "how could he be less?"

Bran's eyebrows lifted. "Long have we known to listen to Arawn Doelguss. Do you also speak as '*the prophet who is and is not?*'"

Reuben quickly shook his head. "I speak only from the knowledge that through the bloodline of his mother, Anna, Caradoc is descended from the line of our great King David."

Until Caratacus slept again, Kimbelinus smothered his rage. When his son's eyelids closed and his breathing eased, the king waved the healer to Caratacus' bedside.

"You heard," he challenged the healer. "I know you heard his words."

"I did."

Kimbelinus smiled, but there was no joy in it. "If my son dies before he can make the accusation, will you stand witness to what you heard?"

Eyes hard, the healer nodded. "I will."

"After all this," the king warned, "he is not to die."

"He——?" Hesitating, the old man nodded. "Yes, Sire."

Kimbelinus had not waited for his answer. Outside, he summoned his guards. "Find Mordag Mor at once. Bring her to me in the hall. Go!"

From the high seat he watched her come and cross the hall. Although she was younger than the king, she was old now, her features deeply lined. But there were few gray streaks in her flame-red hair and her frame was slim, not run to fat. She had once been his consort, mother of his firstborn; never his queen. He had set her aside for another, and she had never forgiven him for it.

On stiff knees, Kimbelinus rose from the high seat. He motioned the guards to escort her to the chamber off the main hall when they could speak without the world hearing.

"Your son poisoned Caratacus," he accused, his voice low, dangerous. "He almost died. I will see that Amminius dies slow and hard."

Mordag Mor glared at him. "*My* son?" she threw back at the king. "You kept him in your house when you cast me aside. I say the acorn did not fall far from the oak."

"Son of mine or no," he argued, "I will see him die for what he has done."

Slow and deliberate, she drew her pouch from her waistband.

Opening it, she cast the bones to the floor. They clattered against the stones, falling this way and that. Mordag knelt quickly, studied the pattern. With a sharp laugh, she gathered the bones, tucked them away, and stood.

"They told me you will not kill my son," she challenged. "He does not die by your hand."

Kimbelinus frowned blackly. He hated her for her insolence while he valued her powers of foretelling the future. If not for those powers, he would have had her strangled long ago. She was passionate enough, he admitted, but she had proved a vixen for a consort.

"What did the bones say?" he asked spitefully. He knew she made this duty burdensome for her own purposes.

"You banish him from *Belerion*," Mordag announced, her lined face triumphant. "You send him away, to the Roman Emperor, to Caligula."

Her prophecy grated on Kimbelinus. Mordag read his face like a pattern of the bones. But she hid from him what else was in the bones. She kept her silence because it troubled her, not because it gave her power over him. Old feelings for him she thought long dead stirred when she read his coming death in the pattern.

"For what he has done, I will not permit Amminius to enter *Camulodunum*," Kimbelinus said stubbornly. "If you believe your pattern true," he glared at her and she looked away first, "find him on the road. Have him take ship elsewhere. Anywhere but *Camulodunum*. If he enters the city after I have forbidden it, he will die."

Mordag nodded. There was still iron in her lost love. Suddenly she was a young maid again and he, the young stag who had won her heart. But rejection and long years wanting him had soured her more than thwarted ambition had him.

She turned away so he would not gloat over the naked heartache and the shriveled longing in her eyes. "Our son will go to Rome," she said simply. "Perhaps I will board that ship and sail with him?"

169

CHAPTER 25

With the dawn Bran the Blessed rose. He found Joseph of Arimathea away from his pallet and standing near the shore, staring across the channel water at the *tor*. With soft steps the Arch Druid approached, loath to disturb his kinsman's concentration.

Joseph knew his coming, half-turned and nodded. "I see you, Bran the Blessed. Approach."

"And I see you," Bran returned. Then he frowned. "What troubles you, my kinsman? Is something amiss?"

"All is well," Joseph assured him. "In the night I dreamed. I saw a humble house of worship," he pointed, "there on the *tor* where the crest is flattest. The remainder of the night I passed too excited to sleep until first light when I could see it clearly across the water."

"You would build a temple there?" Bran questioned. "But the nearest quarries are in the *Mendip Hills*."

"Not a temple of stone," Joseph chided compassionately. "A humble dwelling such as a Celt would build, a round house of wattle and dab. One of a size sufficient for a small gathering to join together in fellowship and prayer. I would see a simple altar built, and anchorite huts, one for each of the twelve who will remain here at Avalon to do the Christ's work."

"Ah," Bran said, smiling. "An *ecclesia*, the Greeks would term it."

"Yes," Joseph confirmed, "a center organized and dedicated to worship and religious work." He turned, faced Bran with the beginnings of a smile. "One that will complement your university, perhaps?"

"Let it be so," Bran agreed enthusiastically. "And our students can help——like they did with the barricades." He pinched his lip with his thumb and forefinger before he continued. "We shall call the construction of your ecclesia——exercises in the *'practical applications of geometry.'*"

They cut timbers for the new buildings from the fastness of the old forest. Arimathea's crewmen kept one eye on their axes, the other on the shadowy places where the *Forest Demon* was said to dwell. One morning they returned to find a cedar tree, cut at day's end and left where it fell, awaiting them on the forest's verge. Afterward, as one would in a holy place, they tread softly and reverently.

With the upright beams in place, the rafters for the high roof raised and set, students began to weave thin branches that formed the wattle between the support poles.

By his choice, Reuben did not take part in the construction. He searched the dark forest where Arawn bade him. On the *tor* Bran stood nearby with Joseph and some of the Judean elders, watching the church's progress.

"Tribesmen mix limestone dust carted from a nearby deposit with clay to hold the mix together," the Arch Druid explained. "To the mix they add aggregates of earth, sand from the shore, and crushed limestone from an exhausted quarry to the mix. Then they reinforce the daub with rushes gathered from the channel and nearby waterways."

Students used wooden trowel-like scoops to imbed the daub in the wattle, infilling the latticework of branches with the mixture.

"Once it has dried," Bran added, "they will whitewash both sides. This increases its resistance to rain. Where gaps form when it dries, they will carefully wedge straw, moss or leaves into the cracks to keep out the wind."

With many willing hands at the old quarry and clay banks, the work progressed quickly. Bran and Joseph disagreed over the size of the church, Bran calling for thirty cubits, Joseph, a meager twenty. When the poles were set in place, the diameter measured exactly thirty cubits.

Beginning at the bottom edge of the rafters, the university students tied hazel batting horizontally to provide a framework for thatching to attach the roof. Word spread quickly among the villages and the nearby tribesmen that the university needed thatching done. Skilled thatchers answered the call. Following them were wains-loads of wheat and rye or a mixture of both.

With deft hands, the thatchers fastened the straw into bundles nearly five cubits long, then laid them on the roof framework with the severed ends facing downward. Layer upon layer followed, until the thatcher skillfully wove the bundles ends together to form the crest. By the time the thatchers completed the main church roof, the first of the outlying huts' roof framing had been set in place and was ready to be thatched.

Noticeably pleased with the progress, Bran told Joseph, "Your disciples will find these roofs easy to repair. With the stable supporting structure that you have, they can easily withstand winter gales and heavy winds."

When the uprights and rafters had been set in place for the twelve outlying huts, Gwydion approached Joseph. "It is in my mind to sail to Thule," the shipsmaster said, "to find my father's people. I would share Broch Gorm's designs with them, but only if you give your blessing."

Joseph smiled. "You and yours have served me well, and I see no need to guard the secrets of our ships any longer. *Judah's Hope* is yours. Go and do as you feel led with my blessing. Since I seek to do the Christ's work, what need have I for ships?"

"You show great faith in one who is unworthy," Gwydion answered. "When I have seen my father's kin, I will return. I choose to remain a bond-servant to Arimathea."

"But Gwydion——" Joseph protested, "I do not ask that of you. You are your own man."

Gwydion shook his head. "There is no need to ask. What I give, I give willingly."

Joseph embraced him, gave him a kiss of peace. "Go swiftly. May the Christ look with favor on your voyage."

On the night before the huts were to be completed, those Christ-Followers who felt called to Gaul came to Joseph—— Lazarus, his sisters, Mary and Martha, and their maid, Marcella, and others were with them. As he had with Gwydion, Joseph heard them out and blessed them, then bade Elvan prepare *Judah's Tears* for a return voyage to *Massilia*.

Elvan did not try to hide his concern. "With Gwydion gone you will have no ship."

"You must not worry," Joseph told him. "Gwydion will return from Thule. He chooses to remain with Arimathea."

A smile tugged at Elvan's lips. "I also am Arimathea. If God wills and I live, I will return."

Joseph shook his head. "But I am no longer a merchant in need of ships."

"Master," he said, staring reassuringly at Joseph, "you are here, and I am no longer a pagan."

"Whatever will I do with a ship's captain," Joseph argued, "who will not obey his Master?"

"Whatever the Christ wills," Elvan answered. "Whatever God wills."

When Reuben sought Joseph and did not find him with the others, he walked the night. He found his master on the shore, hands clasped before him, staring morosely at the moonlight on the dark waters separating them from the *tor*.

"Master, you are here alone. Are you unwell?"

For a moment Joseph did not answer. Then the old man sighed. "I am well, Reuben," he said reassuringly. "It is simply that I feel my age and this new responsibility I have undertaken. It weighs on me."

Reuben did not comment. He let the silence stretch taut, nigh unto breaking. Something indeed pricked Joseph's mood, left him unsettled. Reuben had seen similar moods before; like a bad morsel caught between two teeth, only Joseph could work it out.

"Reuben——" Joseph began, "who am I to inspire such loyalty, from you, Gwydion, Elvan, even Quintus Marcellus Gota and Luke?"

Dumbfounded, Reuben stared at his master. "You who are Joseph, merchant prince of the House of Arimathea, *Nobilis Decurio* for Rome, in charge of Britannia's mines, and now, Apostle to Christ? Why do you ask me this?"

"It is easy to command respect when one has wealth," Joseph retorted. "Respect and even loyalty——if one has coin enough." Then he sighed. "I enter now a realm that sets no store in wealth, and I fear I am no true Apostle. I worry that I will fail those who paint me greater than I am."

Reuben understood his fear. He knew it well. Joseph had given him great responsibility, first as scribe to Arimathea, then as Minister of his House.

"Set your eyes on your calling, Master," he urged. "Whatever else you may have been in your past, you are now bond-servant to our Lord and Savior Jesus Christ, called to His purpose."

"It is as you say," Joseph answered. There was new life in his voice, new determination. "I must never lose sight of that calling. God help me, I must lead and encourage others to spread the gospel of Christ throughout *Belerion*...."

Mordag Mor and her small group of riders found Prince Amminius. Alone and feverish, he was on the road one day's ride west of *Camulodunum*. Mordag barely recognized her son, his wounded face was so swollen and hideous. When they crowded around him, his nervous horse sidestepped, and he almost tipped from the saddle.

"Away, *Demon!*" he croaked, his rust-pitted sword waving weakly about him, fighting shadow enemies no one could see.

"Disarm him quickly," she ordered her guard. "Before he injures himself, or worse, one of us."

With a sure hand the warrior wrested the blade from Amminius' grasp. Unbalanced, the prince slumped over against Mordag's escort. The sudden shift in weight sent both men tumbling from their saddles. Amminius struck the ground jarringly, went limp, head lolling, eyes unfocused.

"We must get him off the road," she ordered, fighting the loathing that gripped her. "Those wounds must be tended, and we must break that fever."

Looking down at him, she felt no pity. *Ah, Amminius,* she thought scornfully, *where is that haughty pride you marshaled against me so few weeks ago? You are sorely wounded, and by rights, from your ill treatment of me, I should ride on by and leave you to your death.*

But she would not. There were few things Mordag Mor believed in, but one of them was the power of the bones. They told her Amminius was to go to Caesar. But from the condition of his face, it would not be the handsome Amminius who rode west from *Camulodunum* on Kimbelinus' order.

Time was against her. Any day Kimbelinus could change his mind and send men searching for Amminius. Ill or not, she had to get Amminius to the ship she arranged.

"Gather wood for a fire," she ordered two of the four remaining men in her escort. Turning to her maid, she said tersely, "Boil water and prepare a poultice for his wound."

Straightening in the saddle, she fixed her gaze on the remaining pair. "Prepare a litter for the prince. We have a half-day's ride before we reach the safety of our ship."

CHAPTER 26

I n the place where the altar would be raised. Joseph of Arimathea bade trusted crewmen from *Judah's Hope* excavate a pit in the floor of the church, five cubits square by five cubits deep. A small flotilla of skiffs had to be constructed to ferry supplies and laborers across the channel from the university grounds.

Tribesmen brought limestone blocks by cart from the nearly-depleted quarry leagues to the south. To transport heavy stones across the channel, Elvan engineered a pair of block and tackle hoists, one on each shore to host the heavy stones onto *Judah's Tears' deck,* then offload them on the other side into carts to be hauled up to the *tor's* crown. There workmen laid the ashlars in the pit as a foundation, well mortared with a mixture of water, sand and lime.

Joseph stood nearby during the construction process, describing what he wanted, assisting where he could, getting his hands dirty when his workers allowed. Time and again, he proudly held up mortar-stained hands to Bran or Reuben or Arawn Doelguss. While the work progressed, Reuben envied his master's boundless energy.

In horizontal courses, crewmen mortared limestone blocks to form firm walls with the necessary niches to support stout oak floor beams that would span the pit. When the four walls were done, along one side, they laid narrow steps, mortared with smaller blocks, to allow access to the tiny crypt.

Across the support beams, crewmen laid a floor of oak planks, secured by hammered spikes. Water rushes, gathered by the students from waterways around the *tor* and carefully dried, were spread over the planks, a half-finger deep. Over the rushes, crewmen laid dressed stone flags, butted and mortared between the stones. A carefully-hewn stone, designed to conceal the descending stairway, was hinged with hidden bronze pins and counter-weighted to swing upward easily, allowing access to the crypt.

Tribesmen from a nearby village crafted an unadorned altar for the church from seasoned oak. Crewmen used the hosts and ship to ferry it across the channel, then hauled it up the winding path of ascending terraces to the *tor's* crest and set it into place.

"Your crewmen did well," Bran told Joseph, a pleased note in his voice. "It is built like our tribesmen would build, with no undue ornamentation. You must be pleased."

"I confess a sense of pride in what they have accomplished," Joseph acknowledged. He ran his hands caressingly over the altar's polished oak, cast his eyes over the white-washed wattle-and-daub walls, the carefully-fitted plank doors, the high-beamed thatch roof. "Even the most humble man will not feel out of place here."

When Bran turned to leave, Joseph laid a restraining hand on the Arch Druid's arm. "At dusk, will you come to the church?" he asked in a hushed voice. "There are things I wish you to see, things most precious I brought from Judea, secrets that must be guarded."

Bran's eyebrow arched. "Ah, that was your reason for the crypt. I wondered——" He grinned. "I will come."

While the last sun's rays bathed the *tor's* dark waters in eldritch gold, Reuben and Joseph climbed the steep path to the summit. Reuben had spent the afternoon patiently supervising students arranging iron sconces and candles within the church, tolerating his master's changing whims.

They were silent, each absorbed in his own thoughts during the long climb. They relived the night the Apostles Peter and John brought their secret treasures to the House of Arimathea and left them in Joseph's keeping.

Reaching the church, Reuben entered the candle-lit interior, tenderly placed the olive wood box on the new altar, and respectfully stepped back. When the box touched the altar, he sensed an indescribable change within the church. It seemed the wide room had somehow been consecrated, had been made wondrously holy.

Eyes rapt, Joseph faced Reuben. When he spoke, his voice was subdued, almost breathless. "Do you feel it?"

Awed, Reuben nodded. "Once before I felt this——"

"In the presence of the Christ," Joseph finished for him. "I felt it when *He* brought me from the Temple cell."

How long that moment lasted, Reuben could not say. Bran the Blessed's shocked voice from the doorway roused them. "Joseph, what is this——?" the Arch Druid demanded. "What have you done?"

Arawn Doelguss stood at Bran's elbow, her stunned expression mirroring her companion's.

"We have done nothing," Joseph answered. "But I tell you, as surely as I live, the presence of the Christ comes to consecrate this church."

Bran approached the altar, saw the box. "Your secrets bring this?" he stammered. "This——this box holds them?"

With reverent hands, Joseph opened the hinged top. He brought forth a nondescript earthenware cup of fired clay about seven fingers tall by five fingers across the mouth. It was a cup of no marked significance, its simple design devoid of handle, its sides unadorned. In his hands the fired clay seemed to glow from within, as if an inner fire burned within the heart of the baked clay. For all its simplicity, it drew the eye, held it.

A choked cry escaped Arawn Doelguss. "*He* held this!" she whispered tearfully, her admission showing pain and wonder. "The Christ held this——*!*"

Joseph nodded solemnly. "The Apostle Peter told us Our Master held this cup to the lips of each of His Disciples so that they might drink at the Passover meal on the night He was taken."

Recalling Peter's words, Reuben faithfully repeated them, "Peter said when *He* had taken a cup and given thanks, *He* gave it to each of *His* disciples saying, *'Drink from it all of you; for this is My blood of the covenant, which is poured out for many for forgiveness of sins.'*"

Tears filled Bran's eyes when he met Joseph's. "You said secrets——"

Joseph's trembling fingers delicately caught the cloth within the cup's mouth, drew it forth. "The Apostle John said this cloth is stained with blood and water from the spear that pierced our Master's heart. The brown stain in the cup also is Christ's blood. While it was still fresh, John thrust the blooded cloth into the cup, and the clay became stained with it."

"Christ's blood——" Arawn murmured. "The blood that healed Reuben?"

Reuben nodded, then told them, "The blood that healed me came from the cross which fell on Jesus in the street when *He* carried it to Calvary. This blood John gathered came from the spear that pierced Jesus' heart. Our Christ shed that blood morning and afternoon of the same day."

Bran's face paled. "Who knows of these secrets?"

"The Apostles Peter and John brought them to us," Joseph answered. "There is Reuben and me, and now——the two of you. There are no others."

"No one else must know," Arawn said suddenly, an odd note in her voice. "It is too dangerous. In ages to come tales will be told about this cup. Legends that place it in *Belerion* near the *tor*." Her gaze centered on Joseph, "Legends that place it in your hands, Joseph of Arimathea. Legends that call Christ's cup '*the Holy Grail*.'"

"For good or ill, we all have become its guardians," Bran told them. "It has great power. We have witnessed it; we feel it here in this church." His eyes swept the others. "There are those who will covet it for that power. Try to use it ill. For that reason, we must guard it jealously."

He reached a hesitant hand to touch it, sealing himself to its defense. Arawn Doelguss did as well. Joseph and Reuben followed those before them.

"Place it in its box, Joseph," Bran urged, "and carry it to the crypt for now. Soon we must devise a more secure hiding place. Too many know the crypt is here."

Before Joseph slid the cup and cloth back into its box, Reuben raised the concealing slab. When Joseph lifted the box with the cup inside from the altar, the presence dimmed, but did not vanish. Even when the box was safely stored in the special chamber below, like an elusive fragrance, that special sense of Christ's presence remained in the church.

Chapter 27

For long days Reuben patiently searched the dim forest glades where ash and oak were old before the coming of man to this island. His senses told him that many who dwelled here knew he roamed their haunts: deer and hog and a host of smaller shadow creatures. He saw their prints in the thick loam beneath the trees: hoof and pad and scurrying foot.

No sword graced his side. No bow fitted his hand. No quiver hung on his back or rode his waist. Reuben went into the old forest unarmed and defenseless.

"Go, and though the wood is wide, Gwyr will know," Arawn Doelguss told him. She had cupped his cheeks in her palms, her concern for his safety open for him to see. "Do not expect the Gwyr you knew. He has changed in these years, grown *feral* like a great cat who holds no trust for man. Only your Christ knows if he will show himself." She shook her head sorrowfully. "Surely I do not."

Reuben had not asked the why of it. Perhaps she did not know. Perhaps only Gwyr knew——

How many leagues he walked he could not say, but having reconciled himself to this purpose, he would trek to the ends of the earth if needs be to see it done. It was no longer about him or his desires. It was about Gwyr.

"Reuben——" Arawn challenged him, "Gwyr saved you. Now you must save him!"

To any eyes other than his own, his path was aimless. And truly it was. But Reuben knew beyond expectation, when Gwyr came near, he would know it.

And suddenly he did!

Reuben shivered when an icy wind chilled his neck. Sweat prickled his forehead. He knew without knowing he was being watched. That eyes tracked his every step.

"Gwyr——" Reuben said loudly, slowly turning about in a circle. "When Damhan told me you were dead, I almost died." He paused, sighed with remorse. "Part of me did. I went mad for a time."

He continued to turn, not trying to spy out the shadow where the big Iceni stood, just letting himself be seen. "For me, your death has been a wound that never healed. If I had been more rational I would have reasoned why. It is simple. We are a blended soul, you and I."

Reuben spread his hands wide, still turning. "In Abyla, in answer to Quintus Marcellus Gota and Titus Antonius Silvanus, you signed to Joseph, *'My reason for life is to carry and protect Reuben. To this end I was born. I obey my God.'* Do you remember that I protested? I held you my dearest friend, my confidant, my brother. I never wanted more than that. Then or now."

Unashamed tears came, slid down Reuben's cheeks. "The Prophet Jeremiah wrote of the Lord, *'Before I formed you in the womb I knew you, and before you were born I consecrated you——'* Before we were ever born, God know even then what lengths you would go to protect me."

He stopped turning, faced a direction that felt right, let his arms fall. "Gwyr, the Lord God also knew me in the womb. He knew before the beginning of time that I would walk again. That I would go to Joseph and witness for the Christ. Just as He knew you would offer yourself as a sacrifice for me, for Joseph, for Damhan and his men."

Reuben's throat was dry, but he would not be silent. "Gwyr, you saved my life. There will always be that debt between us. The Christ nurtured in me a saving faith. *He* healed my legs; *He* also saved my soul."

He raised his hands in supplication. "The Christ lives in me, Gwyr. He has made a place in heaven for those who believe in Him. But I cannot go, Gwyr, not without *you!*"

His voice broke, and he breathed deeply to regain his calm. "Gwyr, do you understand what I am saying? How can I knowingly accept heaven and eternity without you?"

Again his emotions choked him. The forest beyond the glade was strangely silent. No breeze disturbed the high canopies, no twigs crackled. In truth, no one might be near, but Reuben knew Gwyr was nearby. That he listened.

"When I saw the *Forest Demon* fighting the Regni, I knew you lived," Reuben said. "I watched you practice far too often to be deceived. No one fights like you. No one. Silvanus told you that."

He swallowed hard. "From the moment I knew you were alive, I felt betrayed, crushed, and angry. How could you live and sentence me to a life believing you were dead?" Reuben shook his head. "You must have had your reasons. Arawn Doelguss could have told Damhan that you lived, and he would have sent me word. But you did not——"

Bearing his soul sapped his strength, but he could not stop. "In the days I could not walk, the Christ told me I would stand and witness for Him in Judea and beyond. I have and I do. But I tell you this, as surely as I know anything, I was brought into this world for two purposes. My higher purpose was to witness to Joseph about the Christ, to lead him to understand why Jesus could not be the triumphant Christ the Jews sought. That witness set in motion events that would lead to Christ's Resurrection and the redemption of all mankind."

New strength blossomed in Reuben. "My sole purpose now for drawing breath does not involve me. It is not about me at all, Gwyr. It was never about me. It is about *you!*"

His voice grew firm and carried his conviction. "Before we first sailed for Britannia, each time I spoke with Jesus, you were with me. You saw *Him*, felt about *Him* as I did. I beseech you, my Brother, *He* is all we thought and more. *His* blood washes away sin, yours and mine and all who believe. In *His* resurrection, all who believe the Son of Man is the Son of God, the Messiah, are saved."

Reuben sighed heavily. "Arawn Doelguss says you have changed. That you are *not* the Gwyr I knew and loved. That you no longer trust in men. What she says may be true, but the Gwyr I knew had a heart for God, and I tell you as surely as I walk today that Jesus is the Son of God."

He sensed an unbearable tension not born of his mind or his heart. Reuben spoke to that distress, put his heart in what he said. "Gwyr, oh Gwyr, please hear me. The Christ told those who heard *Him* speak, '*I am the way, the truth, and the life. No man comes to the Father but by Me.*'"

Reuben's voice rose with his desperation. "Do you understand what *He* means? If you reject *Him*, you reject the One who sent *Him*. Rejecting *Him* means for all eternity you will be separated from God. Can you endure that?"

With a sigh, Reuben slipped to his knees. "If you intend to reject *Him*, Gwyr, kill me now." He closed his eyes, bowed his head not knowing what to expect. "One quick stroke, and it is done. I shall not blame you, now or in eternity. Do it, Gwyr, and be quick. I simply have no wish to go on living with the knowledge that when you reject the Christ, you are forever lost to me!"

Heartbeat followed drumming heartbeat. Blood flowed through his veins. Breath gave his body life. In those long moments when he waited for death, no sword fell.

Was I mistaken? Reuben wondered. Had his senses betrayed him? *Is Gwyr not here at all?*

With a sigh bordering on desperation, Reuben opened his eyes, lifted his chin. Raw sunlight filtering through the green leaves bathed the glade in gold and peace.

Drained by his witness, his testimony, Reuben remained on his knees, fighting the trembling that seized his limbs. When it passed, he pushed weakly to his feet.

"Where are you, Gwyr?" Reuben asked the silent forest. He wanted to scream it until he had no voice. Would Gwyr hear him? Would Gwyr listen? He did not know, but he knew he would persevere.

"I will walk these woods until I find you. Until you hear me," he promised faithfully. "I will not abandon you," he added. "Now or ever!"

Reuben half-turned and almost stumbled back in shock. Behind him stood death, a silent man with face and body shrouded in black. Death was a giant with two shining swords in his upraised hands.

While Reuben stared wide-eyed, the fingers opened. Released the swords. Let them drop to the forest floor. One hand lifted to the mask. Stripped it away, tossed it aside. An older Gwyr looked down at him. A Gwyr whose fair features now were marred with white scars.

With healed legs and feet, Gwyr signed, *you still are a little man.*

Fighting new tears, Reuben smiled broadly. "And you still are a big ass!"

Gwyr's muscled arms swept down, caught up Reuben. Crushed him breathless against his massive chest. In that embrace and all that followed, the lost years fled, exiled and forgotten....

Arawn bit her lip while she watched Reuben stride purposefully across the moor toward her. She hated when her gift deserted her, now more than any she could remember. Somehow she forced herself to remain where she was. In her current state she doubted if her knees would obey her will.

His face gave no clue to the outcome, and by the time he reached her, Arawn's nerves were hopelessly frayed. Then she could sustain herself no longer. "He came to you?" she cried hopefully. "You saw him?"

Reuben nodded. "He gave me word for you." His fingers faithfully repeated the terse words Gwyr sent to Arawn.

Tears misted her eyes. Then she repeated aloud what he signed, "All is well."

With inarticulate joy, uncaring who witnessed the thawing of

Arawn Doelguss' remoteness, she threw herself into Reuben's arms and cried the relief that filled her against his chest.

Later, hand in hand they walked the *tor*, her familiar ground, well away from the summit where many labored to bring Joseph's dream into reality. Reuben told her all, sharing his sense of hurt and betrayal and how the Christ had healed his heart and reunited two kindred souls.

"Gwyr will not leave the forest," he told her. "It is his home now. He stands guardian over all he loves."

She nodded, accepting what she long expected. Her face took on the haunting expression that said she looked out into a wide expanse of time. "One day he will cradle our little ones is his great hands. They will come to know and love the man who will be legend to others."

"One day, if God allows it," he sighed, "perhaps we too will know and cherish his children."

Arawn blanched. "Forgive me," she whispered. "I thought you knew. Gwyr can sire no children...."

Amminius was mercifully unconscious when Mordag Mor's men hoisted the prince aboard the seedy merchant vessel. A linen wrap held the ground flaxseed poultice against the wound, and she and her maid slept in shifts to see he did not dislodge it. Before it could be stitched, the wound must drain, and the longer it remained open, the worse the resulting scar would be.

Mordag stared at her only son strapped into the bunk, and the only emotion stirring in her heart was scorn.

You will provide me with a better life than your sire, she silently demanded. If he did not, she was certain she could make her way in Rome. The bones told her so.

CHAPTER 28

Just before the sun reached noon, Arviragus approached *Camulodunum's* main gate at the head of his personal guard. Togodurunus, his elder brother, who had been dicing with the guardsmen on duty, abandoned the game to greet his younger brother. They were cut from the same heroic mold as Kimbelinus, though Togodurunus, with his coarser face, was the poorer copy.

"Your horses are hard ridden," Togodurunus said, noting the white lather on their chests and the heaving barrels." He waved to the idle grooms he had stationed near the gate for such as this. "Hand off your mounts to my lads, dismiss your guards, and walk with me."

"When our father is near to death," Arviragus shot back, "and a change of thrones is in the wind, why should I dismiss my guards and walk alone with you?"

"Brother, do not try——" Togodurunus choked off his sharp retort when he saw Arviragus' chiding grin. He shook his head, threatened hollowly, "One day, Arvi, you will say too much, and I will pin your ears between your legs."

Instead, he wrapped his great arms around his brother and embraced him warmly. "I have sorely missed you, boy."

Arviragus took no affront to his brother's assumed agedness. Of all of Kimbelinus' brood, they alone were close in shared affection, and his quip about trust, was only that, an ill-timed jibe he should have left unsaid.

"Your messenger rode two horses near to death to bring me word," Arviragus said. "Kimbelinus has been ill before."

"Not like this," Togodurunus countered. "Judge for yourself when you see him."

"What are these tales we hear of a battle in the west?" Arviragus pressed his brother. "It is said Amminius——"

"Dismiss what you have heard," Togodurunus retorted. "Amminius poisoned Caratacus before he left to lead a foray against the Tribes at the *tor*. He bungled both. Caratacus lives, the Regni assault was crushed, and Amminius was banished to Rome. Thankfully that witch of a mother of his fled with him."

Togodurunus exhaled sharply. "Kimbelinus also has issued a decree should Amminius shows his face in *Camulodunum*, the man who strikes him down would gain a pouch of Roman gold from the King's own hand."

Arviragus' eyes widened, shook his head. "I have been away too long fighting in the north."

"You are home and warmly welcomed," Togodurunus assured him. "Come and judge for yourself our father's health."

They entered Kimbelinus' long house, the king's hall, and though the sun blazed outside the walls, tall fires roared in the great hearths. Arviragus raised an eyebrow at the cloying heat but said nothing.

Kimbelinus sat in the high seat, a cloak about his shoulders, a thick felt drape covering his legs. As they approached, he lifted rheumy eyes to his sons. "Have you come to gloat that I am dying?" he hurled at them in a voice still hale. He waved them away. "Save your pity for lesser men. I will grow strong again and outlive you both."

Arviragus stared at Kimbelinus, hardly believing what he saw. When he left for the north, his father had indeed been old, but tall and strong enough to break lesser men. This old man who growled at him was more than old. His flesh was shriveled and pasty white, and the arm that threatened them, barely skin and bones.

Togodurunus drew his brother to one side. He pressed a finger to his lips, a caution that despite the king's new frailties, Kimbelinus retained his hearing.

"He claims a demon gnaws at his vitals," Togodurunus whispered, his lips close to his brother's ear. "See the fist he continually presses against his side——"

Hesitant to speak, Arviragus waved his brother back the way they came, and their departing footsteps echoed dully on the stones. Outside, he led Togodurunus to a shadowed corner. "When did you last meet with Mordag Mor?"

"I have not," Togodurunus admitted. "I avoid her."

"Then you do not know," Arviragus stated. "I have never slighted her, and she respects me. Before I went north, she called me aside to warn me, war is coming with the Romans. Claudius will invade *Belerion*——"

"But Caligula is emperor and——" Togodurunus rolled his eyes. "The gods preserve us from Rome and its cursed politics. And now, where has Amminius gone? To Rome, of course, with that witch of a mother at his side."

Arviragus held his tongue. His brother was no simpleton. *He can guess the future as well as I——*

"Father had strong friends in Rome," Togodurunus pondered. "They have been influential enough to keep our lands free of the legions' yoke these many years." He stared hard at his brother. "But when Kimbelinus goes to be with his ancestors, that influence also dies."

"Soon you will be King," Arviragus stated, "and you have little time to prepare. If Mordag is right, and I fear she is, we live on sufferance as long as Caligula rules. When Claudius assumes the throne, we must fight to hold what we have or become another insignificant client kingdom under Caesar's rule."

"I have no desire to bend a knee to Rome," Togodurunus replied bluntly. "Now or ever. I will die first."

"Do not speak of dying before you even gain the crown," Arviragus chided. "Instead, make overtures to the Tribes around us, something our Father would never do. Instead of fighting them, let us court allies for the war against Rome. Even the mighty Catuvellauni cannot field sufficient warriors to stand against the legions Rome will throw across the water against us."

Togodurunus scrubbed calloused palms across his braided beard and sighed heavily. "How long do you think we have before they come?"

"We may have months. Years perhaps?" Arviragus shrugged dejectedly. "Mordag Mor could have told us with her bones...."

Years passed. Times of peace giving way to a long war with Rome. One eve, folk gathered around Reuben in the church when the sun sought its rest, a select few privy to many of his secrets. And many of Arawn Doelguss' as well.

Time had misted details they had been too young to know or understand. They asked Reuben many things. How the young church survived the invading legions the Roman emperor Claudius unleashed against *Belerion* after the death of the king of the Britons, the Catuvellauni King Kimbelinus? How the many Tribes were crushed? How many persevered?

Mainly their questions centered on Joseph of Arimathea. How, as Apostle to *Belerion*, he became the first bishop of the church on 'the *Isle of Glass*?' How Joseph, with the help of others, trained and sent disciples throughout the island. Even into Gaul? Missionaries of a new faith many of the Druids and Celts embraced as their own. How Reuben served his mentor and master on many missions throughout Belerion? His time as a prisoner of Rome. Others centered on how he met Arawn Doelguss?

He answered them honestly in every case, except when they pressed him about Gwyr. When those questions came as they must, he glanced at Arawn——who to his shock, answered with a smile and a nod.

"Gwyr has never left his forest," Reuben began. "Even when the Romans came. They never found him, ran him to earth although they tried. In time Arawn and I were blessed to help raise his children."

"Hold! Wait!" Cynan blurted. He was a stalwart young man already mighty in the service of the Christ. "You told us——" he hesitated, raised his head to stare at Arawn who stood behind her husband. "You told us——the Lady of the Lake said he could not sire children."

She nodded. "So he did. And so I did. I told him what I knew, what I had *seen*. But Cynan——" She gave him the smile that Arawn Doelguss reserved for doubters. "My lord husband is living proof that miracles happen."

Their guests left not long after. Arawn stood in the church doorway, watched them descend the terraces encircling the *tor*. Instead of fading, her rare beauty only blossomed more with time. She looked far younger than her years, sufficiently young to enhance her legend of the ageless priestess of *Ynys Wydryn*, though she served the Christ.

Reuben knew he, too, did not look his age. He tried not to dwell on it. Perhaps when the blood of Christ healed his limbs, it brought other blessings as well.

She turned when they were out of sight. "You did not tell them Gwyr's second son wed our second daughter, my husband. That their bloodline will found a dynasty of kings in Belerion."

Reuben went to her, drew her into his arms, kissed the lips that brought him so much happiness. "That, Dear One," he whispered in her ear, "is yet another story. One of many yet to tell...."

Chapter 29

-EPILOGUE-

Year followed year, and the Christ did not return. But the numbers of His followers grew daily. In time they became known as Christians, and they spread their good news throughout the Known World.

Candles burned late in the Arimathea compound in Antioch where Titus the Scribe penned necessary missives to Arimathea factors in other cities. New taxes, mandated by Rome, always forced reassessment of interest calculations and implementation of changes in Arimathea trading policies. Titus cited his recommendations with regard to the spice trade with Arabian South and the Far East, then signed and sealed the missives with hot wax.

Finally, he set aside his quill pen, sighing while he rubbed the ink spots on his hands. He had served the House of Arimathea in Antioch for almost thirteen years. Not knowing the true year of his birth, he guessed his actual age near twenty-five, at most, twenty-seven.

"I have lived in the reign of three emperors," he said softly, "Tiberius, Caligula, and now Claudius. And I survived the great earthquake that stuck Antioch during the first years of Claudius' reign."

He also had witnessed other great and wondrous things. "I followed the Apostle Peter here, arriving in the city in time to work with the church he founded."

Titus held no illusions concerning his contributions to the church. He was a cripple, dependent on others. Like Jacob the Syrian, the

Arimathea bondservant who was his legs. While others witnessed, he ciphered and kept lists and money tallies, wrote correspondence with the other Apostles and disciples.

"What any scribe would do——" Titus murmured wistfully. "One who is devoted to the House of Arimathea."

His normal days were spent in the Arimathea compound library in the eastern district of the city. Late each afternoon, Jacob carried him to the church in the *Kerateion* quarter in the southern portion of the city, cradled between the Forum Colonnades of Herod and Mount Tauris.

But this was no normal day. New Roman taxes had kept him at the compound through the evening and into the night. He was tired, and his twisted legs ached. All he had to do was ring the bell at his fingertips and Jacob would come and carry him to bed. But he did not.

Why do I linger? he pondered. No one drove him in his duties but himself. *If I begin the next assessment, it will require the night to complete it, and with the dawn I must be here at my desk.*

But he knew why. In idle moments such as these, he allowed his dreams to invade his conscious mind. Dreams that would never be realized short of resurrection. Visions of walking on two legs that obeyed him. Running with the wind in his face. Journeying to the ends of the earth to witness for the Lord Jesus Christ.

Resting his elbows on the table, Titus cradled his face in his hands. *Why do I torture myself? I am not wanting for food, for lodging, for brothers and sisters in Christ who love the Lord as I do. It is a sin to lust after what you cannot have.*

In truth through most of his waking hours, he gave no thought to anything beyond his humble state. God had a purpose for him, and he was content with his portion. Only when fatigue wracked him and left him weak and vulnerable, when his legs ached so terribly——his yearnings broke free.

Titus sighed heavily into his hands. "Forgive me, Blessed Christ, for my sin of lust."

"What is it you lust after, my Son?"

Startled that someone had come upon him without his notice, ashamed that anyone overheard him in his private prayer, he wrenched his back straight in his chair and demanded of the shadows——"Who comes?"

A man entered, approached the side of his table, the candlelight barely illuminating him. He spoke Greek with a compassionate voice that carried easily. "Paul, a bond-servant of God, and an Apostle of Jesus Christ."

Shocked speechless, Titus gaped like a fish. His mind blazed bright with horror and shame that an Apostle of the Christ of all people had overheard him. With an inarticulate cry, he threw himself from the high-backed chair, fell painfully to the tiles, face down at the Apostle's feet.

Startled by Titus' actions, Paul dropped to his knees beside the young man. With a tent-maker's strong fingers, the Apostle gripped the young man's shoulders, almost bodily turned him, pulled him to rest against his own thighs.

"What——is this you do, my Son?" Paul demanded. But asking this, the Apostle saw the twisted legs, felt the shuddering breaths and understood.

Paul said softly, "Look at me."

There was such strength and authority in that voice that Titus obeyed with no thought of resistance or rebellion. Paul looked deep into Titus' eyes. For a heartbeat the Apostle saw another lame servant who had witnessed to him about the Christ in the days before he believed. Another student of Gamaliel's. A lame man also healed by the Christ. Reuben ben Ezra——

As quickly as the image flashed through Paul's mind, it faded, leaving only Titus. Through the power of the *Spirit* in him, Paul saw the young man's heart. He knew too the life of humility Titus offered the world was no lie.

In that moment the Savior did not speak audibly, but Paul knew what and who Elias the Penitent was. He also knew the sin of lust the young man confessed was not sin at all. But greatest of these, the

Apostle saw the *Spirit* in him——and that Titus had the faith to be made well.

"Your faith is great," Paul acknowledged. "By the power of the Christ who lives in me, let what your soul desires be done." Then in a loud voice the Apostle commanded, "Stand upright on your feet!"

Without thought, Titus obeyed the absolute command in Paul's voice. He pushed to his feet on legs straight and firm.

Speechless, he stood there. Wonder of that healing reverberated through his mind and his heart like the sound of pealing bells. Stunned, he turned open-mouthed to Paul.

The Apostle shook his head. "Do not look to me. Your faith has made you whole."

In that moment Titus felt his world changing. He knew too his healing served a new purpose. Raising wondering eyes to Paul, he asked, "What shall I do now?"

Paul smiled. "What does the *Spirit* tell you?"

Titus could not help being touched by the Apostle's passion, the urge to share the gospel of Christ with all who would hear. He realized it was something he had groped and fumbled toward his entire life. But hampered by twisted legs, the need to be carried everywhere, he believed it forever beyond his abilities.

But the Lord has answered my unspoken desire, he knew. *Right here in this little room. Not only has He changed my life——* Titus silently affirmed, *the Christ has laid a greater obligation on me as well.*

"My father was Greek," he told Paul. "He abandoned my mother, a poor Jerusalem Jewess, when I was born crippled. Reuben ben Ezra arranged schooling for me in the House of Arimathea. Because of him, I write and speak four languages fluently: Aramaic, Hebrew, Greek, and Latin."

Titus hesitated. He had come this far, he must go farther. "I wish to witness for my Christ. You have much to do. Let me help you in your travels. Let me help bear your burdens."

Paul stared compassionately at Titus. "You do not know what you ask," he warned the young man. "I am to bear His name before the Gentiles and kings and sons of Israel, and *He* will show me how much I must suffer for *His* name sake. I do not wish to have you suffer so, my son."

"I have suffered for a lifetime," Titus countered. "Now I am free to suffer for my Christ. If you will have me," Titus pledged, "whither thou goest, I will go...."

Appendix

-NASB SCRIPTURE PASSAGES USED IN
WHITHER THOU GOEST....

Prologue:

Matthew 26:27-28 NASB
'Drink from it all of you; for this is My blood of the covenant, which is poured out for many for forgiveness of sins.'

Matthew 26: 29 NASB
'But I say to you, I will not drink from this fruit of the vine from now on until that day when I drink it new with you in My Father's kingdom.'

Mark 13:2 NASB
'Do you see these great buildings? Not one stone shall be left upon another which will not be torn down.'

Chapter 3

Jeremiah 31:31-32 NASB
'Behold the days are coming,' declares the Lord, 'when I will make a new covenant with the house of Israel and the house of Judah, not like the covenant which I made with their fathers when I took them by the hand to bring them out of the land of Egypt, My covenant which they broke, although I was husband to them,' declares the Lord.'

Ezekiel 31:26 NASB
'I shall give you a new heart and put a new spirit within you; and I will remove the heart of stone from your flesh and give you a heart of flesh.'

Chapter 4

Acts 4: 19-20 NASB
"Whether it is right in the sight of God to give heed to you rather than to God, you be the judge, for we cannot stop speaking what we have seen and heard."

Ruth 1:16 NASB
"Where you go, I will go, and where you lodge, I will lodge. Your people shall be my people, and your God, my God."

Ruth 1:17 NASB
'Where you die, I will die, and there I will be buried. Thus may the Lord do to me, and worse, if anything but death parts you and me.'

Acts 7:59 NASB
"Lord Jesus, receive my spirit!"

Acts 7:60 NASB
"Lord, do not hold this sin against them!"

Chapter 6

Acts 9:4 NASB
'Saul, Saul, why are you persecuting Me?'

Acts 9:5 NASB
'I am Jesus whom you are persecuting—'

Acts 9:6 NASB
'Rise, and enter the city, and it shall be told you what you must do.'

Acts 9:15 NASB
'Go, for he is a chosen instrument of Mine, to bear My name before the Gentiles and kings and the sons of Israel.'

Acts 9:16 NASB
'For I will show him how much he must suffer for My name's sake.'

Acts 9:17 NASB
'Brother Saul, the Lord Jesus, who appeared to you on the road by which you were coming, has sent me so that you may regain your sight, and be filled with the Holy Spirit.'

Chapter 7

Ruth 1:16 NASB
"Where you go, I will go, and where you lodge, I will lodge. Your people shall be my people, and your God, my God."

Ruth 1:17 NASB
'Where you die, I will die, and there I will be buried. Thus may the Lord do to me, and worse, if anything but death parts you and me.'

Chapter 12

John 18:37 NASB
'You say correctly I am a king,'

John 18:37 NASB
'My kingdom is not of this world.'

Chapter 13

Matthew 22:38 NASB
'This is the greatest and foremost commandment.'

Matthew 22:37 NASB
'YOU SHALL LOVE THE LORD YOUR GOD WITH ALL YOUR HEART AND WITH ALL YOUR SOUL, AND WITH ALL YOUR MIND.'

Matthew 22:39 NASB
'The second is like it, YOU SHALL LOVE YOUR NEIGHBOR AS YOURSELF.'

John 15:13 NASB
'Greater love has no one than this, that he lay down his life for his friends.'

Romans 3:23 NASB
'A**ll** have **sinned** and **fall short** of the **glory** of **God**.'

Matthew 28:18-20 NASB
'All authority has been given Me in heaven and on earth. Go therefore and make disciples of all the nations, baptizing them in the name of the Father, and the Son and the Holy Spirit, teaching them to observe all that I commanded you, and lo, I am with you always, even to the end of the age.'

Matthew 9:37-38 NASB
'The harvest is plentiful, but the workers are few; therefore beseech the Lord of the harvest to send out workers into His harvest.'

Luke 10:16 NASB
'The one who listens to you listens to Me, and the one who rejects you rejects Me, and he who rejects Me rejects the One who sent Me.'

Chapter 26

Matthew 26:27-28 NASB
'Drink from it all of you; for this is My blood of the covenant, which is poured out for many for forgiveness of sins.'

Chapter 27

Jeremiah 1:5 NASB
*'**Before** I **formed you** in the **womb** I **knew you**, And **before you were born** I **consecrated you**—'*

John 14:6 NASB
'I am the way, the truth, and the life. No man comes to the Father but through Me.'

About the Author...

Living in Southeast Texas with his wife Liz, Ben F. Lee is an enthusiastic, dedicated Christian with a special love of the Crucifixion era and a licensed minister of the Gospel. His award-winning professional writing work includes newspaper reporter, manager [resume company office], director of proposal development [major Southeast Texas engineering firm], self-employed writing consultant, freelance articles [various company publications], and ghost writer for novelists.

A long-time member of the Golden Triangle Writers Guild, Lee served in numerous capacities from president to member of the Board of Directors. He is a current member of Texas Gulf Coast Writers.

An active member of the Society for Creative Anachronism, Inc. [SCA] since 1976, a medieval reenactment group where he gained extensive hands-on knowledge of the Medieval Period, Lee is recognized as a fighting instructor for Southeast and Central Texas in chivalric [knightly combat] and rapier fighting.

Printed in the United States
By Bookmasters